W9-CTO-845

PART I:
SURVIVAL
A CLONE WARS SERIES

LUCAS BOOKS

SCHOLASTIC INC.

New York   Toronto   London   Auckland   Sydney
Mexico City   New Delhi   Hong Kong   Buenos Aires

www.starwars.com
www.scholastic.com

No part of this work may be reproduced, stored in a retrieval system,
or transmitted in any form or by any means, electronic, mechanical, photocopying,
recording, or otherwise, without written permission of the publisher.
For information regarding permission,
write to Scholastic Inc., 557 Broadway, New York, NY 10012.

Boba Fett #1: Fight to Survive
ISBN-13: 978-0-439-33927-8, ISBN-10: 0-439-33927-8.
© 2002 Lucasfilm Ltd. & TM

Boba Fett #2: Crossfire
ISBN-13: 978-0-439-33928-5, ISBN-10: 0-439-33928-6.
© 2002 Lucasfilm Ltd. & TM

Boba Fett #3: Maze of Deception
ISBN-13: 978-0-439-44245-9, ISBN-10: 0-439-44245-1.
© 2003 Lucasfilm Ltd. & TM

SCHOLASTIC and associated logos are trademarks
and/or registered trademarks of Scholastic Inc.

12 11 10 9 8 7 6 5 4 3 2 1   8 9 10 11 12/0

Printed in the U.S.A.
ISBN-13: 978-0-545-11621-3
ISBN-10: 0-545-11621-X

First printing, August 2008

CONTENTS

THE FIGHT TO SURVIVE

STAR WARS

BOBA FETT™

THE FIGHT TO SURVIVE

TERRY BISSON

CHAPTER ONE

Rain.

Some hate it.

Some love it.

Some, like Boba Fett, can hardly remember a time without it.

Supposedly, free water is rare in the galaxy, but you would never know it on his planet. It comes down in sheets, day and night, covering this world, which is all seas except for a few cities on platforms.

The world is called Kamino. The city where Boba and his father live is called Tipoca City.

Lived, rather. For this is the story of how they left, and why, and what happened after that . . .

You may have heard of Boba Fett's father. He was a bounty hunter. The fiercest, fastest, and most fearless bounty hunter in the galaxy.

Boba Fett was the kid standing in his shadow or by his side. Or usually, both.

When he was lucky, that is. When his dad took him along. Which was almost always. Boba was ten, nearly but not quite old enough to be on his own.

Boba liked going with his father. Seeing new worlds, experiencing the cold thrill of hyperspace, and even getting to try his hand at the controls of his father's small but deadly starship, *Slave I*, from time to time.

A bounty hunter is an outlaw, a tracker — and sometimes a killer — for hire. He doesn't care who his targets are, or who they're running from, or why. He works for the highest bidder, which means the richest and the most ruthless beings in the galaxy. No questions asked.

Being a bounty hunter's son means keeping your mouth shut and your eyes open.

No problem. Boba Fett was proud of his father and proud of what he did.

"I'm a bounty hunter's son," he would say to himself proudly. The reason he said it to himself, and to no one else, was that he had no one else to say it to.

He had no friends.

How can you have friends when you live and travel in secret, sneaking on and off planets, avoiding police and security and the dreaded, nosy, Jedi Knights?

A bounty hunter must always be ready to go anywhere and face any danger. That was from Jango Fett's code, the rule by which he lived.

Boba Fett had his own, smaller, more personal code: *A bounty hunter's kid must always be ready to go with him.*

At age ten, Boba had seen more of the galaxy than most grown-ups. What he hadn't seen was the inside of a schoolroom (for he'd never been to school). What he hadn't seen was a mother's smile (for he had no mother). What he hadn't heard was the laughter of a friend (for he had no friends).

Just because he hadn't been to school didn't mean Boba was stupid or ignorant.

There were always books. Books to take on trips; books to read at home on Kamino. He could get all the books he wanted ("Two at a time, only, please!") from the little library at the foot of his street in Tipoca City.

The library was just a slot in a doorway, but when Boba rang the bell the librarian passed out new books and took back the ones that were due, the ones Boba had read (or given up on, or decided were boring).

The librarian, Whrr, was almost like a friend. A friend Boba had never actually seen.

Boba had no idea what Whrr looked like — or even if he was a person. He was just a voice through a slot in the library door. In fact, Boba figured Whrr could be a droid, since he could hear him whirring and clicking when he was getting books or hologames.

Mostly books.

Whrr didn't like hologames. "Use your imagination!" he would say. "Find the pictures there! Find the music there!"

Boba agreed. He liked books because the pictures they made in his mind were better than the ones in the hologames.

Boba knew about friends from books.

Lots of books are about friends. Friends having adventures, making discoveries, or just hanging out.

Sometimes Boba pretended to have friends. (Pretending is a form of wishing.)

But his father's voice was always in his head: "Boba, stay unattached. Remember: *No friends, no enemies. Only allies and adversaries.*"

That saying was from Jango Fett's code. Boba's father had lots of sayings, and they were all from his code.

Jango Fett had one friend, though. She was a bounty hunter herself. Her name was Zam Wesell.

Zam could be beautiful but bad. She *liked* to be bad. She sometimes read books about famous outlaws and bloody battles.

It was Zam who first mentioned that Boba should read, even though she herself didn't read much. "Want adventure? Read books," Zam said. "Then when you get tired of the excitement, you can close the book. Better than real life."

Boba's father didn't read much. "Books? A waste of time," he said. "Read maps, Boba. Instructions. Warnings. Important stuff."

Boba read all that — but he liked books better. Especially books about droids and starships, stuff he knew he could use someday.

Sometimes Boba thought Zam had told him to read books just because his dad thought it was a waste of time. Zam liked to tease Jango.

Zam was a changeling, a Clawdite. She changed the form of her body back and forth, depending on the situation.

Mothers didn't do that, Boba was pretty sure. He had read about mothers in books, even though he had never met one.

A mother seemed like a nice thing to have.

*　　*　　*

Once, when he was little, Boba asked his father who his mother was.

"You never had one," said his father. "You are a clone. That means you are my son. Period. No one else, no woman was involved."

Boba nodded. That meant he was exactly like his father, Jango Fett. That meant he was special.

Still, sometimes, in secret, he wished he had a mother.

Boba and his father lived on Kamino because Jango Fett had a job to do there. He was training a special army of super-soldiers for a man named Count Tyranus.

Boba liked to watch the soldiers, lined up in long ranks, marching in the rain. They never got tired and they never complained and they all looked exactly alike — exactly like his father, only younger. Exactly like Boba himself, only older.

"They are also my clones," Jango Fett told him once when he was little.

It was what Boba had expected to hear. But it still hurt. "Just like me?"

"Not like you," said Jango Fett. "They are just soldiers. They grow up twice as fast and only live half as long. You are the only true clone. You are my real son."

"I see," said Boba. He felt better. Still, he didn't go watch the clones march anymore. And he didn't feel quite as special as before.

Tyranus was an old man with a long, lean face and eyes like a hawk.

Boba had never seen him in person — only on holograms when he gave instructions to Jango Fett, or asked about the progress of the clone army.

Jango called him "Count" and was always polite. But that didn't mean he liked him, Boba knew.

Always be polite to a client. That was part of Jango's code.

One night Boba heard his father and the Count talking about a new job on a faraway planet.

The Count told Jango Fett that the job would be very dangerous.

That didn't stop Boba's father, of course. Later on, Boba wondered if maybe the Count had played up the danger to make sure Jango took the job.

You never knew, with grown-ups.

Jango agreed to do the job. He told the Count he

would have to meet up with Zam Wesell and take her along with him.

Boba grinned when he heard that. If they were both going, that meant he might get to go, too.

No such luck.

The next morning, Jango Fett strapped on his battle armor and told Boba that he and Zam were going on a trip.

"Me too?" Boba asked hopefully.

Jango shook his head. "Sorry, son. You're going to have to stay home alone."

Boba groaned.

"*A bounty hunter never complains,*" said Jango, in that special voice he reserved for his code. "And neither does his son."

"But . . ."

"No buts, son. This is a special job for the Count. Zam and I have to travel fast and light."

"I'm fast," Boba said. "And I'm light!"

Jango Fett laughed. "A little too light," he said, patting Boba on the head. "But big enough to stay here on your own. It will only be a few days."

The next morning Boba woke up alone in the apartment. Home alone — but not entirely alone.

His father had left him a bowl with five sea-mice in it. And a note: *We'll be back when these are gone.*

Sea-mice can live in either air or water. They are incredibly cute, with big brown eyes and little paws that turn to flippers when you put them into the water.

They are also incredibly good to eat . . . if you are a sea eel.

Jango's pet sea eel lived in a tank in the bed-room.

CHAPTER TWO

Boba was surprised to find that he liked being home alone.

The apartment was all his. Three squares came out of the cookslot every day, heated to perfection.

Boba could come and go as he liked. He could hang around the spaceport, admiring the sleek fighters and imagining himself at the controls. He could pretend he was a bounty hunter and "track" unsuspecting people on the street. Or, when he grew tired of the endless rain, he could curl up and read on the couch.

It wasn't even lonely. When Boba was with his father, Jango Fett hardly ever talked. But when Boba was alone he could hear his father's voice in his head all the time. "Boba do this. Boba do that."

It was as good as having him actually around. Better, in fact.

*   *   *

The first two days were easy. And in three more days, Jango and Zam Wesell would be back. How did Boba know?

There were only three sea-mice left. The eel ate one a day. Every morning Boba took a sea-mouse out of the bowl and dropped it into the eel's tank.

The eel had no name. Just "eel."

Boba didn't like its narrow eyes and huge mouth. Or the way it swallowed the little sea-mice in one gulp — then digested them slowly, taking all day.

It was creepy.

Jango Fett usually fed the eel. But now it was Boba's job. The note had said it all: *We'll be back when these are gone.*

Boba knew that his dad thought it was important for his son to learn to do what was necessary, even when it was creepy. Even when it was cruel.

The bounty hunter is free of attachments was one of his sayings. Another was: *Life feeds on death.*

On the third morning, when Boba woke up and heated his breakfast, there were three sea-mice left.

He decided to spare one. He felt sorry for the

sea-mice with their big brown eyes. What if he gave the eel his own breakfast — or, say, half of it?

He could hear his dad's voice in his ear: *Vary your routine. Patterns are traps.* (JFC)

"Okay, Dad," Boba said.

Boba broke his breakfast roll in two and dropped half into the eel's tank. It was gone in an instant.

Then he reached down into the bowl and picked up one of the sea-mice. The sea-mouse made it easy, grabbing Boba's fingers with his tiny paws.

Maybe he knows I'm not going to feed him to the eel, Boba thought. But no, each of the others had looked at him in exactly the same way, right before he had dropped them into the eel's tank.

This one has it right, though, Boba thought. *I have to make him gone, but I can do it another way. I am going to give him his freedom.*

That was the plan, anyway.

Boba took the sea-mouse into the hall, down the turbolift, and out to the courtyard behind the apartment building.

He set him down in the weed garden. "So long, little sea-mouse," he said. "You're free."

The sea-mouse looked up at Boba, more terrified than happy. *Maybe he doesn't know what freedom is*, Boba thought. Boba gave him a push with his fingertips, and the tiny creature disappeared into the tall, rain-wet grass. A little wave of movement in the grass showed where he was going.

Then a bigger wave intersected it.

Boba heard a tiny scream — then silence.

CHAPTER THREE

That afternoon Boba went to the library. It always made him feel better to go to the library.

Well, not always, but often.

He stuck the books he was returning into the slot. The light came on, and Whrr whirred and clicked. "Boba!" he said. "How're you feeling?"

"Not great," said Boba. He told Whrr what had happened with the sea-mouse.

"Not great," agreed Whrr, "but at least you tried. Life is hard on the weak and the small, I guess."

"What do you mean, you guess?" asked Boba. "Don't you know?"

"Not really," said Whrr. "That's why I stay in here, out of the way." He whirred his change-the-subject noise. "Ready for some new books? Did you actually finish these?"

"Mostly," said Boba. "I like to read about navigation and starship flying."

"You are reading faster," said Whrr, passing the new books through the slot. "That's good!"

"Why is that good?"

"You can read more books!"

Boba had to laugh.

"Why are you laughing?" Whrr asked. He sounded a little offended.

"My dad says, if you are a pilot, everything looks like a ship," said Boba.

"So?"

"So, Whrr, if you had your way, everybody would read books."

"So? I don't understand what's so funny about that," Whrr said, with a disapproving click.

"Never mind, see ya later!" Boba said, and he took his books and ran.

Time to get rid of another sea-mouse.

Boba woke up determined to try to do the right thing this time. He gave the eel all his breakfast. The eel ate it in one gulp.

There were only two sea-mice left in the bowl. They both looked up at him with their little brown eyes pleading.

"I have to make you gone," Boba said as he picked one up. "But I'm not going to feed you to the eel. I'm going to set you free for real."

He locked the apartment door and took the turbolift down to the street. He stuck the sea-mouse inside his shirt so no one could see it.

It seemed to like it there. When Boba pulled it out it was sleeping.

He held it out in the rain as he walked toward the edge of Tipoca City. He wanted to watch its paw turn into a flipper, but it only turned halfway.

I guess it takes seawater, Boba thought, heading toward the sound of the waves.

Tipoca City is built on a platform over the sea. Huge waves boom and bang and crash, day and night. Kamino is called the "Planet of Storms."

Boba hung onto the railing and leaned over the edge of the platform. He looked down, waiting for a lull in the waves.

Finally, there it was — a long green stretch of smooth water. It looked perfect for a little sea-mouse!

"You're free, little buddy," Boba said as he dropped the tiny creature into the water. The sea-mouse stared up as it fell, as if it wanted one last look at its benefactor, its protector, the great giant Boba who had rescued it from its bowl. . . .

It hit the water with a little *plunk*.

Then Boba saw a dark shape in the water, and a flash of teeth from below.

And the sea-mouse was gone.

Not even a stain on the water was left.

Boba spent the rest of the day playing hologames and staring out the window into the rain. He was tired of books. He was tired of reading about happy families and kids with friends. And pets.

He was tired of being home alone.

He missed Zam's jokes (even the dumb ones). He missed his father's sayings (even the ones he had heard a million times).

The next morning he picked up the last sea-mouse out of the bowl. "Sorry, buddy," he said as he dropped it into the eel's tank. "It's just the way the world works."

Then he sat down to eat his own breakfast and wait for his father and Zam to get home.

CHAPTER FOUR

All day Boba was excited, waiting for a certain sound.

Or a bunch of sounds.

Finally, late in the afternoon, there they were: a symphony of little clicks and clacks, all coming from the locks that hung on the apartment door.

Then the door slid open, and there was Jango Fett, looking strong and bold in his Mandalorian battle armor, standing in a puddle of rainwater in the hall.

"Dad!" Boba said. "Where's Zam?"

"Later," his father said.

Jango Fett took off his battle armor and laid it out on the floor of the bedroom while Boba watched. He called it "the suit." He was much smaller without it.

Jango's face under the helmet was sad and grooved with old scars. The face on his helmet was ruthless and cruel. Boba never wondered which was his father's "real" face. Both were real to him: the worried father, the fearless warrior.

"Where's Zam?" Boba asked again.

"Why are you asking all these questions, son?"

"I have a joke to tell her." He didn't really, but he figured he could always think of one.

"You'll have to save it for somebody else."

Somebody else? There wasn't anybody else! But Boba knew better than to argue with his father.

"Okay," he said. He hung his head to hide his disappointment and started to leave the room. He could tell his father wanted to be alone.

"Zam won't be around anymore," Jango said.

Boba stopped at the door. "Ever?"

"Ever," said Jango.

Only the way he said it, it sounded like *never*.

When Jango Fett wasn't wearing the Mandalorian battle armor, he wore regular clothes. Without the helmet, few recognized him as Jango Fett, the bounty hunter.

The armor was old and scarred, like Jango Fett himself. He always took it off and cleaned it after returning from a job, but he never polished it. He left the scratches alone.

"You don't want it to shine," he told Boba as they worked together cleaning the armor later that afternoon. "*Never call attention to yourself.*"

"Yes, sir," Boba said.

Jango Fett's face seemed even sadder and older than usual. Boba wondered if it had to do with Zam.

Finally he got up the courage to ask.

"She was about to betray us," Jango said. "It couldn't be allowed. There are penalties. She would have done the same if it were me."

Boba didn't understand. What was his father trying to tell him? "Did something bad happen to Zam?"

Jango nodded slowly. "Being a bounty hunter means you don't always make it home. Someday the inevitable will happen. And when it does . . ."

"What does *inevitable* mean?" Boba asked.

"Inevitable means a sure thing. Death is a sure thing."

Suddenly Boba got it. "Zam is dead, isn't she, Dad?"

Jango nodded.

Boba fought back tears. "How — how did it happen?"

"You don't want to know."

Boba felt sadness wash over him like a wave. Followed by a colder wave of fear. If it could happen to Zam, could it happen to his father?

Boba didn't want to think about that. His dad was right: He didn't want to know.

After he had finished helping his father clean the battle armor and reload the weapons systems,

Boba went out and walked all the way down to the end of the street and back.

Zam, dead. No more dumb jokes. No more bright laughter. Boba Fett's lonely world had just gotten even lonelier.

Kamino is a good planet for feeling sad because it's always raining. When you've been in the rain, nobody can tell you've been crying.

When Boba got back to the apartment, he saw that his father had been walking in the rain, too.

Funny, thought Boba. *I didn't see him out there.*

After supper, Jango Fett said, "Boba, listen up."

Boba listened up.

"What happened to Zam could happen to any of us. To any bounty hunter. Do you understand?"

Boba nodded — but his nod was a lie. He was determined *not* to understand. He had promised himself *not* to think about it. He couldn't imagine it, anyway. Who or what could get the best of his father in a fight?

"Good," said Jango Fett. "So, son, I want you to take this."

Jango handed Boba a book.

Boba was shocked. *My dad?! A book?!*

Jango seemed to know what Boba was thinking. "It's not a book, son," he said. "It's a message unit, from me. For you, when the time comes."

Not a book? It looked like an ordinary book, about two fingers thick, with a hard cover. It was black, with nothing on the cover. No words, no pictures. Nothing, front or back.

Boba tried to open it but the pages seemed stuck together. He pulled harder on the cover, and his father shook his head.

"Don't open it," Jango said. "Because when you open it, your childhood will be over. And it is too soon for that. I want you to have what I never had: a childhood."

Boba nodded. Though he was confused. Why had his father given him a book if he didn't want him to open it?

Then his father told him:

"If something happens to me, you should open it. It will tell you what you need to know. Who to ask for. Who to avoid. What to do. What not. Until then, keep it closed, and keep it hidden. Understand, son?"

Boba nodded. He tossed the black book (that was not really a book) into the pile with his library books. He wasn't going to need it. Ever. No way. Like, something bad was going to happen to his father, the fiercest, fastest, most fearless bounty hunter in the galaxy?

No way. Unthinkable. Which simply meant that Boba was *not* going to think about it.

CHAPTER FIVE

The next day, Boba and his father went fishing. The rain was light, so they sat on a rock at the edge of the sea. Boba took potshots at rollerfish with his pocker, a laser-aimed spear-thrower. Jango made him turn the laser off and sight by eye.

Boba knew that the fishing trip was his father's way of trying to make him feel better, so he'd forget about Zam's death. Boba did his best to concentrate.

He kept on fishing even when Taun We, one of the Kaminoans, stopped by to talk with Jango. She was tall and white, like a root that has just been pulled out of the ground. Her dark eyes were as big as saucers, her neck long and thin.

Boba usually liked Taun We, but today it was business, business, business. Something about the clones. Boba tried not to listen. He didn't want to hear about the clone army — his ten thousand twin brothers. It made him feel creepy just thinking about it.

He was glad when Taun We left, and to prove it,

he speared a few more rollerfish. He tried to act excited to please his dad, but the fun had gone out of it.

Boba couldn't stop thinking about the clones. He couldn't stop thinking about Zam.

Boba *did* get excited again, though, when they passed the spaceport on their way back to the apartment. There was a new ship on the landing pad. It was a sleek starfighter he had only seen in pictures before.

"Wow!" he said. "It's a Delta-7!"

"And what of the droid?" Jango asked, pointing to the nav unit behind the cockpit.

"It's an R4-P," said Boba excitedly. While his father listened, he listed the starfighter's features. Extra armaments, extra speed — the Delta-7 with the R4-P was the kind of ship only a few, select pilots could handle.

"Like who?" Jango asked.

"Like you!" Boba said as they hurried home in the rain. He was happy to show off what he had learned from his reading. And even happier to bring a smile to his father's face.

But the smile didn't last. Jango seemed thoughtful. Preoccupied. Even worried.

He went into the bedroom to take a nap while Boba sat down with a reference — *Starfighters of the Galaxy.* He was curious to know how such a sleek ship as the Delta-7 had found its way to out-of-the-way Kamino, where nothing important or exciting ever happened.

Boba had barely started to read when he heard the door buzz. He and his father didn't have any friends, especially with Zam gone, so he was surprised.

It was Taun We again. And this time she wasn't alone. The man standing next to her wore a simple robe and no jewelry. Under his robe Boba could see the outline of a lightsaber.

A Jedi.

All of a sudden, Boba knew where the starfighter had come from.

Cautiously, he opened the door.

"Boba, is your father here?" Taun We asked.

"Yes."

Say no more than necessary. That was a favorite saying of Jango Fett. And Boba knew that it especially applied when the Jedi were around.

"May we see him?"

The Jedi said nothing. Just stood there, watching and listening. Cool and collected. But also a little scary.

Boba tried to be cool himself. "Sure," he said.

Always be polite. Especially to your enemies.

And the Jedi, as keepers of the peace, were the natural enemies of bounty hunters, who operated outside the law.

Boba stepped back to let them in. The Jedi was looking around as if he had never been in an apartment before. *Nosy!* Boba thought. He decided to ignore him.

"Dad! Taun We's here!"

Jango Fett came out of the bedroom. He looked at both of the visitors, and he didn't seem to like what he saw.

"Welcome back, Jango," Taun We said, pretending she hadn't just seen him. "Was your trip productive?"

"Fairly."

Boba listened carefully. Taun We was sounding friendly, as usual. Meanwhile his father was looking the Jedi up and down. To say that Jango didn't seem to like what he saw would be obvious, like saying Kamino is rainy. It was more than that.

Boba wondered if they had met before. He wondered if the Jedi had anything to do with the death of Zam.

"This is Jedi Master Obi-Wan Kenobi," Taun We said. "He's come to check on our progress."

"That right?" Jango said.

The two men stared at each other. It was like a battle fought without words or weapons.

Boba watched, fascinated. It was obvious to him that his father could have whipped the stupid

26

Jedi with one finger. But something was holding him back.

"Your clones are very impressive," said the Jedi with a slight bow. "You must be very proud."

"I'm just a simple man," Jango Fett said, bowing back. "Trying to make my way in the universe."

"Aren't we all?" said the Jedi.

It was like a fight to see who could be most polite!

Meanwhile, the Jedi was looking into the bedroom, where the Mandalorian battle helmet and armor were lying on the floor.

Jango moved in front of the door to block the Jedi's view.

"Ever make your way as far into the interior as Coruscant?" the Jedi asked.

"Once or twice," Jango answered coolly.

"Recently?"

This is one very nosy Jedi! Boba thought. He wondered why his father was talking to him at all.

"Possibly," said Jango, and Boba knew from the tone of the answer that his father *had* been to Coruscant.

And the Jedi knew it, too.

Now Boba knew for sure that the Jedi and Jango had encountered each other before, and that the Jedi had had something to do with Zam's death. How he hated the Jedi's smug little smile!

"Then you must know Master Sifo-Dyas," the Jedi said.

"Boba, close the door," said Jango in Huttese, a language they both knew well.

Boba did what his father asked, never taking his eyes off the Jedi. He wanted him to feel his hate.

Meanwhile Jango Fett was fencing. Using words instead of a sword to block the Jedi's moves. "Master who?" he asked.

"Sifo-Dyas. Isn't he the Jedi who hired you for this job?"

"Never heard of him," said Jango.

"Really!?" said the Jedi. For the first time, he looked surprised.

"I was recruited by a man called Tyranus," said Jango. "On one of the moons of Bogden."

"No? I thought . . ."

Taun We stepped in then. "Sifo-Dyas told us to expect him," she said to the Jedi, pointing to Boba's father. "And he showed up just when your Jedi Master said he would. We have kept the Jedi's involvement a secret until your arrival, just as your Master requested."

The Jedi seemed surprised by all this. And trying not to show it. "Curious," he said.

"Do you like your army?" Jango Fett asked. His cold smile seemed to Boba like a sword thrust straight toward the nosy Jedi's heart.

"I look forward to seeing them in action," said the Jedi. A pretty good parry, Boba had to admit.

"They'll do their job well, I'll guarantee that," said Jango.

The Jedi gave up. "Thanks for your time, Jango."

"Always a pleasure to meet a Jedi," said Boba's father with a slight, sarcastic smile.

The door slid shut and the locks began to snap closed. Boba was thrilled. After winning an encounter like that, he figured his father would looked pleased, even triumphant. Instead, Jango Fett's face was creased with lines of worry, and he seemed deep in thought.

Boba began to wonder if his father had really won the battle. "What is it, Dad?" he asked.

"Pack your things," Jango said. "We're getting out of here for a while."

CHAPTER SIX

While Jango Fett put his battle armor on, Boba threw everything the two owned (which wasn't much) into an expandable flight bag.

"Get a move on, Boba!"

Boba knew his father wasn't afraid of anything. But after the encounter with the strange Jedi, Jango seemed nervous. Worried. Not frightened, but . . . *concerned*, at least.

And he was in a BIG hurry.

After he had filled the bag, Boba threw all the dirty dishes into the cleaning slot. He didn't have to be neat at all. If it hadn't been so scary, it would have been fun.

"Leave the rest," Jango said. "We don't have time."

Be careful what you wish for! How many times had Boba dreamed of having time away from stormy Kamino and living somewhere else, with sunshine — and maybe even friends?

Now it was happening. The having time away part, anyway. Boba was glad, and yet . . .

There was the bed where he had slept and

dreamed. The windowsill where he had sat and read and watched the endless rain. The box where he had kept his books, clothes, and old toys, all in one pile.

It's hard to leave the only place you've ever lived, especially when you don't know when you'll be back. It's like leaving behind little pieces of yourself. It's like . . .

Boba caught himself. This was no time to get sentimental. His father was in a hurry. They had to get going.

And there was one last thing he had to do before leaving Tipoca City.

"Whoa! Where are you going?" Jango asked. His battle armor was on, helmet and all. He was holding what looked like a whip. "Where are you taking that stuff?"

"Uh, Dad . . . library books?"

Boba hoped his father would understand that he had to return them. Who knew when they were coming back? And Boba didn't want Whrr to be charging him for overdue books.

"Make it fast, son," Jango said. "And while you're at it —"

He handed Boba the "whip." It was the eel. "Turn him loose in the sea. Let him try feeding himself for a change."

"Yes, sir!" Boba was out the door before his father could change his mind. The eel was coiled around one arm, and he carried the books in the other.

He ran through the rain as fast as he could. He stopped at the edge of the platform where he had taken the sea-mouse. He leaned over the railing and dropped the eel into the waves.

Plunk.

Boba saw a dark shape, a flash of teeth. And the eel was gone.

"Good riddance!" he muttered as he ran toward the library. "Life is hard for the small and the weak. And it's all relative."

Boba hurriedly shoved the books into the slot. One, two, three . . .

Whrr whirred happily. "How about this batch?" he asked from behind the door, in his tinny voice. "What did you think? Any good?"

"Not too bad," Boba said. "But I don't have time to talk now."

"No? Why not? Don't you want to check out some more books?"

Usually Boba liked talking about books. But today there was no time. "Have to go!" he said. "So long!"

"Hurry back, Boba," Whrr said. "But wait, here's . . ."

"No time to wait!" Boba didn't have the heart to tell his friend that he didn't know when he would be coming back.

So he just turned and ran.

Jango Fett, fierce looking in his full battle armor, was waiting with the flight bag in front of the apartment. Boba could tell his father was mad at him for taking so long. But neither of them said anything.

The two walked quickly to the tiny landing pad where *Slave I*, the bounty hunter's small, swift starship, was parked. Jango stowed the bags while Boba checked out the ship for takeoff.

Boba had just completed the preflight "walk-around" when he heard footsteps. At first he thought it might be Taun We, coming to say good-bye.

No such luck.

It was the Jedi, Obi-Wan Kenobi. The one who had been at the apartment asking all the questions.

And he was running.

"Stop!" he shouted.

Yeah, right! thought Boba.

Jango clearly had the same thought. He drew his blaster and fired, while ordering, "Boba, get on board!"

Boba didn't have to be told twice. He got into the cockpit and watched as his father fired up his battle armor's jet-pack and rocketed to the top of a nearby building. There, Jango Fett knelt and began to fire down at the Jedi with his blaster rifle.

KA-WHAP!

KA-WHAP!

Though he had never flown *Slave I* alone, Boba knew all the controls and weapons systems by heart. Reaching over his head, he switched the main systems on, so the ship would be ready to go when his father got through whipping the Jedi.

Then he got an even better idea. He activated the blaster cannon controls.

Boba had practiced this so many times, he knew just how to do it. He got the Jedi in the sights and pressed FIRE.

SKA-PLANG!

A hit! Or almost.

The Jedi was thrown violently to the ground, his lightsaber knocked out of his hand. Boba was about to fire again and finish him off when his father got in the way.

Jango rocketed down from the building and stood face-to-face with the Jedi.

The Jedi charged.

Jango charged back.

Cool! thought Boba. He had never seen his father in hand-to-hand combat before, and it was awesome.

The Jedi's mysterious Force was no match for Jango Fett's Mandalorian body armor. The Jedi was losing — badly. He got desperate and made a grab, but Jango used his jet-pack to blast up and kick him away.

"Go!" shouted Boba, even though he knew no one could hear.

The Jedi fell and slid toward the edge of the landing pad, where it projected out over the crashing waves. He seemed to be using his so-called Force to get his lightsaber back, but Jango Fett spoiled that plan. From his wrist gauntlet, he shot out a restraining wire, which wrapped around the Jedi's wrists.

Then Jango fired up his jet-pack again, dragging the Jedi toward the edge of the platform — and the water.

"Go, Dad!" Boba shouted.

But the Jedi was able to catch the wire on a column. It stopped his slide and pulled him to his feet. Then he yanked on the wire. . . .

SPROINNGG!!

Jango hit the platform, hard. His jet-pack flared, spat . . . and exploded.

BARRROOOM!

Oh, no! Boba saw the whole thing. He tried to get a shot with the laser, but now both men were sliding toward the edge of the platform — and the huge waves crashing below.

"Dad!" Boba yelled. "Dad!" He banged on the cockpit canopy, as if his fists and his cries could somehow stop his father's slide toward certain death —

But it wasn't over yet. Jango Fett ejected the wire from his wrist gauntlet, freeing himself. Then he used the gripping claws built into his battle armor to stop his slide at the last instant.

Meanwhile, the Jedi slid right over the edge.

Boba fell back in his seat, shaking with relief: His father was safe. And triumph: The Jedi was gone!

Over the edge. Into the sea.

Good riddance! Boba thought.

The ramp was opening.

Boba scrambled out of the pilot's seat just in time.

His father leaped into the seat. The engines roared to life, and the starship lifted off into the storm, which was raging all around.

Boba looked down at the waves. There was no sign of the Jedi, and no wonder. Who could swim in that stupid robe? It had dragged him under, for sure.

"Life is hard for the small and the weak!" Boba said under his breath, and they hurtled upward, into the clouds.

"What, Boba?"

"I said, 'Good going, Dad!'"

CHAPTER SEVEN

Boba had been in space before, traveling with his father. But when you are real little, you don't notice a lot.

Now that he was ten, he understood what he was seeing. Everything looked new and exciting.

On Kamino it was almost always cloudy. The clouds were gray on the bottom, and black as night on the inside. But from above, they were as white as the snow Boba had seen in vids and read about in books.

The sky above was bright, bright blue.

Then, as *Slave I* rose higher and higher, the sky grew darker — blue-black, then inky black. Then Boba saw something even more beautiful than the clouds.

Stars.

Boba knew what they were, of course. He had read about the stars; he had seen them in vids and pictures, and observed them personally on trips with his father to other planets. Yet he had never really paid attention. Little kids don't notice things that are *that* far away. And the stars were almost never visible from cloudy Kamino, even at night. But now he was ten, and now . . .

Boba saw a million stars, each light-years away.

"Wow," he said.

"What is it, Boba?" his father asked.

Boba didn't know what to say. The galaxy was made of a million suns, burning fiercely. Around each sun were planets, each made of a million rocks and stones, and each stone was made of millions of atoms, and . . .

"It's the galaxy," Boba said. "Why is there . . . ?"

"Why is there what, Boba?"

"Why is there so much of it?"

Jango Fett let his son "fly" *Slave I*, which meant just sitting in the pilot's seat while the autopilot flew the ship. He was busy fitting his battle armor with a new jet-pack to replace the one that had blown up in the fight with the Jedi.

When he was done, he got into the pilot's seat, and Boba asked, "Are we moving to another world, Dad?"

"For now."

"Which one?"

"You'll see."

"Why?"

"Why are you asking so many questions?"

That was Boba's signal to shut up. His father

had his reasons for everything, but he usually kept them to himself.

"You don't want to know," Jango Fett said as he hit the button marked HYPERSPACE.

If space was awesome, hyperspace was double awesome.

Double awesome strange.

As soon as *Slave I* shifted into lightspeed and slipped into hyperspace, Boba's head started to spin. The stars were flying past like raindrops. It was like a dream, with far and near twisted together, time and space mixed like oil and water, in swirls.

Boba dozed off, because even strange becomes tiring when *everything* is strange. . . .

Boba dreamed he was meeting the mother he had never had. He was at a big reception in a palace, and he was alone. It was like a story in a book. There was someone coming toward him, making her way through the crowd. She was beautiful, in a white dress. She was walking toward Boba, faster and faster, and her smile was as bright as . . .

"Boba?"

"Yes!?"

"Wake up, son."

Boba opened his eyes and saw his father at the controls of *Slave I*. They were out of hyperspace, back in "normal," three-dimensional space.

They were floating. Directly ahead of them was a huge red planet with orange rings.

It was beautiful, but not as beautiful as the vision Boba had seen in his dream, coming toward him across the ballroom floor. Not as beautiful as . . . Boba felt himself slipping back into his dream.

"Geonosis," said Jango Fett.

"What?" Boba sat up.

"Name of the planet. Geonosis."

As *Slave I* approached Geonosis, it headed toward the rings. Only from a distance were they smooth and beautiful. Up close, Boba could see that the rings were made out of asteroids and meteors, lumps of rock and ice — space rubble.

Up close they were dangerous and ugly.

Jango's hands were dancing over the starship's controls, switching them from autopilot to manual. Flying under the rings would be tricky. As he expertly eased the ship into approach orbit, he said, "Next time, when we get to a planet that's easier to land on, I'll let you fly the approach on your own, son."

"Really, Dad? Does that mean I'm old enough?"

Jango patted his son on the shoulder. "Just about, Boba. Just about."

Boba leaned back, smiling. Life was better than dreams. Who needed a mom when you had a dad like Jango Fett?

Suddenly Boba caught a glimpse of something on the rear vid screen. A blip. "Dad, I think we're being tracked!"

Jango's smile disappeared. The blip was matching their every turn. A ship on their tail.

"Look at the sensor screen," Boba said excitedly. "Isn't that a cloaking shadow?"

Jango switched the sensor screen to higher res. It showed a tracker attached to the hull of *Slave I*.

Boba couldn't believe it. Hadn't he watched the Jedi slide into the stormy sea of Kamino? How could the Jedi have survived to follow them?

"He must have put a tracking device on our hull during the fight," said Jango, with the steel of determination in his voice. "We'll fix that!"

Boba was just about to ask *how*, when his dad pushed him back into his seat.

"Hang on, son. We'll move into the asteroid field. He won't be able to follow us there. If he does, we'll leave him a couple of surprises."

CHAPTER EIGHT

Into the asteroid field! Boba felt a cold touch of fear as his father pulled back on the controls and *Slave I* slid upward, into the ring itself.

Jagged rocks zipped past, on either side. It was like flying through a forest of stone.

Boba couldn't look. And he couldn't not look, either. He knew that if they hit one, they were dead.

Obliterated.

Erased.

They wouldn't even leave a ripple on the galaxy.

Then Boba told himself: *Stop worrying. Look who's at the controls!*

Boba kept his eyes on his father. The asteroids were still zipping past *Slave I* but they didn't seem quite as scary.

Jango Fett was at the controls.

Boba relaxed and checked the rear viewscreen. "He's gone," he told his father.

"He must have gone on toward the surface," Jango replied.

Suddenly the image on the viewscreen wavered

with a rogue signal. In the static Boba saw a familiar outline.

The Delta-7.

"Look, Dad, he's back!"

Jango calmly hit a button on the weaponry console marked SONIC CHARGE: RELEASE.

Boba looked back and saw a canister drifting toward the Jedi starfighter.

He grinned. So long! The Jedi was doomed. . . .

And so was Boba. Because when he turned back around in his seat and looked forward, he saw nothing but stone. *Slave I* was heading straight for a huge, jagged asteroid!

"Dad! Watch out!"

Jango's voice was quiet and cold as he pulled *Slave I* into a steep climb, barely missing the killer rock. "Stay calm, son. We'll be fine. That Jedi won't be able to follow us through this."

That was the plan, anyway. But the Jedi had other ideas. As his father deftly guided *Slave I* through the asteroid field, Boba kept his eyes on the rear screen.

"There he is!" he cried.

The Jedi starfighter was still there, right on their tail. It was as if it were tied to *Slave I*.

Jango shook his head grimly. "He doesn't seem

to be able to take a hint. Well, if we can't lose him, we'll have to finish him."

Hitting a button, he turned the starship and headed straight toward another asteroid, even bigger than the last one.

Only this time, he didn't pull up. Instead, he flew straight toward the jagged surface.

Boba couldn't believe it. Was his own father trying to kill them both? "Watch out!" he cried.

He closed his eyes, waiting for the explosion. *So this is what it's like to die*, he thought. He felt amazingly calm. He wondered how badly it would hurt when they hit. Or would it just be like a flash of light? Or . . .

Or nothing.

With Jango Fett at the controls, *Slave I* never slowed, never hesitated.

It looked like certain death.

The ship dove straight down into a narrow canyon on the asteroid's surface.

At the bottom was a cave, with an opening just big enough for a small starship turned on its side.

Just barely big enough . . .

* * *

Something was wrong.

Nothing had happened. Boba was still alive.

He opened his eyes.

He saw rock everywhere. His dad had flown full speed into a hole in the asteroid, and now *Slave I* was speeding through a narrow, winding tunnel.

But going slower and slower.

At least we're still alive, thought Boba. *But if the Jedi is chasing us, why are we slowing down?*

He soon found out. The tunnel went all the way through the asteroid. When *Slave I* emerged from the stone passage, it was right behind the Jedi starfighter.

The hunted had become the hunter. *Slave I* was on the Jedi's tail.

It was the coolest maneuver Boba had ever imagined. He could hardly control his excitement.

"Get him, Dad! Get him! Fire!"

Boba didn't have to tell his father. Jango Fett was already blasting away. On every side of the Jedi starfighter deadly lasers were stitching streaks of light through the blackness of space.

"You got him!" Boba cried, when he saw the Jedi starfighter rocked by an explosion.

A near-miss, but not a kill.

Not yet.

"We'll just have to finish him!" said Jango. He reached up to the weaponry console and, with two quick flicks of his wrist, hit two switches:

TORPEDO: ARM

and then

TORPEDO: RELEASE

It was *Slave I*'s turn to rock as the torpedo kicked out of the hull and locked onto the Jedi starfighter.

Boba watched, fascinated. The Jedi was good, he had to admit. He zigged, he zagged, he tried every kind of evasive maneuver.

But the torpedo was locked on, and closing.

Then the Jedi starfighter flew straight into the path of a huge, tumbling asteroid —

And it was all over.

There was no way to avoid the collision. Caught between the torpedo's blast and the unforgiving stone, the Jedi starfighter disappeared. Only a trail of debris remained.

"Got him . . ." Boba breathed. "Yeaaaah!"

Jango's reaction was more subdued. "We won't see him again," he said quietly as he guided the ship out of the asteroids and put it into a descent pattern, down toward the giant red planet.

CHAPTER NINE

Boba had thought Geonosis might be different from Kamino, with schools, other kids, and lots to do.

It was different, all right, but that was all.

On Kamino it rained all the time; on Geonosis it hardly ever rained. Kamino was all sea; Geonosis was a sea of red sand, with big rock towers called stalagmites sticking up like spikes, here and there, from the sandy desert.

In fact, the planet looked deserted. At least that's what Boba thought when he first arrived.

Jango Fett landed *Slave I* on a ledge on the side of one of the stalagmites, or rock towers.

Are we going to camp here on this rock? wondered Boba as the ship settled on its landing struts and the engines died.

Then a door in the stone slid open, and Maintenance Droids appeared to service the ship.

Boba was wide-eyed as he followed his father through the doorway, which turned out to be the entrance to a vast underground city, with long corridors and huge rooms, all connected and lighted with glow tubes, echoing with footsteps and shouts.

Yet it still seemed empty. The only inhabitants were hurrying, distant shadows. No one greeted them; no one even noticed a ten-year-old tagging along after his father.

As they climbed the stairs toward the apartment they had been temporarily assigned, Jango explained to his son that the Geonosians themselves were drones who worked all the time. Their planet was a manufacturing center for Battle Droids. "And the people who make the droids aren't much smarter or more interesting than the droids themselves," Jango said.

"So why are we here?" Boba asked.

"Business," said Jango Fett. "*He who hires my hand . . .*"

"*. . . hires my whole self,*" finished Boba, grinning up at his dad.

"Right," said Jango. He rumpled his son's hair and smiled down at him. "I'm very proud of you, son. You're growing up to be a bounty hunter, just like your old man."

The apartment was high in the stone tower, overlooking the desert. Jango went off to meet with his employer, leaving Boba with a stern warning: "Be here when I get back."

After a couple of hours alone in the apartment, Boba knew that his first impressions had been right. Geonosis was boring. Even more boring than Kamino.

Boredom is kind of like a microscope. It can make little things look big. Boba counted all the stones in the walls of the apartment. He counted all the cracks in the floor.

Bored with cracks and stones, he stared out the narrow window, watching the dust storms roll across the plains and watching the rings wheel across the sky above.

Boba wished he had brought some books. The only one he had was the black book his father had given him, the one he couldn't open. It was in a box with his clothes and old toys, not even worth looking for.

He'd have to make his own excitement. But how?

Be here when I get back. That didn't mean he couldn't leave the apartment. Just that he couldn't go very far.

Boba stepped out into the hallway, closing the door behind him. The stone corridor was dim and quiet. In the distance Boba could hear a booming noise. It sounded almost like the sea on stormy Kamino.

Could there be an ocean here, on this desert planet?

Boba walked to the end of the corridor and stuck his head around the corner. The booming was louder. Now it sounded like a distant drum.

Around the corner there was a stone stairway, leading down. At the bottom the stairs, another hall. At the end of the hall, another stairway.

Stone steps, leading down, into the darkness. Boba followed them, feeling his way, one step at a time. The farther he went, the darker it got.

The darker it got, the louder the booming. It sounded like a giant beating a drum.

Boba had the feeling he had gone too far, but he didn't want to turn back. Not yet. Not until he had discovered what was making the booming noise.

Then a last, long spiral staircase ended in a narrow hallway. The hallway ended at a heavy door. The booming was so loud that the door itself was shaking.

Boba was almost afraid to look. He was about to turn back. Then, in his mind, he heard his father's voice: *Do that which you fear most, and you will find the courage you seek.*

Boba pulled the door open.

BOOM

BOOM

BOOM

There was no wild ocean storm, no giant beating a drum. But Boba was not disappointed. What he saw was even more amazing.

He was looking into a vast underground room, lighted by glowing lamps, and filled with moving shapes. As his eyes adjusted to the dim light, he could see a long assembly line, where huge metal machines were stamping out arms and legs, wheels and blades, heads and torsos. The noise was thunderous. The heavy, rust-colored parts, once stamped, were carried on clattering belts to a central area, where they were assembled by grim-faced Geonosians into warlike Battle Droids, which snapped to attention as soon as their heads were screwed on.

The assembled droids then marched in long lines out of the cavern, through a high, arched doorway, into the darkness.

Boba watched, fascinated. What was the purpose of all these weapons of war? It was hard to believe that there was room in the galaxy for so many Battle Droids and droidekas bristling with blades and blasters.

He imagined them all in action, fighting one another. It was exciting to think about — and a little scary, too.

"Hey, you there!"

Boba looked up. A Security Droid was hurrying his way, across a cartwalk toward the open door.

Rather than explain who he was and what he was doing, Boba decided to do the sensible thing.

He slammed the door and ran.

Be here when I get back, Jango had said. Boba was just shutting the apartment door behind him when he heard footsteps in the hall outside.

Barely made it! thought Boba as his father opened the door.

Two men were with him. One of them was a Geonosian, wearing the elaborate finery of a high official over its branchlike body and barrel-shaped head. The other was more simply dressed, but somehow familiar.

"And so you see, Count Dooku, we have made great progress," said the Geonosian.

It was the *Count* that did it. Boba recognized the other man. "Isn't that Count Tyranus?" Boba asked his father, who was hanging up his battle helmet beside the door.

"Sssshhhhh," said Jango. "We are the only ones who know him by that name."

"Ah, so this is the young one?" the Count said. "You'll be a great bounty hunter someday."

He patted Boba on the head. The gesture was affectionate but the hand was cold, and Boba felt a chill.

"Yes, sir," he said, pulling away.

His father shot him a stern, disapproving look as the three men walked into the apartment's kitchen for their conference.

Boba felt ashamed. He had been rude. The chill must have been his imagination. Count Tyranus was Jango Fett's main employer. Boba owed him not only respect, but trust.

You'll be a great bounty hunter someday. The Count's words rang in Boba's head. He hoped someday they would come true.

His father's battle helmet was hanging by the door. Boba took it down and carried it into the bedroom.

He wanted to see what it looked like from inside. He wanted to feel how it felt to be Jango Fett.

He shut the door behind him and pulled the helmet over his head. He opened his eyes and —

"Wow!"

Boba had expected it to be dark inside the helmet, but it wasn't. There were all sorts of displays scrolling down the inside of the faceplate. Most of them were for weapons and survival systems:

ROCKET DARTS

SONIC BEAM

WRIST GAUNTLET

JET-PACK

BOOT SPIKES

COMLINK

RANGEFINDER

It was like being in the control room of a very small, compact, efficient ship. But it was too heavy. Boba could hardly move his head. He was just lifting it off when —

Click.

Boba heard the bedroom door open. Uh-oh. Now he was in big trouble!

But no — Jango Fett was laughing as he lifted the helmet off Boba's head. "Don't worry, son, your own armor will fit you better."

Boba looked up into his father's eyes. "My own?"

"When you are older," Jango said. "This battle armor was given to me by the Mandalores. You will have your own someday, when you become a bounty hunter."

"And you will teach me to use it?" Boba asked.

"When that day comes, I may not be there," Jango said. "You may be on your own."

"But . . ."

"No buts," said Jango. He attempted a smile. "Don't worry. Your time is yet to come."

He reached out and patted Boba on the head.

This time, there was no chill.

*   *   *

Later that night, Boba heard a strange noise. It was not the booming he had heard before. It was not his father's snores, which came from the next bed.

OOWOOOO!

It was something far away and incredibly lonely.

He went to the narrow window and looked out. The night on Geonosis was as bright as day had been on cloudy Kamino. The planet's orange rings shed a soft light over the desert sands.

There was a red mesa right below the stalagmite city. It was crisscrossed with faint trails that glittered, as if they were paved with diamonds.

The mesa looked interesting but it was strictly off-limits. Jango Fett had said that there were fierce beasts called massiffs that prowled the rocks and cliffs.

OOWOOOO!

There it was again — that lonesome, mournful howl. *A massiff,* thought Boba. It sounded more forlorn than fierce.

He knew the feeling.

He wanted to howl back.

CHAPTER TEN

When Boba woke up, his father was gone. On the table there was breakfast and a note: *Be here when I get back.*

Boba was out the door.

He heard the distant booming but he went the other way, down to the landing platform. *Slave I* was no longer the only starship. It looked tiny compared to the others, which came in all shapes and sizes, but were mostly bigger.

Boba made sure no one was looking, then climbed up the ramp into the cockpit of *Slave I*. The seat was a little low, but other than that, it felt right. He had already memorized the flight controls for both space and atmosphere. He already knew the weapons systems, the multiple lasers and torpedoes. His dad had taught him most of it, and he had figured out the rest for himself.

Boba knew how to start the ship, program the navcomputer, and engage the hyperdrive. He was sure that before long his father would let him try a complete takeoff and landing. He wanted to be ready.

He imagined he was piloting the ship while his father was mowing down his enemies with the laser.

"*Beware the wrath of the Fetts!*" he cried in triumph as he zigged and zagged through the enemy fighters. . . .

"Hey —"

Boba sat up — he must have fallen asleep! He must have been dreaming.

"Hey, kid!"

It was a Geonosian guard.

"It's okay," Boba said. "It's my dad's ship."

He got out of *Slave I* and closed the ramp.

The Geonosian had a stupid but amiable expression.

"How come there's nothing to do around here?" Boba asked, just to be friendly.

The Geonosian guard smiled and twirled his blaster. "Oh, plenty to do!" he said. "There's arena! Really cool!"

"What happens in the arena?"

"Kill things!" said the Geonosian.

Interesting, thought Boba. It was something to do. "Every day?" he asked eagerly.

"Oh, no," said the Geonosian. "Only special occasions."

*   *   *

Rules.

Rules are made to be broken.

That was *not* part of Jango Fett's code. *But it is part of the Kids' Code,* thought Boba. *Anyway, it oughta be.*

Boba was making excuses. He was getting ready to break his father's Off-Limits Rule.

He was preparing to slip out of the stalagmite city, to the red mesa.

He was trying to pretend it was all right, that it was something he had to do.

He was looking for adventure.

And he was about to find it.

The first part was easy.

The main door to the stalagmite city was on ground level, down below the landing pad. It was guarded by a drowsy Geonosian sentry, whose job was to watch for intruders, not escapees.

It was easy to slip past him.

As soon as he breathed the outside air, Boba realized how much he hated the musty smell of the stalagmite city. It was great to be outside!

He wanted to explore the glittering trails he had seen from above. He followed the first one he saw. It led down the side of the red rock mesa. The glitter was chips of mica — rock as smooth and shiny as glass that marked the trail and made it easy to follow.

Boba was just rounding a corner on a steep cliff when he heard a scream.

Then a growling noise.

He stopped — then proceeded more cautiously, step by step.

On the narrow trail ahead, two spike-backed beasts were fighting. They were growling, each pulling at one end of what looked like a furry rope.

The rope was hissing in a high-pitched tone.

The rope was a ten-foot snake, covered with fur. Its mouth and eyes were in the center of its long, furry body.

The lizards, which Boba assumed were the dreaded massiffs, were about to tear it in half with their long, razor-sharp teeth.

Then they saw Boba — and dropped the snake.

Boba backed up one step.

The massiffs both moved forward one step. Growling.

Boba backed up another step. The cliff was to his right. To his left, and behind him — nothing but air.

The massiffs moved forward again. Two steps this time.

Snarling.

Boba kept his stare locked on the massiffs' red eyes. He felt that if he looked away for even an instant, they would charge.

They moved forward again, side by side.

Boba knelt down and, feeling with one hand, picked up a slice of mica. Without looking, he tested it with his fingers. It was as sharp as a knife.

Suddenly he jumped up and threw it, spinning, toward the massiff on the right.

YELP!

A hit! But the other massiff was in the air, leaping toward Boba. He heard a snarl, and felt hot breath on his face, and ducked his head, and . . .

OOWOOOO!

The massiff missed him and flew off the cliff, howling as it fell toward the jagged rocks below.

Boba straightened up.

The other massiff was bleeding over one red eye. It was backing up, slinking away. . . .

Then it turned and ran.

The snake lay on the trail, nursing its wounds.

Boba's heart was pounding.

Maybe breaking the rules is not such a good idea, he thought. He was lucky to be alive.

He considered turning back — but decided that would be pointless. He was already halfway around the mesa. So he stepped over the dazed snake and continued on the path.

He had seen the path from above. He knew it would lead back to the entrance. He would sneak back in, and his father would never know he had been outside.

Then he heard something behind him. Something on the path.

The wounded massiff?

Boba felt a sudden chill. He looked back over his shoulder. It was the snake.

It was slithering along after him.

Boba stopped.

The snake stopped.

Its mouth in the middle of its body was smiling — at least it seemed to be smiling. And it was singing, a sort of rushing sound, like water falling. It sounded strange out here in the desert. It reminded Boba of the rain on Kamino, or the waves.

"Go away," said Boba.

The snake kept singing. It slithered a little closer.

Boba backed up. "Go away!"

The snake slithered still closer. Boba picked up a rock — a sharp piece of mica.

"Go away."

The snake looked sad. It stopped singing. It slithered away into the rocks.

Boba was making his way up the path, toward the top of the mesa, when he saw something strange.

There, on a flat ledge under a cliff on the side of the mesa, was a small ship. A starship.

A Delta-7! Could it be . . . ?

Just then Boba heard someone — or something — behind him on the trail.

He ducked behind a rock just in time.

The man who hurried past him along the trail was as familiar as the starship. As familiar, and as unwelcome.

It was the Jedi who had pursued them through the asteroid rings. The Jedi the torpedo had blasted. Obi-Wan Kenobi. Back again!

Boba watched from behind his rock as the Jedi opened his starfighter's hatch and climbed into the cockpit. Boba thought he was about to take off, but he didn't bother to close the hatch.

Whatever the Jedi was up to, Boba knew it was no good. He had to stop him. But how?

From where he was hiding, Boba could see over the rim of the mesa, all the way to the entrance to the stalagmite city. There was the drowsy Geonosian sentry he had slipped past.

The Jedi's starship was hidden from the sentry — but Boba wasn't.

But how could Boba raise an alert?

Boba picked up the biggest piece of mica he could find and wiped it on his sleeve until it shined like glass. Then he used it to reflect the light from Geonosis's sun, which was just peeping over the rings. He tilted the mica slab back and forth until he could see a flash of light across the sentry's eyes.

Then he did it again. And again.

Had the sentry seen it?

He had! He was coming down the path, toward the mesa's edge. Boba couldn't risk being seen, so he left the trail and scrambled up a steep ledge to the top of the mesa. When he got to the top of the mesa, he saw the Geonosian guard at the edge of the cliff, looking down. Boba knew he had sighted the Jedi starfighter, because he was talking excitedly on his comm.

Success! Or so it seemed. Boba ran toward the base of the tower — then skidded to a stop.

The gate was closed. He was stuck outside. How could he get inside without being discovered?

Then he got lucky again. The gate suddenly swung open and out came a squad of droidekas. They were in such a hurry to capture the Jedi that they didn't notice Boba, flattened against the rock wall.

He was able to slip through the door just before it closed behind the droidekas.

Safe! Boba was just about to breathe a sigh of relief when he felt a strong metal gauntlet on his shoulder. It felt gentle, yet stern.

"Where you heading, son?" asked Jango Fett. "Where have you been?"

"Uh, outside. Sir."

"Come upstairs. We need to talk."

Boba followed his father up the stairs and into the apartment. There was nothing he could say. There was nothing he could do. He was found out, and he knew it.

He sat down on the couch and watched while his father took off his battle armor and laid it carefully on the floor.

"Another adventure?" Jango Fett asked with a slight smile as he brewed himself a cup of nasty Geonosian grub-tea.

"I'm really sorry," Boba said. "Really really sorry."

"Sorry for what?" his father asked.

"Disobeying you."

"And that's all?"

"I-I guess," Boba said.

"What about lying to me?"

"I didn't lie," said Boba. "I admitted I was outside."

His father's smile was gone. "Only because you were caught. If you hadn't been . . ."

"I guess I would have," said Boba. "I'm sorry for that, too."

"I accept your apology, then," said Jango. "As a punishment you are confined to quarters until I say otherwise."

"Yes, sir." Boba breathed a sigh of relief. Confined to quarters meant grounded; it meant he had to stay in the apartment. It wasn't as bad as he had expected.

"It would be worse," said Jango Fett, "except that I owe you one."

"You do?!"

"Sure. For our Jedi friend. The one who somehow managed to escape us in the asteroids. He's been captured now, thanks to you. You alerted the sentry, even though it meant you might get in trouble. You did the right thing."

"Yes, sir. Thank you, Dad. I am sorry I disobeyed you."

"I am, too, Boba," said Jango Fett with a smile. "But I'm proud, as well."

"You are?!"

"I would be worried if you didn't disobey me at least once in your life. It's part of growing up. Part of the process of gaining your independence."

Boba didn't know what to say. Did his father really believe he had only disobeyed him this one time?

So he tried to hide his smile, and didn't say anything.

CHAPTER ELEVEN

Confined to quarters.

It could have been worse. But it was still pretty bad. Boba's lonely life got lonelier now that he was stuck in the apartment.

Jango Fett was very busy, talking business with the Count and the Geonosian they called Archduke, among others. Boba knew better than to try to sneak out.

Confined to quarters.

Boba missed his library friend, Whrr.

He was trying to construct a model starfighter from bits of wire when the door suddenly opened.

There in his battle armor stood Jango Fett. "Come, son," was all he said.

That was all he *had* to say!

Boba scrambled to his feet and followed his father down the stairs. He was glad to get out of the apartment, for any reason. And he always felt proud, following his dad. He knew that anyone who saw them was thinking:

That's Jango Fett. And that's Boba, his kid. He'll be a bounty hunter, too, someday.

*   *   *

There was a hush in the dim underground halls. Boba could tell something important was happening. He wondered what it was.

He knew better than to ask. He was lucky enough just to be out of the apartment.

At the end of a long corridor, they encountered a milling crowd of Geonosians. Some had wings on their backs; others didn't. A uniformed sentry waved them through, to the head of the line, and into a huge room with tall ceilings. Though the room was filled with Geonosians, it was so big it seemed almost empty. Every footstep and every cough echoed.

The Archduke and some other officials were seated in a sort of high box at one end of the imposing room, with about a hundred Genosians looking on. Two people stood looking up at them. Something about the way they stood told Boba they were prisoners. But proud, rebellious prisoners.

Jango and Boba squeezed into a crowd of Geonosians at the side of the room.

Somebody banged on something and the room got quiet. Almost, anyway. Everybody turned to look at the prisoners. Boba had to stand on tiptoe to get a good view.

One prisoner was dressed like a Jedi. He was a lot younger than the Jedi called Obi-Wan.

Maybe he's an apprentice, Boba thought. Though why anybody would want to be a Jedi was beyond him.

The other prisoner was a woman. And not just any woman. She was the most beautiful woman Boba had ever seen. She had a kind, gentle face — the sort of face he had always imagined his mother might have had, if he'd had a mother.

"You have been charged and found guilty of espionage," said one of the Geonosians.

Another chimed in: "Do you have anything to say before your sentence is carried out?"

The woman spoke up proudly. "You are committing an act of war, Archduke. I hope you are prepared for the consequences."

The Archduke laughed. "We build weapons, Senator. That is our business. Of course we are prepared."

Senator. Boba was shocked. He pulled his father's arm. "What's a Senator doing here, as a prisoner?"

"Shhhhhh!" Jango hissed.

"Get on with it!" demanded another official, a Neimoidian with mottled green skin and bright red eyes. "Carry out the sentence. I want to see her suffer."

It was the *other* Jedi that Boba wanted to see suffer, not the wannabe — and certainly not the woman. The persistent Jedi. The one they had killed again and again. Jedi Obi-Wan Kenobi.

But where was he?

The Archduke answered Boba's question. "Your other Jedi friend is waiting for you, Senator. Take them to the arena."

The arena! Finally they were going to get to see some action. It was what Boba had been waiting for.

And yet, somehow, he dreaded it.

CHAPTER TWELVE

Like almost everything else on Geonosis, the arena was carved out of solid rock. Yet because it was open at the top, the arena was the brightest place in the entire underground city.

The seats were filled with excited Geonosians, all flapping their wings and screaming with excitement, even though nothing was happening yet.

Vendors in bright costumes worked their way through the stands, singing and whistling to advertise their trays of live insects and other Geonosian treats. Boba loved it, even though he wasn't tempted by the squirming tidbits. He could hardly believe his luck. He was out of the apartment, no longer confined to quarters. He was in the arena, about to see a show. Plus, he and his father had the best seats in the house.

They were sitting with the Archduke and the other officials. Jango Fett and Boba followed the Count into the official box. The crowd started cheering wildly, and, at first, Boba thought it might be for his father, or even for the Count.

Then he looked down toward the center of the arena and saw the entertainment.

The Jedi prisoners.

They were chained to three posts: the young Jedi to one; the Jedi called Obi-Wan to another; and the beautiful woman to the third.

A fat Geonosian official cleared his throat and stood up to make a speech.

"The felons before you have been convicted of espionage against the sovereign system of Geonosis. Their sentence of death is to be carried out in this public arena henceforth."

The crowd was cheering like crazy, and the fat Geonosian sat down, smiling, as if he thought the cheering were for him.

The littlest Geonosian official stood up and waved his stubby arms. "Let the executions begin!"

Boba had mixed feelings. He hated the older Jedi, Obi-Wan, who had gotten lucky and humiliated Jango Fett by escaping twice.

Boba wanted to watch him die.

The apprentice Jedi, he didn't care about one way or the other. The problem was the woman. Boba didn't want to watch her die. Not at all.

One of the Neimoidians did, though. He was rubbing his chubby hands together so hard that they were starting to get red.

Boba looked away, disgusted. *It's guys like him who give executions a bad name,* he thought.

The crowd suddenly roared even louder.

And no wonder! Three barred gates down in the arena were opening. Riders in fancy costumes, mounted on orrays, were poking at monsters with sticks and spears, driving them into the central ring.

And what monsters! Boba recognized them all from books.

The first was a reek, a sort of killer steed with razor-sharp horns.

The second one was a golden-maned nexu with claws and sharp fangs.

And the third was an acklay, a monster with large, clenching claws, big enough to cut an orray in half with one pinch.

The crowd loved it, and why not? This was what the execution arena was all about. Death for fun.

Boba was even starting to get into it, a little bit.

The prisoners weren't, though. The woman had gotten out of her chains somehow and climbed to the top of her post.

Go! Boba thought. Even though he knew it was wrong, he hoped she would escape. He even had a fantasy that he would help her. Then she would join him to enjoy watching the two Jedi get killed.

Of course, Boba knew such a fantasy was ridiculous. No one would escape. What was happening down in the arena was an entertainment, but it was also an execution.

The reek was running around the arena, slashing at the air with its horn and, it seemed to Boba, enjoying the wild cheers of the crowd. Then the great beast got serious. It charged the young Jedi's post.

WHAM! The reek hit the post a smashing blow, while the Jedi dodged sideways as far as his chain would let him. Then the Jedi jumped up, chain and all, onto the reek's back, which was, for him at least, the safest spot in the whole arena.

Cool move! Boba thought, in spite of himself.

Then the young Jedi did something even cooler. He wrapped the chain around the reek's horn, so that when the beast backed up and shook its head, the chain was torn free from the post.

Now the Jedi had a chain he could swing like a whip.

Boba cheered. Like the rest of the crowd, he was cheering for the reek.

The other Jedi, Obi-Wan, shifted deftly as the monster knocked the post flat, snapping it in two — and breaking the chain at the same time.

The nexu was after the woman. Its long fangs were bared, and it was trying to claw its way to the

top of the post where she was perched, barely holding on.

Boba closed his eyes.

This one he did *not* want to watch.

The crowd groaned. AAAAAWWWWWW!

Boba opened his eyes. The Jedi Obi-Wan had
grabbed a spear somewhere. He was using it to
pole-vault over one of the orray riders. The acklay
chasing him rammed into the rider and his orray,
knocking them both flat. The acklay opened its
huge claw, and then —

CRRRRRRUNCH!

It was the rider, an employee of the arena, who
had been pinched in half. But the crowd of
Geonosians didn't care. They just wanted to see
blood. They didn't care whose blood it was.

Meanwhile, the young apprentice Jedi was riding
the reek. He was using the chain for a bridle, con-
trolling the beast.

The woman was still trying to get away from the
nexu, which had ripped her shirt. Using her chain
like a swing, she flew through the air, kicking the
nexu into the sand and injuring its leg. Then she
landed back on top of the post, out of reach.

Go! Boba thought again. Only to himself, of
course.

The apprentice Jedi rode up on the reek, the
beast completely under his control. The woman

jumped on behind him. The nexu spat and snarled with rage — and then was attacked and killed by the reek. The Jedi called Obi-Wan jumped up behind the woman, so there were three of them on the reek, charging around the arena.

The crowd went wild. They weren't exactly cheering the gang of criminals — but they loved the excitement.

Boba cheered, too. He was glad to see the woman get away. So far, anyway.

It was all too much for the Neimoidian, though. He turned to Jango Fett. His beady little eyes were filled with rage.

"This isn't how it is supposed to be. Jango, finish her off!"

Boba watched, wondering what his dad would do. Jango didn't move.

The Neimoidian stared.

Jango Fett stared back.

The Count broke the silence.

"Patience, Viceroy," he said. "She will die."

A cheer went up and Boba looked down toward the arena.

The gates were opening again, all four of them this time. Droidekas rolled in, unfolding as they surrounded the prisoners, their blades gleaming wickedly in the light from the hole above the arena.

Before Boba could even blink, the droidekas had completely surrounded the three prisoners on their reek.

It was over.

Boba closed his eyes. He didn't want to watch. Then he heard a noise behind him.

A very slight clicking sound. He opened his eyes and turned, and saw a terrible sight.

A Jedi, standing behind his father.

The Jedi's face was dark, like fine wood. His eyes were narrow and cruel. His purple lightsaber was drawn, and ignited.

And held across Jango Fett's neck.

CHAPTER THIRTEEN

The Geonosians stopped cheering. The droid-ekas stopped advancing.

The reek, with the two Jedi and the beautiful woman on its back, stopped prancing and bucking and rearing. A hush fell over the entire arena and all eyes turned away from the Jedi and the droidekas. All of a sudden the show was not in the ring, but in the stands.

Everyone was staring at the officials' box, where the Jedi held the lightsaber to Jango Fett's neck.

We are the show! Boba realized with horror.

Jango Fett stood perfectly still. His Mandalorian battle armor was useless against a Jedi lightsaber. One flick of the Jedi's wrist and he would be decapitated.

Boba was scared.

As usual, the Count kept calm. Boba had noticed that he liked to turn everything into a game, even a bad situation. Even an emergency.

The Count seemed to know the Jedi.

"Master Windu," he said, in a smooth, oily voice, "how pleasant of you to join us. You're just in time for the moment of truth. I would think these two new boys of yours could use a little more training."

"Sorry to disappoint you," said the Jedi. "This party's over."

The Jedi gave a little hand signal. It looked to Boba as if lights were coming on all over the arena.

Lightsabers.

There were at least a hundred of them — some in the corners down by the ring, others up high in the stands. They came on all at once.

And each was in the hands of a Jedi.

Where had they come from? How had they all gotten in?

Boba was amazed at how bad the Geonosians' security was. And he was beginning to understand his father's grudging respect for the Jedi. They had their ways.

The Count, as always, tried to seem unimpressed. That was his style in a crisis.

"Brave but foolish, my old Jedi friend," he said. "You're impossibly outnumbered."

"I don't think so," said the Jedi called Windu.

He scanned the crowd with his hooded eyes. "The Geonosians aren't warriors. One Jedi has to be worth a hundred Geonosians."

But the Count came right back at him. "It wasn't the Geonosians I was thinking about."

It was the Count's turn to give a hand signal, even slighter and more subtle than the one the Jedi had given. Boba heard a sound like a storm on Kamino — a low rumble. Suddenly all the doors in the arena opened and every aisle in the stands was filled with Battle Droids.

The Battle Droids ran down the aisles with their lasers flashing, firing at the Jedi and scorching whatever else was in their way.

Lasers flashed overhead, and Boba ducked. The Jedi called Windu had gone from offense to defense in an instant. He was deflecting the droids' lasers with his lightsaber; it was like fencing with the air.

That was all Jango Fett needed. He crouched and fired the flamethrower that was built into his battle armor.

WHOOOOOSH!

Windu was engulfed in a torrent of orange flame, and his robe caught fire. It flared behind him like the exhaust of a rocket as the Jedi jumped out of the stands into the ring.

Jango let him go. He turned and went into action with the Battle Droids and the Geonosian troops, toasting the Jedi with vicious laser fire.

The Jedi all began to clump in the center of the arena, back-to-back, around the reek with the apprentice Jedi, Obi-Wan, and the beautiful woman still on its back.

The fight was on!

The reek wanted no part of it. It leaped into the air, throwing the three off its back. Then it ran in wild circles, snarling and snorting, stomping and stamping, crushing droids, Geonosian troops, Jedi, and bystanders under its hooves.

"Go!" Boba shouted, out loud this time. It didn't matter which side he was on — it was exciting to watch. Blood and bodies were flying. And the only person down there in the ring that he liked, the pretty woman, was unhurt, at least so far.

She was standing in the middle of the ring with the Jedi. Somebody had tossed her a blaster rifle. She was pretty good with it, too, blasting droids and Geos on all sides.

Jango was standing right beside Boba, taking a heavy toll from the stands, firing with deadly accuracy into the Jedi. It was the first time Boba had ever been in such a big battle with his father.

And he loved it!

"Stay down, Boba!" Jango ordered, and Boba knew better than to disobey. But he was able to peek over the railing and see down into the ring.

In the middle of all the confusion, Boba saw the Jedi called Mace Windu, the one his dad had scorched. He was mowing down droids and Geonosian troops with his lightsaber, rallying the Jedi with his boldness.

The reek saw him, too. The big, horned beast singled him out and started chasing him around the arena. Boba had to laugh. The Jedi had gone from hound to hare in about one second.

Mace Windu tried to make a stand. He skidded to a stop and slashed out at the reek with his lightsaber. But the reek kept coming — and knocked the lightsaber out of his hand.

It went flying, and the Jedi took off running again.

Jango Fett put his big, gloved hand on his son's head and growled, "Stay here, Boba. I'll be back!"

That turned out to be the last thing he ever told his only son.

CHAPTER FOURTEEN

Jango Fett used the jet-pack on his Mandalorian battle armor to rocket down into the arena. He landed right in the middle of the fighting. The runaway reek, which made no distinction between friend and foe, tried to stomp him.

From the stands, Boba saw his father dodging and rolling, trying to get out of the way. He bit his tongue to keep from screaming out. Those hooves were as sharp as knives.

But Boba needn't have worried. His dad rolled free, jumped to his feet, and proceeded to kill the beast. A couple of blasts and the reek was no more.

Then Jango Fett and the Jedi Mace Windu faced off, one-on-one, while the fight raged all around them.

Boba stood on tiptoe, trying to see, and at the same time dodging the bolts that were filling the air like angry insects. Super Battle Droids, more powerful than the Battle Droids, were now dominating the battle.

The dust rose in a cloud. The arena was filled with screams and shouts, the clash of lightsabers and bolts of laser fire. Boba yelled "Dad!" as he tried to see.

And then he saw.

He saw.

He saw the Jedi's lightsaber swing in a deadly arc. He saw his father's empty helmet go flying. He saw his father's body drop to its knees, as if in prayer.

Boba watched in breathless horror as Jango Fett fell lifeless onto the bloody sand.

"No!" Boba cried. *No, it can't be!*

The concussion from a nearby blast of laser fire knocked Boba down. He stumbled to his feet, ears ringing, and saw that the arena below was littered with bodies and pieces of droids and droidekas.

The acklay and the reek both were dead. The Jedi were outnumbered but still fighting. And the beautiful woman was right in the middle of it all, blasting droids and Geonosians alike.

Boba couldn't see his father or the Jedi he had been fighting. Had he dreamed it all? The swing of the lightsaber, the helmet flying off; the warrior falling to his knees, then toppling over, like a tree.

A bad dream, Boba decided. *That was it!* His father was somewhere back up in the stands. Boba knew that he didn't like to fight alongside droids. Jango Fett scorned the droids because they had no imagination. *Imagination*, he often said, *is a warrior's most important weapon.*

A bad dream, Boba thought, pushing his way down the stairs, toward the arena.

Even without imagination, the Super Battle Droids were winning. They were programmed to win, or at least to never give up. And even with all their losses, they far outnumbered the Jedi.

The droids in the stands kept firing, and the droids in the arena kept advancing, and soon there were only twenty or so Jedi left.

They stood in a clump in the center of the arena, back-to-back, lightsabers and lasers drawn. Trapped!

The aisles were full, so Boba climbed down from seat to seat, toward the arena. The Geonosians were cheering as the droids moved in for the kill. Then the Count raised his hand.

"Master Windu!"

Silence.

Boba stopped. *What's this?* He watched as the Jedi his father had been fighting stepped forward, covered with dust and sweat.

"You have fought gallantly," said the Count. "Worthy of recognition in . . ."

Boba didn't wait to hear more. He knew it was all a lie. It had to be.

He continued to jump from seat to seat, down toward the ring, pushing and shoving his way through the crowd.

He couldn't think. He didn't *want* to think. He just wanted to get into the ring and find his father, Jango Fett, who would tell him: *Don't worry, Boba, it was all a dream. A bad, bad dream.*

"Now it is finished," said the Count. "Surrender, and your lives will be spared."

"We will not be hostages for you to barter with, Dooku."

"Then I'm sorry, old friend," said the Count. "You will have to be destroyed."

The Count nodded and the droids were just about to fire into the little clump of Jedi, ending the whole thing, when all of a sudden the woman looked up.

All around the arena, the Geonosians started looking up.

Boba stopped and looked up, too.

Gunships were descending from the sky.

One, two, three gunships . . . six altogether.

They landed around the Jedi survivors. Doors in the ships opened and troops poured out, running down the ramps, firing at the droids. Boba knew the troops well, although he was surprised to see them. The Jedi began backing into the ships, still blocking laser blasts with their lightsabers.

The battle was on again, but Boba hardly noticed. He was running again, jumping from seat to seat, down toward the arena, as the gunships took off, with the Jedi still running up the ramps. Some were barely hanging on by their fingertips as the ships rose.

They were getting away. Not only the beautiful woman, but the Jedi he and his father hated. The Obi-Wan Jedi; the apprentice Jedi; the dark-faced fighter called Mace Windu. They were all escaping!

Boba didn't care. All he cared about was finding his father. He ran down the last aisle, pushing his way through the stunned crowd.

He climbed over the wall and jumped into the arena.

"Dad! Dad! Where are you?!"

The dirt and sand under his feet were soaked with blood. Bodies lay in heaps on all sides.

A droid that had been blasted in half was thrashing around in a circle, kicking weapons, droid pieces, and bodies in every direction.

One piece rolled toward Boba, hit his foot, and stopped.

Boba looked down and saw — Jango Fett's battle helmet.

Dad! With its narrow eye-slits, it was as familiar as his father's face. More familiar, in fact.

It was bloody. It was empty. It was as blank and as final as the period at the end of a book.

Over. End of story.

As he fell on his knees and picked up his father's battle helmet, Boba knew that the nightmare he had seen from the stands had been no dream.

It was real. All of it.

CHAPTER FIFTEEN

No one notices a ten-year-old kid, especially in the midst of a battle.

Especially when he is wandering in a daze, stepping over bodies and trails of blood, oblivious to the laser bolts whining through the air near his head or spinning into the bloody sand at his feet.

Especially when he is ignoring the shouts of the living and the screams of the dying; ignoring even his own cries.

Boba was invisible.

He was invisible even to himself. He didn't know what he was thinking or what he was feeling or what he was doing. He was numb. It was like walking through somebody else's dream.

He carried his father's empty battle helmet cradled in both arms, while he stumbled around the arena in the remains of the battle; while the troops were fighting the last of the droids and the gunships were departing with the rescued Jedi; while the panicked Geonosians were evacuating the arena in a stampede.

He carried the broken piece of his father's armor through the broken pieces of his world.

Did he think he could put his father back together?

Did he think he could put his life back together?

Boba didn't think anything. He was numb.

It was all gone, all shattered.

It had all come to pieces. Pieces lay everywhere. Pieces of droids, body parts, the dead and the dying. Those who were still alive, and some of those who weren't, were firing their blasters wildly.

Boba walked past a spinning droid, its right leg shot off. It was firing around and around as it spun, spraying the upper tiers of the arena and the panicked crowd of Geonosians.

Laser bolts hit the ground around him, throwing up geysers of sand. Boba didn't care. Boba walked on.

Crouching troops in battle armor hurried by, firing as they ran. One grabbed Boba's arm and threw him to the ground. "Get down!"

WHARROOOMM!

An explosion ripped through the air where Boba had been. He hit flat on his belly.

WHARROOOMM!

Another explosion — and Boba felt sand stinging his cheeks. He buried his face in his arms, next to the empty helmet. When he opened his eyes and looked up, he saw —

Dad! It was his father, Jango Fett, looking down at him! Boba reached up for his father's hand, and —

Then, suddenly, Boba saw how wrong he was. It was not his father. It was the trooper who had saved his life, or one of the others. For they all looked exactly alike beneath the armor. It was his twin, only older. It was his father, only younger.

It was one of the clones.

As he stumbled to his feet, Boba realized clearly — and with horror — that the troops that had poured out of the gunships were the clone army that his father had trained on Kamino. Here they were, in action for the first time, on Geonosis. And unbeatable, just as his father had predicted. But they were fighting on the wrong side. Fighting for the hated Jedi!

No! Boba thought, clenching his fists. His disappointment was replaced by feelings of betrayal and rage.

"Just a kid!" the trooper said. "Thought you were one of us." He ran with the other clones toward a departing gunship.

"I'm not one of you!" Boba muttered angrily. "And I never will be. I am Jango Fett's *real* son."

The arena was almost empty. The Archduke was nowhere to be seen. The Count was nowhere to be seen. The fighting was almost over. The last gun-ship was leaving, blasting upward through the opening over the arena.

Boba hardly noticed. He was looking down, not up. He didn't care about the clones anymore. He had a job to do. One last job for Jango Fett.

It was getting dark. The rings of Geonosis filled half the sky with an orange glow. With the helmet in his arms, Boba was walking in circles, stumbling through the blood-damp sand. Finally, he found what he was looking for. Stumbled across it, in fact.

It was his father's body, still clothed in the remaining pieces of Mandalorian battle armor, scuffed and bloodied.

Boba placed his father's helmet on his father's chest, then sat down beside him. He was tired and it was time to rest. He noticed a tear slowly making its way down through the gritty sand on his cheek. He wiped it away with his fist.

It was too soon to cry. Boba still had a job to do.

It was dark, or as dark as it gets on the ringed planet. The battle had moved out of the arena and had covered a wide part of the land.

The Geonosians — now under the control of the victorious Jedi — sent in squads of drones to pick up the dead. They were tossed on a fire. The smashed and broken droids were luckier. They were picked up by a scoop to be taken outside to a scrap pile, for recycling.

Boba was sitting by his father's body when the scoop rolled by, on its second pass through the bloody arena.

Boba knew what he had to do. He was not like the clones. He was Jango Fett's *real* son. It was his job to take care of his father's body. And as long as he did his job, he could put off feeling the feelings that he didn't want to feel.

The scoop whined and jerked as it moved from place to place, blindly scouring the sand for more parts. Boba dragged his father's body into the scoop's path, where it would be picked up. In his Mandalorian battle armor, Jango Fett felt to the scoop just like a droid. A broken droid.

Boba got on the scoop and sat beside his father. He held the battle helmet in his arms as the robot scoop headed out of the arena, down a long passage leading out to the desert.

Boba was doing his job. That was all that mattered.

For now.

The droid scrap yard was under the mesa where Boba had spotted the Jedi in his starfighter. It was an immense heap of broken circuits, busted arms and legs, wheels and heads and steel knives and torsos.

The scoop made its dump and headed back into the stalagmite city, through an underground passage. Boba dragged his father's body off the scrap pile and onto the rocky mesa.

The mesa seemed a better resting place. More peaceful, and certainly more beautiful.

Boba removed his father's battle armor and set it aside. He took one last look at the strong arms and legs that had protected him. Then, using a broken droid arm for a shovel, Boba buried his father in a sandy grave overlooking the desert.

The broken droid arm made a "J," and Boba found another that he bent to make an "F." He arranged them on top of the grave.

JF. Jango Fett. Gone but not forgotten.

Boba suddenly felt very tired. He sat down beside his father's battle armor. He wished he had something to eat.

He shivered. The wind off the desert was cold.

Boba leaned back against the helmet and looked up at the great orange rings that encircled the planet. It was if they were holding it in their arms. It was a peaceful sight. . . .

Boba slept peacefully all that night. His dreams (and he forgot them) were of the mother he had never had, and the father he had been lucky enough to have. He awoke in the morning, rested and surprisingly comfortable. Then he saw that a furry sand snake had wrapped itself around him as he slept, keeping him warm.

Startled, Boba jumped to his feet. The sand snake yelped in alarm and slithered away in a panic.

The same one? Boba wondered.

It didn't matter. What mattered was that his job was done, for now. His father was buried. The little grave with the *JF* on it was proof of that.

Looking at it, Boba realized how much he was going to miss the father who had protected him, guided him, watched over him — and loved him. Now he was alone, all alone.

And for the first time, and for a long time, he wept.

CHAPTER SIXTEEN

It was time to think clearly, time to make plans. Time to swing into action.

First things first, Jango Fett always said.

First was taking care of the Mandalorian battle armor: the suit, the helmet, the jet-pack, and all the weaponry. *It will be yours someday*, his father had said.

But for now, Boba was too small to wear it or even carry it around. So he cleaned it, then hid it in a small cave under a cliff. He would reclaim it later.

Second was the black book his father had left him; or rather, the message unit that was not-a-book.

It will tell you what you need to know.

Boba had to get back into the apartment to get it. That presented a problem, given the chaos created by the battle that had spread from the arena. He had been confined to quarters by his father, which meant that his retinal print might not open the door.

Boba got the battle helmet out of the cave to

bring with him, just in case. Since Jango almost always wore it, it would contain unlocking codes.

The next problem was getting into the stalagmite city. *I can do it,* he thought, hearing the crash of broken droid parts being dumped below the mesa.

First load of the morning.

So far so good, thought Boba as he rode the scoop through the underground passage. Dad would be proud.

He felt a sad thought approaching but he waved it away. There would be time for all that later. For now, the best way to honor his father was to learn and live by Jango Fett's code.

That would take some doing, but it would be worth it. It had been Jango's plan for his son. Now it was Boba's plan for himself.

Carrying the battle helmet, Boba ran up the long stairs toward the apartment. He passed only two or three Geonosians, and they hardly noticed him.

There are certain advantages to being ten. One is that no one ever thinks you are doing anything serious.

The door clicked open as soon as he touched it. The apartment was almost empty. Jango Fett had always traveled light. Boba looked for the black book in the box where he kept his few clothes and old toys.

It wasn't there.

Suddenly, he remembered his last trip to the library in Tipoca City. He realized, with horror, what he had done. He had gotten the black book mixed up with his library books. It looked just like a book, after all. He had returned it with them!

That's why Whrr had tried to call him back. But Boba had been in too much of a hurry to listen.

The information Boba needed was on Kamino!

Boba threw a few clothes and the battle helmet into his father's flight bag. Trying not to be noticed, he made his way along the vast halls of the stalagmite city, toward the landing pad where *Slave I* was parked.

He had learned that the best way not to be noticed was not to worry about being noticed. That was easy. He had something else to worry about.

Could he fly the ship alone, without his father watching over his shoulder?

There was only one way to find out.

Boba hurried on.

There was a guard at the door to the landing pad. Even though the Jedi had taken over the planet, the Geonosians were still guarding their property.

It was easy enough to slip past the guard while he was busy shooting the breeze with another Geonosian.

Or so Boba thought.

"Where are you going?" The guard blocked the door with his blaster.

"My dad," Boba said. He held up the flight bag. "He told me to put this into the ship for him."

"Which one?"

Boba pointed to *Slave I*. It was the smallest ship on the landing pad. Its scarred and pitted surface belied its great speed and maneuverability.

"Okay, okay," said the guard, turning back to his friend and his gossip. "But you only get five minutes. Then I'm running you off."

There was no time to check to see if *Slave I* was loaded and fueled. Jango had schooled Boba in all the flight checks, but he had also let him know that there are times when they had to be overlooked. Times when one had to trust to luck.

Boba hurried. The guard might come looking for him at any moment now.

Once he was in the cockpit, Boba pulled the helmet over his head and sat on the flight bag. To an outside observer, he looked like an adult. He hoped.

He kept his fingers crossed as he started the engines and engaged the drive, just as he had been taught.

So far so good. The guard at the door even

flipped him a lazy "good-bye" wave as Boba lifted *Slave I* off the platform and soared into the cloudless sky of Geonosis.

The ship felt familiar, almost like home. Boba was thankful for all the time he had spent practicing, and even pretending. Pretending is a kind of practicing.

The fuel was low, but sufficient to get him to Kamino. He was on his way. *Wish Dad were here to see me*, he thought. *I know he would be proud.*

That thought, instead of making Boba happy, brought a sudden sadness. He tried to shake it off.

He had other things to worry about.

Like the blip in his rear viewscreen.

It was a Jedi starfighter, on his tail.

The Jedi must have left him behind to watch for stragglers, Boba thought. *Is he here to follow me, to force me down, or to blast me out of the sky?*

Boba wasn't about to find out.

He knew he couldn't outrun the starfighter. And since he barely knew *Slave I*'s weaponry, he couldn't outfight him. That left only one option.

He had to outsmart him.

Instead of heading for space, Boba dove into the canyons and mesas that surrounded the stalagmite city. Using all the maneuverability of the craft, he sliced through the narrow canyons, turning right, then left, as fast as he could.

The starfighter was gaining. But that was okay. That was part of Boba's plan.

He remembered a trick his dad had told him about. A trick that had been used on Jango Fett once, and once only. (No trick ever worked on Jango Fett twice.)

Boba slowed where the canyon forked, left and right. He fired a missile at the canyon wall on the right, then turned left and landed on a narrow ledge under the shelter of a cliff.

Boba shut off his engines and waited. And waited.

If the trick worked the Jedi starfighter would see the marks of the explosion of the wall, and turn back. If it didn't . . .

If it didn't, the starfighter would appear around the corner, lasers blazing. Or call for backup, and the sky would fill with starfighters. Or . . .

Finally, Boba quit waiting and restarted his engines. The trick had worked. The Jedi starfighter had seen the explosion and turned back.

Boba grinned with satisfaction as he took off again. *He thought I hit the wall!*

Boba pushed *Slave I* up into the rings and beyond. He had never been alone in space before.

He had felt alone on the planet after his father's death, and particularly after burying him. But this was different. There is alone and there is *alone*.

There is no place more lonely than the vacuum of space. Because space is No Place.

In space, there is only Not. Zero. Absence. And the absence of absence . . .

Welcome to The Big Isn't.

Boba shivered at the thought of the emptiness around him—then pushed the thought aside. He had no time for The Big Isn't. He thought of his father and his code: *A bounty hunter never gets distracted by the big picture. He knows it's the little things that count.*

Boba had a job to do. He had to find the black book.

Boba slipped into high orbit, above the rings.

Geonosis below looked almost peaceful. It was hard to believe it had just seen the fierce fighting that had killed his father — and hundreds, perhaps thousands, of others.

It was a beautiful sight, but Boba didn't intend to spend time enjoying the view. He was already preparing the ship for a hyperspace jump.

For a return, this was a simple process. Since Kamino was the last place *Slave I* had been, all

Boba had to do was reverse the coordinates on the navcomputer.

The ship would take care of the rest.

So he did.

And so did it.

CHAPTER SEVENTEEN

In hyperspace, all sectors of the galaxy are connected. Near is far and far is near.

The ship was falling into a hole. No, out of a hole.

Boba was back in "normal" space.

He was floating in orbit around what looked like a ball of clouds stitched together with lightning.

Stormy Kamino!

Home. Or as much of a home as Boba Fett had ever known.

Boba rubbed his eyes, stretched, and put *Slave I* into descent trajectory. Gray clouds whipped past like torn flags. Lightning flashed on all sides; thunder boomed. As the little starship slowed below supersonic speed, rain splattered the cockpit's transparisteel.

Boba adjusted his speed and circled down slowly toward the lights of Tipoca City. He had watched his father do it several times, but this was his first time at the controls.

The funny thing was, he didn't feel alone. It was almost as if Jango Fett were right there behind him. Boba could almost feel the big hand on his shoulder.

Smooth! He cut the engines and eased onto the landing pad with hardly a bump.

The weather in Tipoca City was normal, which meant there was a big storm in progress — which was all right with Boba. He didn't want to be noticed.

He had worn the battle helmet, so that anyone watching *Slave I* landing would think there was an adult at the controls. But he needn't have bothered.

The landing pad was deserted. There was no one around.

Boba threw on a poncho and scrambled out of the cockpit, after setting the ship's environmentals on INPUT to take on air and water, both plentiful on Kamino.

Especially water — it was pouring rain!

The little library at the end of the street corridor was dark. Boba banged on the door.

"Whrr, are you there?"

Was he too late? Or too early? Boba was warp-lagged from hyperspace, and he realized he had no idea what time it was in Tipoca City.

"Whrr, please. Open up!"

The light behind the slot came on.

Boba wished the door would open so that he could go in, out of the rain, but the library was only a branch.

An awning slid out, though, to protect him from the rain. And he heard the familiar whirring and clicking inside.

"Whrr, it's me."

"Boba? You're back! Where have you been? What happened?"

A short question with a long answer. Boba told Whrr the whole story, from the time he and his father had left the planet in a hurry, to the horrible scene in the arena, where he had seen his father killed.

"Oh, Boba, that's terrible. You are an orphan, at only ten. Do you have enough to eat? Do you have any money?"

"Not exactly," said Boba. "A few crackers. An extra pair of socks."

"Hmmmmmm," whirred Whrr.

"I'll be okay," said Boba. "But I have to get something my father left with me. By accident I left it with you."

"A book?"

"Yes! You remember! It looks like a book, anyway. It's black, with nothing on the cover. I returned it by mistake, with the last books I brought back right before I left."

"I will be right back."

There was a whir and a click, a clank and a clatter. Soon Whrr was back — with good news!

"Here you are," he said, passing the black book through the slot. "But there is a fine, you know."

"A what!?"

"There's money due on this book. Quite a bit."

"It's not even really a book. Besides, I didn't check it out. It's *mine*! I left it with you."

"Exactly," said Whrr. "Which means the library owes you, let's see, two hundred and fifty credits."

"That's impossible —" Boba began.

"Sorry," said Whrr, passing the money through the slot. "A fine is a fine and must be paid. Now go on about your business, Boba, and good luck. Come and see me sometime. If you're ever around."

I get it, Boba thought. *I'm a little slow, but I get it.*

"Thank you, my friend," he said. "Someday I will come back to Kamino. I'll come by and see you then, I promise."

"Good-bye, Boba," Whrr said through the slot. The light went off and Boba heard a strange snuffling sound.

Must be the rain, he thought, *because everybody knows that droids don't cry.*

* * *

Boba could hardly believe his luck! Two hundred and fifty credits would buy groceries and supplies, even clothing, with some left over for fuel. This was vital — since he didn't know how to access his father's accounts.

And he had the black book! He patted it under his poncho, where he was carrying it out of the rain.

Before heading off-planet, Boba wanted to make one stop.

He wanted one last look at the apartment where he and his father had lived, where he had spent the first ten years of his life (although, of course, he didn't remember most of it).

Fortunately, it was on the way back to the landing pad.

As Boba rode up in the turbolift, he wondered about the locks. Had they been changed? Would they still recognize his finger and retinal prints?

He never found out. The door was wide open.

The apartment was dark. It was spooky. It no longer felt like home at all.

Boba closed the door and was just about to turn on the lights when he heard a voice behind him.

"Jango."

It was Taun We.

Boba could barely see her in the dim light from

the window. She was sitting on the floor with her long legs folded up out of sight under her long body.

"I saw *Slave I* come in," she said.

Boba crossed the room and stood in front of her.

Taun We looked up, startled. "Boba!? Is that you? Where's your father?"

Boba had always regarded Taun We as a friend. So he sat down and told her.

"You poor child," she said, but her words were cold and mechanical. Boba realized she wasn't such a friend after all.

"What were you about to tell my father?" he asked.

"The Jedi," she said. "They came and took the clone army, after you and your father left. They also wanted to question Jango Fett further. Now that he is dead, they will want you."

"My father hated the Jedi."

"I have no feelings for the Jedi," said Taun We. "Of course, we Kaminoans have few feelings for anything. It is not in our nature. But fairness requires that I tell you that they are after you. Just as I have told them that *Slave I* has landed in Tipoca City, and that you and your father would probably be coming here."

"You did *what*!?"

"I must be fair to all," said Taun We. "It is in my nature."

"Thanks a lot!" Boba said, heading for the door. He didn't bother to shut it after him. He couldn't believe Taun We had betrayed him to the Jedi. And he had thought she was a friend. Then he remembered his father's code: *No friends, no enemies. Only allies and adversaries.*

But what about Whrr? he thought as he pressed the button for the turbolift. *Wasn't Whrr a friend?* It was all too confusing to think about!

Boba was still lost in thought when the turbolift arrived. Then the door slid open, and —

It was a Jedi. A woman, young and tall.

Boba ducked aside and let her walk past. He kept calm, kept walking.

"Siri? You're too late," said Taun We from inside the apartment.

"You bet I'm gone!" said Boba as he opened the garbage chute and dove in. He closed his eyes and held his breath as he fell — down, down, down. . . .

It wasn't the fall he feared, it was the landing. The trash pile at the bottom would either be hard or . . .

OOOMPH!

Soft! Luckily, it was all old clothes and paper.

Boba was surprised to find himself grinning as he brushed himself off and ran out the door, toward the safety of *Slave I* — and flight!

CHAPTER EIGHTEEN

One good thing about stormy Kamino — there are lots of electrical disturbances to cover your tracks, even from radar.

Boba Fett knew that once he had lifted off the landing pad, he would be hard to follow. He buried *Slave I* in the thick, gray clouds, changed course a few times just to be sure, then punched up through the atmosphere into the quiet of space, and a long, slow orbit.

Back into The Big Isn't.

At last it was time to check the black book. The message that his father had promised would guide him after he was gone.

He grasped the cover tightly, prepared to pull hard. But the cover opened easily. Instead of pages and print, Boba saw a screen.

It was just as Jango had said. It was not a book at all, but a message screen. An image was coming into focus, a planet . . .

No, a face. Becoming clearer.

Boba's father's face.

It was dim but it was him. Jango Fett's eyes

were wide open. He looked sad, though; sadder than ever.

"Boba."

"Father!"

"Listen up, Boba. You are only seeing this because I am gone. Because you are on your own. Alone."

Boba didn't have to be told that. He was feeling very alone.

"That is the way. All things must end. Even a parent's love, and I am even more than a parent to you. Remember me, and remember that I loved you."

"I will, Father," Boba whispered, even though he knew his father could not hear. "I will never forget you."

"There are three things you need, now that I am gone. I can only point you toward them. These three things you must seek and find on your own."

On your own. The words had a cold, familiar sound.

"The first is self-sufficiency. For this you must find Tyranus to access the credits I've put aside for you. The second is knowledge. For knowledge you must find Jabba. He will not give it; you must take it. The third and the most important is power. You will find it all around you, in many forms. But beware, sometimes it is dangerous. And one last thing, Boba . . ."

"Yes, Father! Anything!"

"Hold onto the book. Keep it close to you. Open it when you need it. It will guide you when you read it. It is not a story but a Way. Follow this Way and you will be a great bounty hunter someday. I was sure of it when I was alive, and I am sure of it still. . . ."

The picture was fading. "Father!"

The screen was blank. Jango Fett was gone.

Boba closed the black book. The cover sealed with a soft click.

Wow.

Boba didn't know whether to smile or cry, so he did both, while he sat with the black book on his lap. It was just a message screen, just a recording. But to him it was something very precious. It was his only connection with his father.

It was home and family.

He felt less alone.

Boba gave the black book a little pat and slipped it into the flight bag for later.

Then he stretched, and looked around.

Slave I was in high orbit. The planet Kamino was covered with storms far below. It looked like a marble made of mud and snow. On all sides, above and below, the stars beckoned.

Boba scanned through *Slave I*'s energy and environmental systems. Enough for one more hyperspace jump. Then he would have to refuel and re-fit.

Boba leaned back and planned his next step.

First things first, Jango always said. And according to Jango, or Jango's memory, Boba's first task was to find Tyranus. The Count. The man for whom Jango had created the clone army.

Boba had seen him in person, for the first time, on Geonosis. But he was sure that Tyranus had fled in the chaos of the battle in the arena. He didn't seem like the sort who would submit to being captured by the Jedi.

Where would he have gone?

Boba closed his eyes and remembered his father's voice, talking to the Jedi in Tipoca City: "I was recruited by a man called Tyranus on one of the moons of Bogden. . . ."

The moons of Bogden. That was a start.

Boba did a search in the ship's database. Bogden was a swampy, uninhabited planet in a far sector, surrounded by "numerous tiny satellites."

The moons of Bogden . . .

Boba punched in the coordinates. Then he hit the hyperdrive switch, and hoped for the best.

The stars started to dance as hyperspace wrinkled around the starship. Boba leaned back and crossed his fingers for luck.

"Here goes, Dad," he breathed as he closed his eyes. "I'll do my best to make you proud of me."

CHAPTER NINETEEN

Even though Boba had looked up Bogden in the database, he wasn't prepared for what he found when *Slave I* came out of hyperspace. "Numerous satellites" indeed!

He was orbiting what looked like a handful of pebbles someone had tossed into the air.

Bogden was a small, gray planet, surrounded by a swarm of tiny moons. Boba counted nineteen before he quit. It was hard to keep them straight. They were all shapes and sizes. The smallest was barely big enough for a ship to land on, while the largest had room for mountains, a city or two, and even a dry sea.

Day and night were erratic on these tiny circling worlds. Some were in darkness, some in light. Several had atmospheres; most did not. Boba scanned them all, looking for a city with a spaceport; or at least a town with a spaceport; or at least a town.

Many of the moons seemed uninhabited. Boba rejected one pear-shaped lump that oozed volcanic fumes, and another that was covered from pole to pole with gravestones. He decided against one that was covered in ivy that looked carnivorous. He passed on one that was all ice and one that was all ash and smoldering embers.

Finally Boba located a moon that was roughly spherical, half in light and half in darkness. At least it looked occupied.

He aimed for the largest cluster of lights he could find. The atmosphere was thin and shallow, and soon *Slave I* was in an approach trajectory over what looked like a small city scattered through several rocky valleys.

The ID-scan gave the moon's name as Bogg 4.

Boba aimed for a wedge of lights that looked like a landing pad. He clicked *Slave I* out of auto and began to set her down.

Smoothly and easily, and then . . .

Whoa! Something was rocking the ship, almost like a windstorm.

Boba fought the controls, trying to slow the descent.

Later he remembered a joke that went, "It wasn't the fall that was bad. It was just the last centimeter."

So it was with Boba. He made a perfect landing except for the very last part.

CRUNCH!

Slave I was tipped over on its side. Boba tried to right it, but it wouldn't move. According to his damage control panel, he had bent one of the landing struts.

At least no one was watching. The landing pad seemed deserted. Boba got out of the cockpit to survey the damage.

He felt dizzy. It looked bad. Two struts were good but the third was bent almost double.

He had no idea how to fix it. He got the flight bag down from the cockpit and looked through it for a repair manual. But there was only the black book his father had left him.

Boba pulled the black book out of the flight bag. Maybe there would be something in it that he could use. If he ever needed it, it was now!

The book opened easily. On the screen inside were two lines, looking like something out of Jango Fett's code:

Never tell the whole truth in a trade.
A favor is an investment.

Darn! Nothing about landing gear, Boba thought, closing the book.

He was putting it back into the flight bag when he heard a high-pitched voice behind him: "Whose ship?"

Boba turned.

A small humanoid was approaching. He had beady eyes, a long snout, and narrow, hooved legs.

Boba recognized him by his chin beard and purple turban as a H'drachi from the planet M'Haeli. But modified: His right arm had been replaced with a multipurpose tool extension.

He wore coveralls with words stitched over the pocket:

HONEST GJON
STARSHIP SERVICE
"we will warp you"

"My ship," Boba said. Then he remembered that he was just ten, and looked it. "I mean — it's my father's."

"And where mmight this father of yours be?" asked the H'drachi.

"Unavailable at the moment," said Boba. "But you can talk to me."

"Honest Gjon at your service," said the H'drachi. "This is mmy landing pad. Which mmeans you owe me a landing fee. And it looks like you mmay need repairs as well."

"Looks like it," Boba admitted. Still feeling dizzy, he checked in his pocket for the credits Whrr had given him. He had planned to spend them on food and fuel. But now . . .

"How much to fix a strut?" he asked.

"How mmuch you got?" asked Honest Gjon.

Boba was just about to say two hundred and fifty credits, when he remembered the black book:

Never tell the whole truth in a trade. "Two hundred credits," he said.

Honest Gjon smiled at him. "Mmy mmy, what a coincidence. That's exactly how mmuch it costs."

So maybe the book helps with repairs after all, Boba thought as he gave Honest Gjon two hundred credits. He still had fifty for himself.

Plus, as a courtesy, the H'drachi agreed to waive the landing fee.

Boba gave Honest Gjon the access codes to *Slave I* and headed toward the lights of the little town. As soon as he started walking, he understood why the landing had been so difficult. Something was shaking Bogg 4. He had hardly gone ten steps before he ended up in a ditch.

He scrambled to his feet — then fell to his knees again. He felt dizzier than ever. It was as if the ground were rocking under his feet — and yet everything looked stable.

The rocks stayed stationary. The ground didn't move.

Boba stood up again, carefully. He took a step, then another. So far so good. The dizziness came and went, and, finally, Boba realized what it was that felt so strange.

It was the gravity itself! It was strong one moment, weak the next; now tilting him forward, now back. It came and went in waves.

Boba started off again, uneasily, holding onto a stone wall that ran along the road. By the time he got to the edge of the town, he was walking in a more or less straight line.

Or so he thought.

"I see you're a newcomer," said a voice from behind him. "A newcomer, yes."

Boba turned and saw a skinny male in a long black coat. He looked almost human except that he had white feathers instead of hair on his head, and his long fingers were slightly webbed. His face had a pinched, worried look, as if it had been shrunk.

"I can tell by your walk," said the being in the long black coat. "By your walk, yes."

"So what?" Boba said. The dizziness was making him sick to his stomach, and he wasn't feeling too friendly. "And why does the gravity here come and go like the wind?"

"Why, you have it exactly," said the man, or whatever he was. "It's the moons crisscrossing, now cancelling one another, now doubling their pull. It makes walking hard. That's why we locals prefer to soar, yes."

Boba looked for wings under the long coat, but he didn't see any. "You are a native, then, of this world?"

"Bogg 4? No. Of all the moons, of all the moons, yes. Say, you're pretty good, kid. Pretty good, yes."

"Huh?"

"At the walking. You've almost got it down, yes."

*　　*　　*

They introduced themselves to each other and walked together into the town.

Aia (for that was his name) explained to Boba that the moons of Bogden were a kind of outlaw heaven, where no warrants were served and no questions were asked.

"What does that mean?" Boba asked.

"It means that no one wonders why a ten-year-old boy is wandering around on his own. No one, yes."

And it was true. Boba was even more invisible here on Bogg 4 than he had been on Kamino or Geonosis. The streets in the town were crowded with creatures from every corner of the galaxy, all walking with the same rolling gait, and none paying the slightest attention to Boba and his companion.

The gravity came and went in waves as the moons overhead (and unseen "below") slid in and out and around one another, sometimes dark, sometimes bright. Boba was still dizzy. But he was getting used to it.

"So tell me," said Aia. "Why are you here, yes?"

"A short visit," said Boba cautiously. He wasn't sure who he could trust and who he couldn't. "I'm looking for a certain man who hired a certain bounty hunter."

"Lots of bounty hunters on Bogg 4," said Aia.

"Dangerous characters, yes. They come here to hang out and trade info. To get new jobs. They usually only associate with one another, yes. Never with their prey. You don't have a bounty on you, do you, yes?"

Boba laughed. "No way. I'm the son of a bounty hunter."

"Here, then," said Aia, stopping in front of a low tavern that fronted on the narrow street. A wooden sign said THE BONNY BOUNTY. "This is where the bounty hunters hang out, yes."

Boba looked in the window. The place was almost empty. He could see long tables, guttering candles, and a smoky fire. "I will wait here, then," said Boba, "while my ship is being repaired by Honest Gjon."

"Honest Gjon?" said Aia. "Oh dear, yes."

"Is something wrong?"

"I mean, no, nothing. Never mind. I'll leave you here, yes."

"You're not coming in?" Boba asked. Aia was his only guide. The last thing he wanted was to be alone in this strange place.

"No, my, uh . . . religion forbids it, yes."

"Religion, my reptilian foot!" Suddenly two figures were standing in the open door of the Bonny Bounty. "He's not coming in because he's a thief!" said one. "And he knows that we know it!" said the other.

On the right was a birdlike humanoid with leathery skin and a broad beak. Boba recognized him as a Diollan. On the left was a green and reptilian Rodian. Boba knew that members of both species often became bounty hunters.

"This man is wanted for picking pockets!" the Diollan said.

"He stole from me, too," said the Rodian.

They grabbed Aia, each taking one of his skinny arms. "Oh, no, yes, no!" cried Aia, excitedly. He twisted and turned but couldn't get free.

Boba thought of the black book: *A favor is an investment.* Maybe if he did Aia a favor, it would pay off. At least he would have a guide. "How much does he owe you?"

"Twenty credits," said the Diollan. "Same here," said the Rodian.

"Here." Boba counted out forty credits, twenty for each. That left him ten. He wondered if it would be enough to buy something to eat.

The Rodian and the Diollan let go of Aia while they counted their money. As soon as his arms were free, Aia opened his black coat like a kite, bent his knees —

And jumped. Straight up. He soared up, over the rooftop, and out of sight.

Boba watched, dismayed. There went his investment.

The Rodian and the Diollan barely noticed. They turned and went back inside the tavern.

Boba followed them. Surely they owed him

something. He had done them a favor, after all, by giving them their money back. "Maybe you can help me," he said. "Are you bounty hunters?"

"Sure are," said the Rodian, with a laugh. "Are you bounty?"

"I am Jango Fett's son," said Boba. "Perhaps you knew him?"

The Diollan and the Rodian both looked at Boba with new interest. They took him to a table and signaled for the innkeeper, who brought food and tea. The tea was bitter but it made Boba feel less dizzy.

In fact, the more he drank the less dizzy he felt.

"We knew your father," the Rodian said.

"A great bounty hunter and a great man," said the Diollan.

Boba told them the whole story of how his father had died and everything that had happened since. He hoped he could trust them because they were his dad's colleagues.

Somehow, talking about his father's death made Boba feel better. It made it seem less like a tragedy and more like a story. Boba wondered if that was why people told stories — to get over them.

"My father mentioned a client," Boba said. "I thought I might find him here."

"His name?"

"Count, uh . . ." Boba suddenly remembered

that Tyranus was a name no one was supposed to know. "Count Dooku," he said, using the name the Count had used on Geonosis.

"Dooku?" said the Diollan.

"Not here!" said the Rodian.

"You must go to — Coruscant!" they both said together.

"Are you sure?" Boba asked, confused. Coruscant was the planet where the Republic and the Jedi had their headquarters. Why would Tyranus be there?

"Yes, yes, absolutely sure!" said the Rodian.

"Positively. Go to the Golden Cuff tavern in Lower Coruscant," said the Diollan.

"Tell the bartender who you are looking for," they both said together. "He'll know immediately what to do!"

"Thanks!" said Boba. He tried to pay his bill but the bounty hunters insisted on treating him. Boba thanked them again and headed back to the landing pad where he had left his starship with Honest Gjon.

As soon as he had left, the Diollan and the Rodian turned to each other and grinned.

"That's the best kind of bounty," said the one.

"The kind that delivers itself and saves us the fuel . . . *and* the trouble!" said the other.

*   *   *

The tea was wearing off, Boba could tell, as he headed back for Honest Gjon's landing pad. He felt dizzy again. Not as dizzy as before, but a little bit.

The moons of Bogden were wheeling across the sky. Some were small, some were large; some were dark, and some were bright.

Boba could hardly believe his luck. He had picked the right moon, Bogg 4. He had found the right bounty hunters, the Diollan and the Rodian. And on his very first try, he had located Tyranus. He had even eaten dinner, and it hadn't cost a credit!

A favor is an investment. He had meant to do the favor for Aia. Instead he had done it for the bounty hunters, and it had paid off.

Now all he had to do was get in his starship and go to Coruscant.

There was only one problem. The landing pad was empty.

Slave I was gone.

CHAPTER TWENTY

Boba sat down on the ground, under the wheeling, spinning Bogden moons. He was dizzy again. The tea had worn off completely.

His starship was gone. So was the black book that contained Jango Fett's code. So was his father's battle helmet — his legacy.

Even his money was gone, except for ten credits.

Gone, all gone. How could he have been such a fool? How could he have let his father's memory down? How could he have trusted Honest Gjon? He put his head in his hands and moaned in dismay and self-disgust.

Then he heard a clucking sound. "Tut, tut, yes."

It was Aia. "I was afraid of this," the skinny moon-being said. "That's why I ran back. But I was too late. That Honest Gjon is a crook, yes."

"So are you," Boba pointed out. "You steal things."

"Only my fingers steal," said Aia, holding up both webbed hands. "And only what I need, yes. To prove it, I will help you find Honest Gjon. Not so honest, yes."

Boba felt a glimmer of hope. "Where did he go?"

"His shop. He tears ships down for parts. So they can't be traced, yes."

"Then we must hurry," said Boba, jumping to his feet. "Before he begins to tear *Slave I* apart. Where is this shop of his?"

Aia pointed straight up, toward a jagged, spinning moon.

"Oh, no!" Boba sat back down. "He has taken it to another world."

"Yes, of course. He thinks you can't follow, yes."

"But he's right! I can't!"

"But you can," said Aia. "Come. Come with me, yes." And he took Boba's hand and pulled him to his feet.

"If you were any older or any bigger, this would be a problem, yes," said Aia as he led Boba up the path. "As it is, we may just make it, yes."

"Make what?" The path twisted and turned up a rocky hill overlooking the landing pad.

"You will see, yes."

Boba saw — and didn't like what he saw.

The path ended at a cliff.

Boba gripped Aia's big hand and leaned out, looked up, looked down. Above, he saw darkness, a few moons, and many stars. Below, he saw only darkness.

He was dizzy again.

"The gravity waves rise and fall with the moons, yes," said Aia. "If you get high enough, and if you know what you are doing, you can ride them. Like a bird on the wind, yes."

All of a sudden, Boba got it. And he didn't like it.

He backed away from the edge of the cliff, but not fast enough. Aia was already stepping off into thin air — and pulling Boba with him.

Boba was falling.

Then he wasn't.

He was rising, soaring, slowly at first and then faster, faster, faster. Rising up through the air.

"You have to ride the vectors, yes," said Aia, whose coat was spread wide like a kite, like wings. He squeezed Boba's hand. "When one vector gives out, we cross to another, yes."

Let's hope so, thought Boba.

Aia pulled Boba with him. They plummeted down, then started to rise again.

They were heavy one moment, weightless the next.

Boba ignored the lump rising in his throat for as long as he could.

Then he lost it.

"Yu-ck!" said Aia. "If I had known you were going to do that . . . I would have . . . yes . . ."

"Sorry," said Boba.

He was feeling less dizzy. The higher they soared, the easier it got. All Boba had to do was hang on to Aia's hand and follow. Other figures darted in and out of the clouds. All of them were small like Aia.

Aia waved at them.

"We are the couriers, yes," he said to Boba. "We are the only ones light enough to travel from world to world. You too, yes. As long as you stay with me."

Don't worry, Boba thought, squeezing Aia's hand. *I'm sticking with you!*

It was getting cold. Boba looked down. He immediately wished he hadn't.

Bogg 4 was a tiny lump of stone and dust, far away. The stars were too bright. It was hard to breathe.

We're almost in space! Boba thought. *We have soared too high!*

"There, Bogg 11, yes," said Aia, pointing up ahead to where a smaller, darker moon was about to cross Bogg 4's orbit. Gravity was pulling at both moons, tangling their clouds together in long streams, like seaweed.

"The foam is where the atmospheres brush one

another," Aia said. "That is where we make the jump, yes."

"And if we miss . . ."

"Space is cold," said Aia. "Eternity is cold. Hang on, hold your breath, yes!"

Boba held his breath. But he couldn't hold on.

His fingers were numb and stiff with cold. He felt Aia's hand slipping away.

"No!" cried Boba silently, since there was no air with which to shout or scream.

No air to breathe.

He closed his eyes. He was spinning, weightless, drifting away into The Big Isn't. The nothingness of space. Of death.

Here I come, Dad, he thought. It was almost a peaceful feeling. . . .

Then he felt gravity pulling at him like fingers, gently. Slowing his spin. Pulling him down.

Boba could hold his breath no longer. He gulped, expecting the cold rip of vacuum in his lungs.

Instead, he tasted air. It was hardly sweet but it tasted great to Boba.

He opened his eyes.

Aia had him by the hand again.

They were soaring in the sky of a different world. A smaller, smokier world.

"Bogg 11, yes," said Aia.

They circled down toward Bogg 11 in long loops.

Boba saw *Slave I* parked in a rocky little valley, surrounded by piles of spaceship parts.

"Luckily he's just getting started," Aia said. "We made it, yes."

They landed on the side of a small, steep hill. Boba fell and rolled to a stop. He got up, dusted himself off, and started running down a rocky path, toward *Slave I*.

Honest Gjon saw them coming and stared.

"What if he won't give it back?" Boba asked. He picked up a rock. He wished he had a blaster.

"Don't be silly," said Aia. "Put down the rock. Thieves have honor, yes?"

Yes. It seemed so. Sort of, anyway.

"Can't blame a guy for trying!" said Honest Gjon, throwing up his hands. The bearded H'drachi's smile seemed genuine.

Boba shook his head in exasperation and looked into the cockpit. The flight bag was still there. The battle helmet and the black book were inside it. Maybe there was honor among thieves after all.

Boba tried the book, and it opened.

Money is power.

*   *   *

Not much help, Boba thought, *since I don't have any.* He closed the book and put it back into the flight bag.

Honest Gjon was watching Boba's every move. "What does it say?"

"It says you're supposed to give me my money back."

"No way!" said Honest Gjon. "I fixed your strut, didn't I?"

"He did, yes," said Aia.

"Can't blame a guy for trying," said Boba.

They all shared a laugh.

But while Boba laughed, he tried to think of his next move.

CHAPTER TWENTY-ONE

Boba found that he liked these outlaws of the moons of Bogden. Crime was just a game to them. They were like bounty hunters, in a way.

"Coruscant's a dangerous place," said Honest Gjon, when Boba told him where he was going.

"And expensive," said Aia. "You have no money, yes?"

"I have ten credits," said Boba. "I guess that'll have to be enough."

"There are ways to get money, yes," said Aia.

"Such as?"

"Such as crime," said Honest Gjon. "I happen to know of some mmoney being smuggled from Bogg 2 to Bogg 9. A few fellows with a good ship and a little luck could take what they needed."

"You could be one of those fellows, yes," said Aia.

Boba was intrigued. *Money is power.* "You're talking about a hijacking? A robbery?"

"An interception," said Honest Gjon. "Not exactly a robbery, since it isn't real mmoney, yes. It's counterfeit credits. They are made on Bogg 2, then sent by light-air balloons to Bogg 9 when the align-ment of the mmoons is just right."

"The atmospheres brush together and the bal-loons pass from world to world," said Aia. "Like we did, yes."

"A smugglers' trick," said Honest Gjon. "And if we pick off one balloon on the way, no one will mmiss it."

"They will think one just got away, yes," said Aia. "Of course, catching it on the fly requires a *very* good pilot with a *very* good ship. You may be too young, yes."

"I want a third," said Boba. "When do we go?"

"In about ten minutes," said Aia. He looked at Honest Gjon and winked. "I told you he would do it, yes?"

From space, Bogg 2 looked like a dry dirt clod, spiked with mountains. Boba cruised over slowly, then put *Slave I* into a slow holding orbit just above the atmosphere.

"No lights, no electrics, no radio," said Honest Gjon. "That way we can't be seen. The trick is to try to catch the balloon as it rises. If you get close, I will hook it into the hatch."

"We should let the first one go, so they don't suspect anything, yes," said Aia. "Then grab the next one."

"Sounds like a plan," said Boba.

"Look," said Honest Gjon. "Here comes number one."

He handed Boba a viewfinder. Boba saw a red balloon rising out of a mountain valley.

He handed the viewfinder to Aia. The balloon rose swiftly in the low gravity. It streaked past, into the stormy space between the moons. A gondola hung below it, packed with bales of credits.

Money! thought Boba with a grin. *Money is power!* If only his father could see him now. He knew he would be proud.

"Here it comes," said Honest Gjon. The second balloon was on its way. It had an even larger gondola hanging beneath it. *Even more money*, Boba thought.

Aia tracked it with the viewfinder and then with his naked eye, while Boba operated the ship. "Back up a hair, yes. Now forward. Now up, yes. Whoa!"

Honest Gjon opened the ramp and pulled in the balloon. "Got it!"

"Great," said Boba. "Now let's close the ramp and get out of here."

"One more," said Aia.

"I thought two was the plan," said Boba. "They will see us if we stay too long. They'll send someone up after us."

"One mmore can't hurt," said Honest Gjon. He held up a fistful of brand-new credit notes.

Why not? thought Boba. *More is better.* If the black book didn't say that, well, it should!

He pulled the ship back into place and held it steady, adjusting for the varying gravity of the spinning moons.

"Number three!" said Aia. Honest Gjon went to open the ramp.

The red balloon was getting closer and closer. Honest Gjon went down to open the ramp and pull it in. The gondola underneath it was even bigger than the one before.

More money! *More is better*, Boba thought, with a grin.

"Ooooops," said Honest Gjon. "Slight problem."

"You're all under arrest for counterfeiting," said a gruff voice.

Boba turned and saw Honest Gjon in the doorway. He was not alone. Standing beside him was a trooper in a security uniform, holding a blaster.

Oh, no! thought Boba.

"It's not our money," said Aia. "It's all a mistake, yes. We'll give it back!"

"Who cares about the money?" said the trooper, with a cruel smile that was all teeth. "I'm officially confiscating this ship in the name of the law. It's contraband."

Boba was thinking: *No way!* Give up *Slave I*, his father's ship? But what could he do with a blaster pointed at his face?

Then he remembered a trick Jango had taught him.

"Move over, kid," said the trooper. "And put your hands up where I can see them. Now!"

"Yes, sir." Boba set the power on FULL AHEAD and punched in DELAY 4. Then he stood up with his hands over his head and slowly backed away from the controls. He counted silently: four, three —

The trooper grinned. "That's better," he said, motioning with his blaster toward the open hatch. "Now grab some air, all three of you."

Two, one —

Boba lunged, grabbing the back of the pilot's seat as the engines roared to life and *Slave I* suddenly sprang forward. The trooper, Aia, and Honest Gjon all flew through the air and hit the back wall in a clump.

WHACK!

THUMP!

Boba held onto the seat and threw the ship into a sharp turn. Honest Gjon and Aia grabbed the dazed trooper, one on each arm. They dragged him to the still-open hatch — and shoved him out!

Boba grimaced as he brought the ship back under control. "Murder of a security trooper. Now we're in big trouble!"

"He's got a parachute, yes," said Aia.

"He's no trooper, anyway," said Honest Gjon. "That uniform was as counterfeit as the credits. That was a hijacking that failed."

*   *   *

"We did it!" said Boba as he set the ship down on Honest Gjon's landing pad. His heart was still pounding, but he had saved *Slave I*. And made some money, too.

"How many credits do we have?" he asked. "Let's divide them three ways, so I can get out of here."

"That's the bad news, yes," said Aia. "They all flew out the door when we shoved him out."

"All but one," said Honest Gjon. He handed Boba a hundred-credit note. "Take it, you deserve it all. And you're going to need it on Coruscant."

Boba put the money into his pocket with the pathetic little ten. Even though he had only made a hundred credits, he felt that Jango Fett would have been proud.

He had found out what he needed to know on the moons of Bogden. He had even made a few friends (or, as Jango would have called them, allies. *No friends, no enemies. Only allies and adversaries*).

Now it was time to head for Coruscant and find Tyranus.

He shook hands with Honest Gjon, but Aia insisted on giving him a big hug. "Boba, continue your quest, yes. But take care. You are too trusting. Watch your back, yes?"

"Yes," said Boba. "Thanks, Aia."

They hugged again, then Boba got into *Slave I*

and took off. It was only after he was in deep space, preparing to shift into hyperdrive, that he noticed that the hundred-credit note was missing from his pocket.

And so was the ten.

CHAPTER TWENTY-TWO

In the endless, intricate web of civilized and half-civilized worlds that make up the Galactic Core, some planets are obscure and hard to find. And others are hard to miss.

Coruscant is in the second category.

The coordinates are easy to remember and even easier to punch into a starship's navigational computer:

zero zero zero.

It is here that civilization begins. At the heart of the Core Worlds. At the very center of the Known Universe.

Coruscant. The planet that is a city; the city that is a planet.

Boba awoke when *Slave I* shuddered out of hyperdrive and slid into normal space.

He shook his head to clear it of the dreams that always crowded in during hyperspace jumps.

And there it was. The legendary city planet, covered by pavements and roofs, towers and balconies, parks and artificial seas. Coruscant was one immense metropolis from pole to pole.

Not a green spot nor an open field; no wilderness, no forests, no ice caps. Coruscant was one enormous planetwide city, covered by slums and palaces, parks and plazas. It spun below in all its glory, welcoming *Slave I* as it had welcomed pilgrim and pirate, politician and petitioner, wanderer and wayfarer since the Republic's first beginnings millennia ago.

And now it awaited Boba Fett. An orphan seeking only to please his father's ghost.

Hopeful again at last, Boba eased *Slave I* into suborbital approach, past the big orbiting mirrors that gathered and focused the light of Coruscant's faraway sun.

The starship hit the atmosphere and began to slow. Boba descended in big looping turns, past the towers of the wealthy and powerful, past the hanging gardens, and into the commercial zones reserved for uninvited visitors. With traffic crowding in on all sides, this was a much more harrowing approach than on Kamino or the moons of Bogden. Boba's heart tightened in his chest. Would they find him here?

He felt a slight bump and let go of *Slave I*'s controls. The ship was locked into autopilot, being flown "by wire" on a microbeam. It would land itself.

That was fine with Boba. He had other things to worry about. Money, for starters. He would need to pay his landing fees before he could take off again. Then there was the problem of the Jedi. If they were really after him, as Taun We had warned, they might have a warrant out on *Slave I*. He could be arrested as soon as he touched down.

He needed some guidance. Maybe the book would help. It seemed to open when he needed it, or at least when it had something to say.

He pulled it out of the flight bag. Sure enough, it opened. But the message was even more mysterious than usual:

Watch out for things that go too well.

That's hardly my problem! Boba thought. He closed the book, disgusted, and put it away. He watched nervously as the ship eased in toward the spaceport, slipping smoothly between the towers and under the lighted walkways and gardens of Coruscant.

Slave I bumped down, light and easy. No alarms went off.

Boba lowered the ramp. He scanned the landing pad, ready to run if need be.

Nobody was watching. Nobody was around.

This was Coruscant. Nobody cared about an insignificant little ship like *Slave I*. Or its insignificant little ten-year-old pilot.

Boba's first emotion on landing was relief.

His second was fear. The Jedi had eyes and ears everywhere. And especially on Coruscant. Would they find Boba before he found Tyranus?

Boba didn't fear the Jedi as much as he feared failure. Would he disgrace his father's memory by failing in his first test, the search for Tyranus — and self-sufficiency?

"Welcome to Coruscant," said a disembodied droid voice.

"Sure, whatever," muttered Boba.

Carrying his flight bag with the black book and the battle helmet, plus a few extra pairs of underwear and socks, he climbed down out of the ship. He started down the escalator toward the streets.

Boba had read enough about Coruscant to know that it was arranged in layers according to class and function.

The upper levels were for the rich and powerful. Looking up, Boba could see their towers and gardens reaching up into the clouds.

The middle levels, where he had landed, were for both business and pleasure. The streets were filled with creatures from all over the galaxy, rushing around, buying and selling, or just sightseeing.

The lower levels were said to be dangerous. They were the outlaw zones, filled with fugitives, pirates, and criminals — all the denizens of the underworld that lay beneath the Imperium.

Boba hoped all would go well on the lower levels when he went to find the Golden Cuff. He'd had quite enough adventure, thank you. He just wanted to find Tyranus.

Boba was in luck.

The Golden Cuff was a little hole-in-the-wall on the upper layer of the lower levels, just under the lower layer of the middle levels.

It was far enough down that the light was dim and the neon signs could glow all day. But not so far down that one had to hire a posse of armed guards to cross the street.

Boba walked in through the sliding door.

The bar was deserted except for the bartender, a four-armed being who was using two of his arms to wash glasses, one to count credits, and one to wipe the bar with a wet rag. His skin was a dark crimson, and a proprietor sign named him as Nan Mercador.

Boba put his flight bag on the floor and sat on a bar stool.

"No kids allowed!" said Mercador, wringing out the rag and tossing it onto the bar. "And that means you!"

"I'm not a customer," said Boba. "I'm not looking for a drink. I'm looking for a — uh, relative. Named Dooku."

The bartender's face brightened. "Dooku!" He looked at Boba with new interest. "Dooku. Oh, yes, of course. Absolutely. He's a good friend of mine. Let me give him a call."

Mercador started punching numbers into a comm unit. "Dooku? Is that you?" he said. "Somebody here to see you." Static came up on the comm screen behind the bar, as if it were a long-distance planet-to-planet call. The bartender smiled at Boba. "How about a juice while you are waiting?"

"I don't exactly have any money," said Boba.

"It's okay," said the bartender, wiping the bar with one hand and filling a mug with two others. "It's on the house!"

The juice was cold and tasted great. Boba could hardly believe his luck. He had only been in Coruscant for an hour or so, and already he had met a friendly bartender who actually *knew* Tyranus (excuse me, Dooku!), and now he was drinking a free juice!

Suddenly he remembered the black book: *Watch out for things that go too well.* Could it be that —?

The static on the comm screen went away, and Boba saw two familiar faces. Neither was Tyranus. The one on the right was the Diollan; the one on the left was the Rodian. The two bounty hunters from the moons of Bogden.

"That's him!" said the Rodian. "Grab him! You can bring him to the Jedi for the reward." Boba tried to slide down off the stool and run. But it was too late. Strong hands grabbed his right arm.

And his left arm.

And his left leg.

And his right leg.

Nan Mercador came out from behind the bar and lifted him off the stool, into the air.

"Hey!" Boba yelled. "Let me go!"

"Not a chance," said the bartender, holding Boba over his head. "You're worth money!"

"This is a mistake!" Boba said.

"No mistake, kid," said the Rodian on the comm screen.

"You're bounty," added the Diollan.

"The Jedi know you're coming," said the Diollan to Mercador.

"They will give you your share in cash," said the Rodian.

"I should get half," said the bartender as he started toward the door holding Boba over his head with all four arms. "I saved you both the trouble of coming here."

"Too late for that," said the Rodian.

"It's already been arranged," said the Diollan as they hung up.

The screen went black.

Think fast, thought Boba, squirming and kicking helplessly near the ceiling. *And if that doesn't work, think faster!* He stopped squirming. "Don't be a fool," he said. "Count Dooku will pay twice as much as the Jedi. And you won't have to split it with anybody."

"I won't?" Nan Mercador stopped. But he didn't let go of Boba. "Are you sure?"

"Positive," said Boba. "Set me down, and I will call him myself. You can ask him."

"You must think I'm a dope," said Mercador, still holding Boba so high above his head that he almost scraped the ceiling. "Besides, you don't know his number. You asked me to find him, remember?"

"I was just testing you," said Boba, looking at the ceiling light near his left foot. It was only centimeters away. "But you don't have to believe me. You can call him yourself. The number is . . ."

He rattled off a string of numbers, hoping they would sound right. Apparently they did. The bartender let go of Boba's left foot and began punching them into the comm unit on the bar.

Boba was ready to move. As soon as his foot was free, he kicked the light as hard as he could.

CRASH! It shattered, showering glass down onto the bar, the stools, the floor. . . .

Mercador lifted his hands to protect his head

from the falling glass. Boba fell, straight down, headfirst. At the last moment he managed to twist in the air like a diver and land on his feet. He scrambled toward the door, which slid open —

And revealed two gleaming boots, blocking his way. Above them were two shapely legs. And above them —

It was a woman, holding a vicious-looking blaster. She grabbed Boba's arm with one hand. She raised the other hand and fired.

ZZZ-AAA-PPP!

The bartender howled with pain and sat down on the floor in the middle of the broken glass.

"It's set on stun," she said. "But one false move and it goes to kill."

"Cool," said Boba, looking up at his rescuer. She looked dangerous. That made her even more beautiful to him. "Who are you?" he asked.

"Aurra Sing," she said. "But never mind that. Let's get out of here."

Boba didn't have to be asked twice. He grabbed his flight bag and followed her out onto the street, toward a parked hovercraft that was idling quietly on the narrow street.

"Bounty hunters," he explained breathlessly. "They betrayed me. I never should have trusted them!"

"Bounty hunters can always be trusted," Aurra Sing said. "Trusted to do what they are paid to do." She opened the door of the hovercraft. "I know, because I am a bounty hunter myself. Get in, young Boba Fett."

"You know my name?"

"Of course. The bounty hunter always knows the bounty's name."

Boba backed up, ready to run.

"Get in!" Aurra Sing patted the blaster in the gleaming holster that matched her boots. "It's very painful, even set on stun. Don't make me try it on you."

Boba gave up and got in. He groaned as the hovercraft lifted off. He'd thought he had been rescued. Instead, he had been captured again!

As the hovercraft rose higher and higher, winding through the towers and hanging gardens of Coruscant, Boba sat back in his seat and sulked, disgusted with himself.

"Watch out when things go too well." I should have known better, he thought. *I will never trust anybody ever again!*

He was surprised when Aurra Sing landed the hovercraft at the spaceport, right next to *Slave I*.

"Aren't you taking me to the Jedi?" he asked. "I thought you were a bounty hunter."

"I am," she said. "But I would never work for the Jedi. My client lives on another planet altogether. That's why we are taking your ship. You can fly it, can't you?"

"What if I say no?"

She patted her blaster again.

Boba opened the ramp and checked out *Slave I*'s systems. To his surprise, Aurra Sing paid off the landing fees, and even tipped the droid.

"Low orbit first," she said. "Then hyperspace. And no funny business. I'm not known for my sense of humor."

"No kidding," Boba said under his breath. Then he asked, "Do you mind telling me who put out a bounty on me, and where we're going?"

"You'll find out the *who* soon enough," she said. "The *where* is an outer rim world called Raxus Prime."

"Excuse me? I must have heard you wrong. I thought you said Raxus Prime."

"You heard right."

"But — that's a seriously uninhabitable planet."

"I know. And we're late. So drop us into hyperspace, and let's go."

CHAPTER TWENTY-THREE

Boba had read about Raxus Prime, but he had never seen it, not even in pictures. Few had. Who would want to?

Raxus Prime was the most toxic planet in the galaxy. It was the dump for all the debris and detritus of a thousand civilizations.

It didn't look so bad from a distance. *Sort of like Kamino,* Boba thought, as he dropped out of hyperspace, into orbit. It was all clouds. Beautiful, swirling clouds, all tinged with scarlet, green, and yellow.

But as *Slave I* descended through the clouds, Boba saw that they were actually made of smoke and steam and toxic gas. The smell was so bad that it even penetrated the ship's systems. The stink was terrible but the colors were beautiful as *Slave I* crossed the line from the dark side of the planet into the light.

Pollution makes for great sunrises.

The smell didn't seem to bother Aurra Sing. Nothing seemed to bother her. "Fly slow and low," she said. It was the first thing she had said in hours. The entire trip from Coruscant had been silent.

That suited Boba fine. He had nothing to say to her, either. She was not his ally but his adversary.

As *Slave I* dropped lower, Boba saw the surface of Raxus Prime for the first time. It was covered with rubble, trash, junk, and garbage, piled in huge twisted heaps and rows like grotesque mountain ranges. Rusted, busted starships, scorched weaponry, mangled machinery, gobs and stacks of glass and steel lay half buried under heaps of slag. And all of it oozed and steamed and smoked, fouling the air above and the water below.

Though it all looked dead, it was alive. Boba saw tiny brown-robed creatures scurrying through the oily wasteland. He saw birds the color of dirt, like smears against the sky. There were no cities, but every few kilometers a smokestack belching fumes marked the site of a refinery or recycling plant, run by scurrying oil-smeared droids.

"Slower, kid."

Aurra Sing consulted a code on her wristwatch. "It should be along here somewhere. Look for a lopsided hill and a lake — there it is!"

The "hill" was a heap of foul refuse a thousand meters high. Twisted, leafless, mutant trees grew from its ravaged slopes, fed by the continual rain that oozed from the stinking clouds.

The "lake" was a pool of iridescent liquid the color of bile. Following Aurra Sing's instructions, Boba set the ship down on a flat spot between the lake and the base of the hill.

"Don't shut it off."

"Huh?"

"The ship. Leave it running. I'm getting out of here. You're staying. This is it."

"You can't leave me here! You can't steal my ship!" said Boba.

"Who says? The ship is my pay," said Aurra Sing. She opened the hatch and lowered the ramp. "There is a door in the side of the hill. As soon as I leave, it will open for you. My client is waiting for you inside. Don't forget your flight bag."

She tossed it out, onto the stinking, steaming "ground." Boba ran after it. She closed the ramp behind him.

"You can't just leave me here!" Boba yelled, banging on the hull of the ship. "I'll run away!"

"Look around — I don't think so!" she yelled back. "I'm gone. Good luck, Boba Fett. I hope you can live up to your father's reputation. He was the genuine article. Who knows, maybe someday you will be, too. I liked the way you handled that bartender."

Boba could hardly believe it. She had rescued him, then betrayed him, then robbed him, and then complimented him! And now she was about to leave him alone on the foulest planet in the galaxy. He banged on the hatch in a rage, but instead of opening, it sealed with a hiss.

He felt truly alone now. There was no one he could trust.

Slave I's engines whined. Boba knew that sound. He stepped back, out of the way. He watched helplessly as the starship — *his* starship! — rose into the noxious clouds and disappeared.

Once again, he felt dangerously close to tears. At the same time, he could barely breathe. Suddenly, he heard a sound behind him.

He turned. A door in the hillside was sliding open. Inside, Boba could see a brightly lighted hall, leading to a carpeted stairway.

Boba didn't wait to be invited. Coughing and gagging, he ran inside.

Now what? Boba thought as the door slid shut.

Before he had a chance to answer his own question, he heard a voice behind him. "Welcome to Raxus Prime, Boba Fett."

The voice was familiar. So were the lean, lined face and the hawklike eyes.

"Count Tyranus! I mean, Count Dooku!"

"You are among friends now, Boba," said the Count. "You can call me anything you please. Count will do."

"My father told me to find you," said Boba.

"And I made sure it happened," said the Count. "I see that Aurra Sing did a superb job and delivered you here safely."

"Yes, sir," said Boba. "I mean, no, sir. You see, she stole my ship, and it's . . ."

The Count smiled and raised his hand. "Don't worry. Your ship is safe. Everything will be fine from now on. You must be very tired."

Boba nodded. It was true.

"Don't worry about a thing," said the Count, placing his cold hand on Boba's head. "Come, let me show you to your room. Let me carry your bag."

Boba followed him up the long stairs. The carpets were deep and soft. Who would have imagined that there was such an elegant palace on the planet of garbage? Even the air was sweet. There was only a very faint foul smell from the planet outside.

"I have big plans for you, Boba," said the Count. "Plans that would have made your father proud. But first you need to rest. You must be tired after all your travels."

Boba nodded. He had packed a lot of adventures into just a few days. The escape from the Jedi starfighter on Geonosis, the escape from the Jedi woman back on Kamino, the recovery of his ship and the robbery gone wrong on the moons of Bogden, the struggle with the bartender on Coruscant . . .

He had lost the ship, but he would get it back. The Count had promised, hadn't he? Something like that.

A lot of stuff for a ten-year-old, he realized. He *was* tired. But he was also confused. He knew he should be happy. He had been lucky. He had completed the first part of his quest. He had found Tyranus. Now he would find Wisdom.

So why had he felt a cold chill when the Count put his hand on top of his head?

Probably just nerves, Boba thought as he followed the Count up the stairs, toward his room.

And his unknown future.

CROSSFIRE

STAR WARS

BOBA FETT

CROSSFIRE

TERRY BISSON

CHAPTER ONE

"Hello!"

Silence.

"Hello!?"

No answer. The hallway outside his door was quiet.

Boba Fett was all alone.

That was okay. Boba was used to being alone.

Ever since he had buried his father, he had been by himself — a ten-year-old against the galaxy. He missed his father but he didn't mind being alone. Sometimes.

Sort of.

. . . *whrr* . . .

Movement! Boba ran to a bend in the corridor. "Hey! Hey!"

. . . *whrrr* . . .

It was just a droid. A small, shoe-sized house droid, the custodial kind that dusted and cleaned continually. While other creatures bustled in other corridors of the Count's underground lair, only the custodial droids came into this hallway.

That explained why Boba felt so isolated. But it didn't explain why he had been brought here, and what was going to happen to him. Only the Count could do that.

The Count, a tall, thin, powerful man with a cold smile, was known as Tyranus — or Dooku, depending on whom you were talking to. Boba's father, Jango Fett, had left instructions that Boba was to find the Count if something happened to him.

Something *had* happened to Boba's father. He had been killed in a battle with a Jedi. Boba had buried his father on the planet Geonosis. He had gone to his home planet of Kamino only to find that it wasn't home anymore. With his father gone, there was no security. With his father gone, there was no safety. There was only the need for escape.

Boba's father had left him a book. *Find Tyranus*, it had told him, *to access Jango's credits and find self-sufficiency.*

That suited Boba. He wanted to learn how to become a great bounty hunter like his father. To start out he'd need credits — then he'd earn more. But Boba hadn't had time to find the Count. The Count had found him first, sending a bounty hunter named Aurra Sing to capture him on Coruscant and bring him to this underground hideout on Raxus Prime. She'd taken his ship, *Slave I,* as payment.

But she hadn't explained why the Count wanted Boba.

Only the Count could answer that, and Boba couldn't find him. The Count had welcomed him to this hideout — sort of — and had given him a room with a table, a chair, and a bed. Boba had immediately gone to sleep, exhausted. Now that he was awake, the Count was nowhere to be found.

"Hello?"

No answer.

Walking around, Boba had seen rooms half-empty or filled with mysterious equipment, some of it still in crates. He had heard strange sounds in the distance. Voices, many languages. He passed figures half-seen as they scuttled down dimly lit corridors, hurrying around corners.

There was something going on. But what?

Clearly, the Count wanted to keep him separate from others. Boba hoped this was because the Count was going to train him, was going to employ him like he had employed Boba's father.

That was his hope.

The room Boba had been put into was painted white and lighted by glow panels set in the ceiling. Like everything he'd seen so far in the compound, it was thrown together, ramshackle. Clearly the Count had just moved in. And he might not be planning on staying for long.

Boba knew the lair was underground — he had

entered through a hillside, after being dropped off by Aurra Sing — but that was all he knew. He was far from the outside world, and even farther from any place he had ever known. He was isolated. The Count controlled everything.

Boba knew he couldn't stay in the room all day. If he'd learned anything from the terrible days following his father's death, it was that he couldn't hesitate to take action. Boba kept walking down the hallway, which led to another dim hallway, the far-off voices a little closer. *How will I find my way back to my own room?* Boba wondered. The room where he had slept was where he had left his flight bag. It was his only property, the legacy from his father.

He would worry about that later. *First things first.* That was a lesson his father had taught him. First he had to find the Count and figure out what was going on.

"Hello?" Another empty room. But wait . . . this room was different.

It had a window.

The window overlooked a lake, surrounded by woods. A blue sky overhead was flecked with white clouds. But how could that be?

Raxus Prime was the most toxic planet in the

entire galaxy. Boba had seen the skies, thick with smoke; the hillsides piled high with wreckage and garbage; the oily waters choked with debris and waste. Everything on Raxus Prime was foul and filthy. So what was this lake out the window? Had it all been cleaned up while he slept? Or had he been moved somewhere else?

Boba crossed the room toward the window. He was just about to try to open it when he heard a stern, forceful voice behind him.

"Not allowed."

Boba turned. Someone — or some*thing* — was standing in the doorway to the room, making the empty space seem suddenly filled. He was huge, his bald, reptilian head crowned with a clawlike crest. He wore a gray jumpsuit with gold braiding and buttons. His broad mouth was filled with too many big square teeth, and his tiny eyes were cold.

"*Not allowed,*" the giant in the doorway said again, this time with a stomp of his tall, heavy boots. The ground shook beneath his statement.

Boba felt a chill of fear, and remembered his father's words: *Welcome your fear as a friend, but never show it to others.* He made his voice sound casual, almost friendly. "What's not allowed?" he asked.

"The unpermitted," was the terse reply. "Now come with us, young sir."

Us? There was just him, just the one giant. But that was enough. "Come — where?" Boba asked.

"The Count, ready to see you. Follow us, please."

Boba knew he had no choice. The creature wasn't going to move until Boba did as he said.

CHAPTER TWO

Boba followed the giant past more closed doors, to an ornately carved door at the end of a long hall.

The giant knocked, then entered to a signal Boba hadn't heard. Inside, the room was larger than the others. It had furniture, too. A desk with carved legs had a holoprojector on it. A holographic comm unit was ready for transmissions in the corner of the room.

Behind the desk was a tall picture window. The window faced a different direction than the window in the other room, but overlooked the same view, surrounded by the same woods. *What's going on?* Boba wondered.

A man in a long cloak was standing at the window, looking out. He turned when Boba entered the room. A smile as thin and as sharp as a dagger creased his long, narrow face, slicing his white beard in two. In a single glance, Boba could feel his dark presence. This was something more than strength. It was power.

"Young Boba Fett," the Count said in a

sonorous voice. "I hope you slept well. I see you found the clean clothing that was left beside your bed."

Boba nodded, fingering the coarse tunic. "Yes, sir."

"And the accommodations?"

Boba nodded again. The breakfast hadn't amounted to much, only a shuura. But he wasn't about to complain.

"Excellent," said the Count. "And I believe you have met Cydon Prax. He assists me with all things."

The hideous giant bowed and Boba bowed back. His father had taught him to spot a killer when he saw one. And Prax looked like he could easily be a killer, if pushed the wrong way. Boba felt a tinge of anger, too. Prax now stood where Boba's dad had stood before, at the Count's side.

"Prax will look after you and take care of your needs," the Count continued. "You must let him know if there is anything you desire. Anything at all."

Boba nodded. "Yes, sir. Thank you, sir." He wanted to seem agreeable — almost subservient. He wanted Prax to think of him as an obedient little kid. That way, neither Prax nor the Count would know what was really going through his head.

"Since the unfortunate death of your father, I have been pleased to take on the responsibility for your care and upbringing," said the Count. "As you no doubt know, that was Jango Fett's last and fondest wish."

It was? Boba thought. The Count's words were kind, but why was his voice so cold?

"I have many obligations that may, unfortunately, prevent me from giving you my total attention," continued the Count. "However, I welcome you to my quarters here on Raxus Prime. You may find them a little primitive. We are engaged in an important archaeological project here. I will expect you to respect my rules and stay out of the way."

"Yes, sir," said Boba. It was easy enough to please adults. All he had to do was nod and agree.

"Good." The Count's smile was as bright and cold as an icicle. "Cydon, leave us."

Cydon Prax gave a nod and lumbered out of the room. The Count slowly approached Boba and asked, "Have you ever heard the name Tyranus?"

Boba nodded. It was a simple question, but the Count's tone was ominous.

"Your father may have mentioned it to you in connection with his work on Kamino, developing the clone troopers. I believe I've heard you say that he and I were the same person. When you were on Geonosis, you looked at me and said, 'Isn't that Tyranus?' Do you remember that?"

"I remember," said Boba. *Where is this going?* he wondered.

"You might ask, why would someone have two names, Tyranus and Dooku?" the Count suggested mildly.

"I learned from my father not to ask too many questions," Boba said. He could see from the Count's eyes that this was the right answer.

"Excellent," said the Count. "Your father was very discreet. I believe you will be, too."

"Yes," said Boba, wanting to reassure the Count.

"A useful man, your father," said the Count. "And I see you are your father's son. I am sure that with the proper training, you will be as useful some-day."

"Yes, sir," said Boba. Training! Now they were getting somewhere. "Also, my father left a mes-sage about some credits that belonged to him. He said you would give them to me."

"Ah, yes, Jango Fett's savings. I suppose, if you prove worthy . . . but we will discuss all that later, this evening."

"I will prove worthy!" said Boba eagerly. "I want to be a great bounty hunter like my dad."

But the Count was no longer listening. He was studying some strange images on his holomap. He had turned all of his attention away from Boba, as if Boba had never been there.

Boba heard the door open and felt a grip on his shoulder. "Come with us," said Cydon Prax.

As he was being led out the door, Boba heard

the Count behind him, talking on his comm device. "Keep digging," he said in his icy voice. "Expand the search. Spare no expense. What we are looking for is more powerful than you can possibly imagine."

CHAPTER THREE

As Boba followed Prax down the long halls, back to his lonely room, he thought of the Count's cold dismissal. *Can I trust him? Do I have a choice?* Maybe the Count wasn't going to turn out to be such a good friend after all. Jango Fett had always said that in a bounty hunter's life, there was no such thing as a friend. Boba knew this was probably true. But still he hoped . . .

"Stay here," said Prax, when they arrived at the room. "No wandering. Unpermitted."

Boba nodded his agreement and closed the door. His original clothes were back, clean, folded at the foot of the bed. He changed into them, glad to shed the rough tunic.

His flight bag sat on the floor beside the bed. It contained everything Boba owned — except his father's ship, *Slave I*. Boba fully intended to get it back. Meanwhile, the bag contained all his worldly possessions:

A helmet and a book.

When Boba had buried his father with his armor on Geonosis, he had kept his scarred and pitted battle helmet. It was Mandalorian. Boba took it out of the flight bag and looked at it longingly. The faceplate of the helmet was as familiar, as stern, and, in its own strange way, as loving as his father's actual features.

In fact, Boba was beginning to fear he would forget his father's face. *This* would become more familiar — this harsh visage, like a T, with an eye slit at the top.

Boba put the helmet beside him and took out the book.

The black book contained Jango Fett's final messages to his son. Sometimes they were the same, from day to day. Sometimes they changed.

The most recent message had been about the Count, credits, and self-sufficiency. Boba opened the book to see if it had changed. It had, but only a little. Today it read:

> *Self-sufficiency you will*
> *learn from the Count.*

Sometimes the book wasn't much help. How was he going to learn *self-sufficiency* from the Count, who wasn't even interested in talking to him?

Boba had lots of questions. Why was the Count so cold and mistrustful? What was he digging for? But it was clear that if he wanted answers, he was going to have to find them himself — even though *wandering* was *unpermitted,* according to Prax.

He closed the book and put it back into the flight bag. It was time to explore.

Boba clenched his fist and held it in front of his face, making a vow. "Self-sufficiency means do it yourself!" he muttered. He picked up his father's helmet — it was his only possible disguise, just in case he needed one. Carefully, as quietly as possible, he opened the door. . . .

CHAPTER FOUR

Boba looked right.
Boba looked left.
No Cydon Prax.
Good — all clear!

He started his exploration, staying close to the wall, so he could duck out of sight if necessary. He followed the hallway to the end, then rounded a corner; then another corner — always heading toward the noises and commotion he could hear in the distance.

The halls around his room were empty, but those farther away were filled with noise and activity. Soon Boba found himself sharing the corridors. Droids of all shapes and sizes bustled about, carrying equipment in and out of the small storage rooms. Their whirrs and clicks sounded almost like speech.

There were other creatures, too. Boba saw a Geonosian warrior armed with a sonic blaster at a distance and a Nemoidian in colorful robes, looking angry and harassed.

The whole place had a temporary, provisional

air, like a construction site. There was dirt on the floor and scars on the walls, where they had been bumped and scraped. There was a sharp smell, either of the outside air or of the oil-like sweat glistening on the limbs of the busy droids.

The equipment in some of the rooms looked like it was for digging or drilling. Most of it was covered with muck, but some was bright and gleaming, as though it hadn't yet been used.

And under it all was a low hum, a constant buzz of activity. Boba heard two Nemoidians talking about "the dig" and "the harvester," but they turned a corner and were gone before he could hear more.

Boba made his way down the halls and around the corners, trying to remain as inconspicuous as possible. He had learned that it was easy for a ten-year-old to be invisible, as long as he stayed out of the way.

The droids and workers were all intent on their tasks. And none of them knew or cared who Boba was, except for Prax. All Boba had to do was avoid him.

The air in the corridor was growing colder. The toxic smell was stronger. Ahead, Boba saw a large opening to the outside. Droids and workers streamed in and out, some carrying strange-looking tools, others riding on square all-terrain vehicles.

He was trying to get a better look when he heard a familiar voice: "Give us results!"

That harsh, booming sound was familiar. Cydon Prax? Boba wasn't taking any chances. He ducked into a nearby room and flattened himself against the wall.

To his surprise, he was facing a window. The view was just like the ones he had seen earlier. The window overlooked a lake surrounded by woods, with a clear blue sky overhead.

Again, Boba wondered how such a view could exist on Raxus Prime. And why was the view exactly the same every time he saw it? How could three rooms in different places have the same view?

He approached the window and reached out to touch it. It was soft, like a plastic curtain. As soon as he touched it, the scene changed. Now he saw bright blue-green water lapping against silvery sands.

He touched the window again.

Snow-covered peaks watching over an icy planet.

Now I get it! Boba thought. It was all a display, a virtual window showing a virtual scene. A series of illusions installed by the Count.

Boba touched the viewscreen one last time and saw toxic steam belching from piles of trash and slag, under a reddish, smoke-stained sky. This was the real world — Raxus Prime. The beautiful views were just fabrications.

In the distance was a tower with huge arms, moving up and down. It looked like a giant robot. Was it real, or an illusion? Boba couldn't tell. Here in the Count's lair, it was impossible to tell the truth from a lie.

Suddenly, Boba heard a distinctive set of footsteps in the hallway — the heavy tread of Prax patrolling. In the blank room, there was nowhere to hide. Boba held himself close to the wall, next to the doorway. If Prax peered in, Boba would be fine. If Prax walked inside, he'd be caught.

The footsteps came closer. Then stopped. Right outside the room. Boba held his breath. The door opened. Prax stuck his head into the room.

The window is wrong, Boba realized. Too late. There was no way to hide the scene of Raxus Prime.

Prax was no more than a meter away from Boba. If he turned his head, it would all be over.

For a long second, everything remained still. Then Prax grunted and pulled his head out of the room.

Boba waited a few minutes, until he was sure Prax was gone again. Then he slipped back out into the hall and headed toward the other creatures near the exit.

Boba stood to one side and looked out the giant

doorway. Through the swirling mists he saw the tower he had seen through the "window." The tower was definitely real. It was the focus of all the activity; a crude dirt road from the door to the tower's base was crowded with vehicles, droids, and workers carrying equipment, some coming and others going out.

Boba was fascinated. This must be the Count's "dig."

What was he digging for? The Count had made it sound like something very powerful . . . which would make it something a bounty hunter should know about.

There was one way to find out the truth.

CHAPTER FIVE

Whew! What a stink! The sky was dark with swirling smoke; the ground was heaped with the trash and garbage from a thousand planets. The twisted wreckage of hundreds of crashed ships stretched into the distance. The air was almost too foul to breathe.

Luckily, Boba had brought his father's battle helmet. He put it over his head as he started out on the road, toward the tower. The helmet was surprisingly light, and it made breathing easier; though it had no independent air supply, its filters removed the worst of Raxus Prime's poisons.

Self-sufficiency, thought Boba, *begins with the right equipment.*

The road angled up a ridge of oozing slag. Boba slogged along, his boots slipping in the soft terrain. At the top, where the road crested the ridge, he stopped to rest.

From here he could see the tower much better. It was a crane. The arms were equipped with drills and vats, which dipped deep into the muck of Raxus Prime. Lights from the top of the tower illuminated a great pit, where droids and workers toiled in and out of the vapors and the darkness.

All around were ruined walls and arches, like the remains of a great city that had been buried and forgotten, and was being dug up again.

Boba descended the ridge until he was at the edge of the enormous pit and looked down. Remote diggers and salvage droids rattled and bumped through the muck, far below. Well-armed "spider" droids stood watch at the perimeter of the pit, and Boba saw AAT tanks idling nearby, hovering off the ground. But none of them seemed interested in him.

A lot of firepower for a hole in the ground, especially on the galaxy's garbage planet. Boba wondered again what could be so valuable, buried in the mire and muck of Raxus Prime?

As if in answer to his unspoken question, a gruff voice said, "Getting close to it, huh?"

Boba jumped. He hadn't seen the Givin driver, who had stepped out of his drilling vehicle and walked up to stand beside him.

"Guess so," Boba asked. He didn't want to admit that he didn't know what "it" was.

"About time." The driver bit off a piece of radni root, and offered it to Boba. "Have a chaw?"

Boba realized that in his helmet, he was being

taken for an adult. Another advantage of his father's legacy.

"No, thanks, I don't chew," he said. Then he ventured: "So that's it — the treasure?"

"Treasure?" The Geonosian laughed and spat into the pit. "Not unless you call death a treasure. No one's supposed to know, but the Count is after something called a Force Harvester."

Boba had heard about the Force. The Jedi used it, his father had told him. But the Count wasn't a Jedi . . .

"But don't mind me," he said, heading back to his mud-laden craft. "I just work here."

"Security check!" said a gruff, familiar voice in the near distance. Boba ducked behind a rock just as Cydon Prax strode into view.

"All systems secure?" Prax asked. "No intruders?"

"Who'd intrude on this planet?" asked the driver, swinging up into his seat. "Not exactly a resort."

"Keep an eye open," growled Prax. "The Count does not want anyone nosing about his digs. Got it?"

"Got it, got it," said the driver.

I'd better get out of here, fast! Boba thought. Prax might recognize him, even in his helmet, because of his size. He waited until Prax was out of sight, then started back down the road.

The problem was, the road was too exposed,

too narrow. Prax could come along at any moment. Boba decided to take what he hoped was a short-cut. A path veered off through the wreckage, but Boba thought he saw it emerge back by the Count's base.

After getting off the road and rounding a few bends, Boba realized he'd already gone far. Like most shortcuts, it turned out to be the long way.

CHAPTER SIX

It was hard going. Up one stinking slag heap, and down another.

Boba tried to keep the big tower straight behind him, and the distant light of the door ahead. That would be the shortest, fastest route back to Dooku's underground lair.

The stinking ground sucked at his boots where it was wet, and crumbled into toxic dust where it was dry.

Raxus Prime was all ruins and debris. Boba passed through forests of broken machinery and shredded wire. He climbed cliffs of soggy, discarded fabric and slid down steep mountainsides of muck. Brown steam spewed from the steep piles, while foul-smelling liquids oozed down their sides.

The helmet helped him breathe but it couldn't mask the smell of the noxious atmosphere. Still, Boba pushed on. He had no choice; he had to beat Prax back to the Count's lair. Otherwise, the Count might find out he had broken his rules and gone outside. Even though Boba wasn't sure what he had discovered. The Force Harvester? What was that?

"Ugh!" Boba slipped on a particularly foul-smelling piece of refuse and slid to a stop. He was at the edge of a wide pond of bubbling, greenish-brown liquid. It looked *very* nasty. A mist rose from the surface that smelled like rotten rikknit eggs.

Unless Boba turned around, the only way through was by way of the pond. He walked straight into the liquid — first one step, then another. The nasty goop sloshed over the tops of his boots, but what did he care? Boba was not going to let any-thing get in his way. A bounty hunter was not de-layed by revulsion.

Boba shook the slime off his boots and trudged up another steep ridge of dripping slag. Even through his helmet, the smell was terrible. But from the top, he could see that the brightly lighted doorway of the Count's lair was only a few hundred meters away. He was almost there!

There was only another pond to cross, and this one was long and narrow — just a few meters across. Boba slid down another slope slick with oozing slime, to the edge.

The pond was ringed with foul-smelling ferns. It was a brighter green than the last one, and it looked deeper. A lot deeper.

Boba summoned up his courage and stepped off the edge, into the ferns. His boots sank into the ground. He took another step and sank up to his boot tops. Boba tried to pull his left leg free; it sank even deeper.

Another step, and it was up to his knees. Boba was more than halfway across, but he was stuck. The ooze felt like hands, pulling him down deeper and deeper.

Boba tried to take a step back, but he couldn't. Instead, he slipped farther into the greenish muck. Now it was up to his waist.

He tried again to pull his legs free, but thrashing around only sank him deeper into the stinking, gluelike mud.

He quickly sank in up to his neck.

The mist was rising into his mask, and he could hardly breathe. He could feel a burning sensation in his knees and feet. It felt as if he were being dissolved by the acid gunk.

I am being digested!

Only the helmet allowed him to breathe, to survive. It seemed to have stopped the sinking and the digesting for some reason. But for how long? His chin sank into the muck. In a moment his mouth and nose would be covered, too. The mask was clearly being rejected by the horrible mass . . . but how long would that last?

Boba searched frantically for a means of escape. He saw a coil of wire sticking out of a slag heap on the other side of the pond, but it was too far away. A stick lay closer, on the bank below the wire, but still out of reach. The reeds were all around, but they were too thin and frail to hold his weight.

Then Boba remembered: *self-sufficiency*. It meant using whatever was available.

He managed to get one arm out of the muck and grabbed the longest reed he could find, pulling it up by the roots. It felt slimy, even through his gloves. He used it like a long flexible hook to snag the wire, inching it across the mud until it was within the reach of his hand.

Yes! The wire felt plenty strong. Boba wrapped it around his hand and began to pull.

It was almost too late. His eyes were burning and he could hardly breathe. His arms were weak. He gathered all his strength and pulled. . . .

The wire was coming loose from the slag pile. It dislodged a tiny clod, starting a small land-slide down the slippery slope of slag and garbage. Then it jerked tight again. It had snagged on some-thing.

Boba pulled again, but more carefully this time. The wire was barely caught on the edge of an old piece of machinery. If it slipped off, he was a goner.

This was his last chance. Hardly daring to breathe, he pulled himself toward the shore of the pond. One leg was free . . . then the other . . .

Boba grabbed a handful of reeds and pulled

himself out of the stinking liquid, onto the slimy shore. "Whew!" Plain old slime had never felt so good before.

He was free.

Boba blended in with the crowd of droids, warriors, and workers streaming in the wide, brightly lighted doorway. No one noticed him, and Prax was nowhere to be seen.

Even the filth that covered him didn't give him away. Many of the others were filthy as well, from the dig.

Boba took off his helmet and wiped it clean. It had saved his life, that was for sure. He now realized why it was so important to his father . . . and why it would be important to him.

Boba joined the "dig" workers in the shower that steamed the worst of the slime off his clothes and his boots, and then dried them instantly. Now all he had to do was make it back to his room and no one would know he had been outside.

He stepped out of the shower, his clothes already dry — and grimaced in pain as a rough, strong hand gripped his shoulder.

"Come!" The voice was unmistakable. Boba opened his mouth to explain that he hadn't *meant* to break the rules, that it was all a mistake. But what was the point?

Cydon Prax wasn't listening as he dragged Boba down the corridor, toward the Count's inner sanctuary.

CHAPTER SEVEN

The Count wrinkled his finely arched nose. "We shall have to clean you up," he said dismissively.

Boba tried to keep from shaking. He knew it was best never to show fear. He gripped his father's helmet in his hands.

"Your father didn't teach you very well," said the Count. "You have been sticking your nose where it does not belong."

"I didn't see anything," Boba said. He could feel the Count's power turning steadily into wrath.

"Oh, really?" The Count was scornful. He stood behind his desk, in front of the "window" that showed a blue lake under a blue sky. Anything but the real filth of Raxus Prime.

"*Really,*" said Boba. "I just stepped outside the door. I didn't go far."

"Perhaps I should take on your training, after all," said the Count. Boba felt a moment's hope. But the hope was dashed by the Count's next words: "If I did, the first thing I would teach you is how to lie. You are not very good at it."

"I am sorry I broke your rules," said Boba. *And especially sorry that I got caught.*

"Sorry?" said the Count with a smooth, cold grin. "You have broken my rules. And that is not all . . ."

Not all? Wasn't that enough?

"I've decided that you know too much at a time when information is a valuable commodity." He turned to Cydon Prax, who stood by the doorway. "Isn't it ironic that one small boy should be the only one who knows such a great secret?"

Prax didn't answer, of course. Boba wasn't sure what the "great secret" was that he was supposed to know about. But the Count's remark gave him an idea that he hoped just *might* save his life.

"What makes you think I'm the only one who knows?"

The Count raised his eyebrow — the most surprise Boba could imagine the Count betraying. "What do you mean?"

"Just what I said," said Boba. He tried to keep his voice calm, cool, *Jango Fett–style.* "I have already told someone else."

He had the Count's attention now . . . barely. "May I inquire who?" the older man asked.

"That's my secret," Boba bluffed. "And she knows who to tell if anything happens to me."

"*She?*" Boba could hear a slight undertow of un-
certainty. "Might you be insinuating the bounty
hunter Aurra Sing?"

Boba was making it up as he went along. "I do
mean Aurra Sing," he said.

"Young fool. Are you threatening me?"

"No, sir. I simply want what is mine. My freedom — and my father's credits."

"Freedom? Credits?" The Count's eyes blazed
like cold fire. "I do not bargain with children. Especially those who are a nuisance."

I went too far! Boba realized. His last chance
was lost.

"Cydon Prax, you know what to do with him."

Boba knew it was useless to resist. He closed
his eyes as Cydon Prax picked him up. Boba
dropped his helmet as his arms were pinned. His
father's voice came to him. *If you must die, do so
with valor.* That is what Jango Fett had done, fighting to the last moment.

The memory inspired Boba. He was done with
pleading and pretending. Whatever was coming, he
would face it with the courage of the son of Jango
Fett.

Suddenly the Count raised his hand. For the first
time, Boba saw genuine concern cross his face.

"What is it, sir?" Prax asked.

"The Jedi have found us," the Count answered.

Boba strained to hear something beyond the silence of the room. *How did the Count know?*

"Finish him off, then join me," the Count said tersely as his hand seemed to instinctively find the curved lightsaber handle that glistened beneath his cloak.

BAR-ROOOM! An explosion shook the floor.

Quickly picking up a holopad from his desk, the Count left the room. As if on cue, a second explosion rocked the room. This one was closer. Small rocks started to fall from the ceiling.

Cydon Prax hesitated for a moment and his grip on Boba loosened just a little as he looked after his master. Boba saw his chance. He kicked out with all his strength against the nearest wall. Prax was propelled backward, into the desk. Boba's elbows slammed into him as they landed.

"You little . . ."

Prax's words were lost in a series of explosions outside. The floor pitched up like the deck of a ship being tossed by a giant wave. The door cracked and fell to the ground. The sound of blaster fire and confused voices filled the air.

Boba lunged and twisted free from Prax's grip. He scooped up his battle helmet from the floor where he had dropped it. And then he did what his father had taught him to do whenever he was in a bad situation he didn't expect to get any better.

He ran.

CHAPTER EIGHT

The once dim corridor was filled with light, and no wonder!

The Count's underground hideout had been blown wide open. Large parts of the roof were missing, and Boba was standing on top of a pile of smoking rubble.

He looked up. The filthy sky of Raxus Prime was even filthier than usual. It was filled with explosions, blossoming like deadly flowers.

The noise was deafening. A battle was raging. Blaster fire screamed past. The Count's automatic defense system was firing into the air, rapid-fire lasers filling the already smoky air with bursts and clouds of brightly colored smoke.

Through the clouds, Boba saw the approaching gunships. They bore the eight-spoked insignia of the Republic. The Count had been right — it was a Jedi-led attack! Republic assault ships were unloading clone troopers in their gleaming white battle armor. They fanned out in impressive military order through the slag heaps, smashing the Count's defenses.

My brothers! Boba thought scornfully. His father had helped create the clone troopers; the Kaminoans had used his dad's genetic material to make millions of them. So why were they fighting on the side of the hated Jedi — again?

Battle droids followed what Boba instantly recognized as GAT tanks, closing in on the clone troopers from behind — until a Jedi on a speeder-bike streaked over the horizon, mowing them down with deadly laser fire. And here came what looked like a new kind of tank, its telltale red markings signifying it belonged to the Jedi, lurching through the same slimy ponds that Boba had survived.

Jedi gunships were closing in on the ruins that surrounded the crane tower and the pit. One gunship dodged a missile's streak; another was hit and spiraled down to crash unseen over the horizon.

Yes! Boba watched, fascinated. He hated both sides — the Jedi and the Count. But he loved the action.

It was chaos, and it was just the diversion he needed to help him escape. He looked down and saw his reflection in a puddle. His face was streaked with dirt again, but he was grinning from ear to ear.

Anything was better than being the Count's prisoner. He was free!

*　　*　　*

Boba heard a noise behind him and turned just in time to see a huge starship rise from the other end of the Count's hideout.

It was the Count, making his escape. Boba wondered if he had managed to rescue the dark treasure that he had come to Raxus Prime to find.

Two Jedi starfighters raced over the horizon, zeroing in on the Count's starship. The pursued and pursuers both vanished into the thick clouds.

KABOOM!

KABOOM!

Even though the Count had fled, his defense system was still working. It would keep firing until his slave droids were dead and the lasers ran out of energy. Boba kept his head down as he crawled through the rubble, looking for an opening that would lead back down into the hallways of the abandoned hideout where he had to go to get his father's book.

Wearing his helmet for protection, Boba crawled through a smashed opening in a wall. The hallways were choked with smoke and rubble. The dust, the explosions, the noise, made everything difficult to see.

As he grasped his way through the abandoned corridor, Boba found that he felt very little fear. He had escaped the worst fate imaginable, and now he felt like a new man, or at least a new boy. What could happen to him worse than what he had escaped?

He saw a familiar-looking door. His room!

There was his bed, turned on its side by an explosion. But where was the flight bag that had been under it?

Frantically, Boba dug in the rubble with his hands until he felt the familiar curve of a handle. He pulled, harder and harder, until it came free.

Safe! He threw the helmet into the bag and sealed it. With the troopers around, it was best to keep Jango Fett's mask out of sight.

CHAPTER NINE

Boba crawled toward the open air — and found himself face-to-face with a squadron of clone troopers bursting through the wreckage. As soon as they saw Boba, they leveled their blasters at him.

"Come with us," the trooper said, extending a white-gloved hand.

Boba wondered if the trooper knew who he was. The trooper soon answered that question with his next words:

"Are you one of the orphans?"

"Uh, sure," Boba replied. He *was* an orphan, after all.

"Name of missing or deceased parents."

"Oh, uh — Teff," said Boba.

"Orphan Teff, age, please?"

"Ten."

"Under guidelines," said the clone trooper. "Follow me for food and shelter."

Food and shelter? That didn't sound so bad.

Boba didn't trust the Jedi, but this clone trooper

was not a Jedi, even though he was probably working for them.

"Sure thing," said Boba, picking up his flight bag and noticing the trooper's number — CT-4/619.

Explosions still rocked the building. Even though the Count had escaped, the battle raged on. The Count's slave droids were continuing the fight — and Boba was now caught in the crossfire.

The clone troopers paid little attention to the explosions as they lifted their blasters to repel the super battle droids. For a split second, Boba felt an echo of the past — the clone troopers' movements were almost exactly the same as Jango Fett's. The way they held their blaster rifles. The way their heads turned to take in the full scope of the battle. The fierce stealth of their steps. *He trained them as well as he trained me.*

No, better.

Boba knew he had to snap out of these thoughts. The battle droids were pushing forward against the troopers' ranks, relentlessly firing their blasters. They had been programmed to kill or be destroyed. There would be no surrender, no retreat.

They aimed their fire at the troopers and at the top of the rubble's entrance. Boba dashed out into the open just as the doorway began to cave in. The troopers inside died without a sound. The air was suddenly choked with dust. The other troopers did not look back.

An eruption of blaster fire landed at Boba's feet. *A close call.* A trooper at his side was knocked off his feet, crashing into the rubble. The droids, too, were being torn apart by the shooting. *A bloodbath — without the blood.*

There was nowhere for Boba to hide. No way to get out of this.

He picked up a fallen trooper's blaster and chose a side. The clones were his only chance of getting off the planet. He had to help them win.

Boba had never fought in a battle before. Whenever he'd held a blaster, his father had been at his side. Watching. Checking. Instructing.

Boba looked again at the troopers, the echo of his father. He raised his rifle like they raised theirs. He aimed at the controls of one of the battle droids. Without hesitation, he fired. The droid exploded into parts.

Another trooper fell — there were only four left with Boba. He could hear the sound of other battles close by. *Who is winning?* CT-4/619 leaped —with Jango Fett's dexterity — toward a fallen excavation rig. Boba understood at once — *protection.* As the second and third troopers ran for cover, Boba kept in their shadow. The fourth trooper followed and was cut down by a rapid barrage of blaster fire. His mask went flying as he hit the ground. Boba knew if he looked he would see his father's face, replicated once more in death.

He did not look back.

Instead he positioned himself at CT-4/619's side, aiming his blaster rifle as the troopers made their last stand. One battle droid down. Then another. Still, it wasn't enough. There were at least a dozen left.

CT-4/619 did not falter. He did not look at Boba. He did not say a word. He kept his focus. He kept his aim. Boba knew this concentration well.

Boba fired again. A miss. The droid returned his fire, tearing a hole into the excavation rig — the only protection left.

Two more droids down. But the remaining droids were not deterred. They turned all their fire onto the third trooper the next time he moved into blasting position. He didn't have a chance.

This is it, Boba thought. *There's no other way out.*

Out of the corner of his eye, he could see another form approaching. Not a clone. Not a droid. A female Bothan, bearded and small. Wearing the robes of a Jedi.

With one sharp, quick movement, the Jedi activated her lightsaber and began to repel the droids' fire. As the droids turned their attack on her, Boba and the two remaining clone troopers had an open shot.

The droids began to fall. The Jedi expertly destroyed them with their own fire. The remaining clones rallied with cold precision. And Boba did his part. He was not as experienced or as focused as his clone brothers. But he had a desire to survive that they couldn't match.

The firing from the droids slowed . . . then stopped. There were none left. Boba looked over to see the Jedi's reaction — but she was already gone. Off to the next skirmish in order to complete this invasion.

Eventually, the laser cannons fell silent. Some of the gunships left the perimeter, their mission complete. A few more circled, the remains of the attack force. Jedi and clone troopers combed the ground for survivors — and prisoners. CT-4/619 led Boba forward. There was no time to stop and mourn for the dead. There were no congratulations, no expressions of relief. Just the task at hand — getting back to the ship, finishing the mission.

They walked across the smoking rubble toward a sleek gunship idling in the swirling, stinking mists. Boba followed resolutely. Even though he was walking into the hands of the Jedi, it was worth it to be walking out of the grasp of Raxus Prime. CT-4/619 took away Boba's blaster rifle as he walked on board the gunship — but luckily he was allowed to keep his bag. Boba followed the trooper into the pilot area. The trooper got into the pilot's seat and Boba sat in another seat.

"Not for seating," said the trooper. "For my partner, CT-5/501. Detainees sit on the floor. We'll wait here for the others."

Boba wasn't about to protest. He sat on his flight bag while the trooper powered up the vehicle.

Where's the food? Boba wondered. He suddenly realized how cold and hungry and tired he was.

The gunship seemed awfully comfortable, even on the durasteel floor. He could still hear the last gasp of explosions and commands being given over the gunship's comm unit, but for some strange reason, he felt safe. He knew he had survived.

"Impossible!"

Boba opened his eyes. Had he dozed off?

There was a face on the viewscreen. Angry, violet eyes peered out from under long ash-blond hair and over a cream-colored beard that had been braided into points. But it wasn't the face that bothered Boba, or even the harsh, demanding voice.

It was the uniform.

Even though this Jedi had just saved Boba's life, she was still the enemy. Boba knew he had to remember that.

"Impossible!" the Jedi said again. "There are no humanoid orphans on Raxus Prime, only Jawas. The planet is nothing but a toxic dump."

"Nevertheless, General Glynn-Beti," said CT-4/619. "I rescued one and brought him into the gunship, as per intructions."

"Bring him up and stick him with the others, then. We will check on him just like the rest."

Boba tried not to show the emotion in his face. The troopers were easy enough to fool; or perhaps they didn't care. But the Jedi would see through his deception. They were looking for him; he had almost been apprehended on Coruscant. He was starting to think it was better to stay on Raxus Prime, foul as it was.

But wait! Boba's new wisdom took over. The Jedi thought he was a war orphan. He would be put with other orphans, as she had said. If he kept his mouth shut, he would get food, shelter — and transportation to another planet, where he could begin the search for Aurra Sing and *Slave I*.

Self-sufficiency was all about using the opportunities that presented themselves. The Jedi wanted orphans — so Boba Fett would be Orphan Teff!

CHAPTER TEN

Boba stared out the narrow viewscreen as the powerful gunship rose above the slag heaps of Raxus Prime and into the clouds. He was glad to see the last of the galaxy's most toxic planet!

A droid fighter closed in on them, but the craft's automated turret targeted it and annihilated it with withering turbo fire. Below, skirmishes continued as clone troopers cleaned out the slave droids and continued their work in the Count's compound.

As he watched the clone troopers work together to fly the ship, Boba felt pangs of jealousy. He yearned to get his hands on the controls of a ship. He missed flying; it was all he had ever cared about or wanted to do.

"Entering high orbit," said CT-5/501. "Request permission to approach *Candaserri*."

"Permission granted."

The clones worked well together, executing the small tasks of maneuvering and communications with hardly a word among them. They flew the ship skillfully, avoiding fire and making precise judgments, but without any particular joy or style.

Boba found them fascinating, but slightly repellent. It was just too weird. They were his brothers, though they didn't know it. Like him, they were clones of Jango Fett, but they had matured at twice the normal rate. They looked and acted twenty years old, not ten.

Their rushed maturity and other engineering meant that they were very narrow in their interests and enthusiasms. They seemed to have no fear, and no excitement, either. They weren't the least bit interested in Boba, which suited Boba fine.

The less I see of these guys, the better.

Boba retreated to a back corner of the cockpit and he opened the black book his father had left him. He needed some advice. He needed to feel that he wasn't entirely alone.

But there was no new message. Only the message that had brought him here:

*Self-sufficiency you will
learn from the Count.*

The Count who had wanted to kill him? Who had stolen his father's credits and cheated and betrayed him?

Yes. Boba suddenly understood what his father's cryptic message meant.

The Count had taught Boba never to trust anyone again. The Count had taught him that he could rely only on himself.

The Count had taught him *self-sufficiency.*

And with that came confidence.

Boba returned to the viewscreen. Stars! He greeted them like old friends, with a fierce joy. He hadn't realized how much he had missed them on Raxus Prime, which was so polluted that the stars were never visible.

Space, cold and empty as it was, felt like home.

The gunship soared in silence through the void until an assault ship came into view — first as a single far-off dot of light, one among millions; then as a galaxy, spinning slowly; then as a dagger shape, larger and larger, festooned with dozens of turbo lasers. "Awesome," said Boba. "What's its name again?"

It was the biggest ship he had ever seen — as big as a city, floating in space.

"Starship *Candaserri*," CT-4/619 reported. "Republic troopship, *Acclamator*-class. Seven hundred fifty-two meters long. Crew seven hundred, military and support personnel fifteen thousand five hundred."

"And Jedi?" Boba asked.

"Only a few. They are in command, usually on the command bridge."

"Any names?" Boba wondered if they would include the hated Obi-Wan Kenobi, or Mace Windu, who had killed his father.

"Glynn-Beti is the Jedi general who works with us," said CT-4/619. "You will meet her or her Padawan, who is in charge of the orphans as well."

"Padawan?"

"A Padawan Learner is an apprentice Jedi."

Oh, thought Boba, remembering the young Jedi, Anakin Skywalker, who had also been present at Jango Fett's death.

Boba felt a mixture of excitement and apprehension as they drew closer to the *Candaserri*'s rear docking bay.

Tiny figures could be seen behind the ports and windows: crew members going about their duties, clone troops drilling.

And somewhere, on the bridge perhaps, the hated Jedi.

Soon, Boba knew, he would face a stern test. If he could conceal his true indentity, the Jedi could help him by taking him far away from Raxus Prime. He could then begin the task of tracking down Aurra Sing and recovering the stolen *Slave I*.

After a few more maneuvers, they were ready to

land. Airlocks hissed, ramps dropped, doors slid open.

Boba followed the two clone troopers out into a huge enclosed space. The rear docking bay was filled with gunships and starfighters, lined up in neat rows. Clone troopers in fours and sixes walked among them, guarding them or servicing them — it was hard for Boba to tell.

Boba heard footsteps approaching. "Where is the orphan?" a serious voice called out. "Let's see!"

"Over here," said CT-4/619.

Boba saw two robed Jedi approaching. Both were small, no taller than he was.

This was it. Boba turned to CT-4/619 and CT-5/501. They had saved him from Raxus Prime. He wanted to say good-bye, and thanks.

But they were already gone. Was that them, in the clone group servicing a *Cord*-class starfighter? Or were they among the four walking out the door in formation?

There was no way to tell; the troopers all looked exactly alike.

"Orphan Teff?"

Boba nodded, looking down.

The Jedi who stood in front of him was only about a meter and a half tall, but radiated power and command. Boba would have felt it even if he hadn't seen her in action on the battlefield. She had violet eyes and a pointed beard. Boba was not surprised by the beard. He knew her as a Bothan, and all Bothans, male and female alike, were bearded.

The younger Jedi, the Padawan, had three eyes and horns, but a friendly look.

"We didn't expect to find orphans on Raxus Prime," said the elder Jedi. "I am Glynn-Beti. This is my Padawan, Ulu Ulix."

The younger Jedi bowed. Boba bowed back.

"You sure you're an orphan and not a Separatist spy?" asked Glynn-Beti gruffly. She didn't seem to expect an answer. "Teff, huh? Account for yourself, Teff! How did you get on Raxus Prime?"

Boba put his hands behind his back, so she wouldn't see them trembling. This was harder than he had thought!

"Speak up, Orphan Teff! What are your parents' names? What's in the bag there? Open it, please."

Boba panicked. If he opened the flight bag and the Jedi saw the Mandalorian battle helmet, they would know he was Jango Fett's son. They would arrest him immediately. He didn't know what to do. *Self-sufficiency, don't fail me now!*

Instead of opening the bag, Boba decided to burst into tears. He covered his face with his hands and began to sob.

"Oh, bother!" said Glynn-Beti, visibly uncomfortable. "Ulu, take him to the Orphan Hall. But stop by the bacta baths first — he stinks of Raxus Prime, and who knows what contagion breeds there."

She turned on a tiny, pointed heel, and was gone.

"Come with me, Teff," said the Padawan, putting a gentle arm around Boba's shoulder. "Don't cry. Let's get you some clean clothes and something to eat. You'll feel better then, I promise. You don't seem like a spy and we'll hear your story later."

Boba sniffled as he followed Ulu Ulix. He kept his face covered to hide his true feelings.

It worked! he thought.

CHAPTER ELEVEN

Boba figured that taking a bacta bath was one of the galaxy's most intense experiences. He breathed through a mask while he was submerged in a synthetic gel that did a search and repair over every centimeter of his body, *inside and out*, healing, restoring, and refreshing every organ.

It took hours.

It made him tingle all over.

And it got rid of the stink of Raxus Prime.

Much better, Boba thought as he allowed the air scrubber to dry him. He put on the clean coveralls that had been set out for him by Ulu Ulix.

He was glad to see that no one had opened his flight bag.

"You look like a new person," said Ulu when he returned. "As you can see, Teff, there's no need to cry. Lots of kids have been separated from their parents during this war. Most of them will be reunited, I am sure. Meanwhile, all you orphans — *temporary* orphans — are being taken to a temporary clearing site in the beautiful Cloud City of Bespin."

Bespin! Boba perked up. The gas giant was fairly remote but a minor hub of the galaxy, and a good place to start his search for Aurra Sing. *Things are looking better already.*

Boba and Ulu walked through the halls of the vast ship. It was like Coruscant, levels and levels interlocked with ladders and chutes. But the halls were not teeming with hangers-on and tourists from all over the galaxy, all in different brightly colored outfits. Rather, there were only two basic types:

— the crew, who represented every sentient race or life-form. Diverse in color, stature, and shape, they were united by their magenta tunics.

— and the clone troopers, all looking alike, whether they were in their white battle armor or their red coveralls. With their helmets off, their blank faces showed neither emotion nor interest in anything outside their own ranks.

I hope I don't look that blank when I'm twenty, Boba thought with a shudder.

Ulu Ulix was very friendly, for a Jedi. He seemed to lack that aggressive arrogance that Boba associated with the order.

He'll probably flunk out, Boba thought.

They went into what must have been one of many small kitchens set up to feed the around-the-clock patrols. "The other kids will be at dinner," said Ulu Ulix. "You must be starving. What would you like?"

All the food was unfamiliar. Boba pointed to what looked like a meat pie that was sitting behind a pane of glass.

Ulu pressed his palm against the glass, and the meat pie made itself in a swirl of laser light, then floated out, released temporarily from the ship's artificial gravity.

"Thanks!" Boba said, catching it. It tasted better than good — it had been a long time since he'd had a full meal.

Boba didn't like Jedi — at all! — but it was hard to hate Ulu. He was different. Almost cordial. "Aren't you going to eat some?" Boba asked. "You can have a bite of mine."

"Not hungry. I just ate the day before yesterday."

At the end of a long hallway in the depths of the ship, they found a dormitory. It was empty of people, but filled with beds, all of them short.

"Grab an empty bed, Teff," said Ulu. "The other kids will be back from dinner soon. They'll tell you the drill. It mainly involves staying out of the way."

"That's it?"

"That's it," said Ulu. "I'm in charge of the Orphan Hall. It's part of my training. I try to make things as easy for you kids as possible. If there's anything you need, just let me know."

Ulu smiled and left, and Boba lay down on a bunk by the wall. This was going to be something new: a roomful of kids. Was he finally going to have a chance to make some friends? That would be something new for sure! His father had warned him about friendships and making himself weak to so-called friends. But Boba was still curious.

For now, Boba was too tired to think about it. He lay down and closed his eyes. It seemed that his head had barely hit the pillow when he was awakened by a hideous cackling noise, as if he were being attacked by a flock of birds.

He sat up, terrified. A nightmare?

He opened his eyes. No nightmare. It was kids — shouting, screaming, laughing, jumping on and off the beds. Boba looked at them and groaned. They were incredibly loud, and diverse. The only older kids (his age) he saw were separated into two groups, a small group of girls, looking suspiciously at a small group of boys.

The rest of the kids were squalling, laughing, and crying. The chaos was unbelievable. Boba groaned again. This was far worse than he had imagined. Boba Fett, the bounty hunter's son, who could fly a starship and survive a Count's attack . . . stuck with a bunch of underage brats!

I don't belong here! Boba put his pillow over his

head, hoping he would go to sleep before he went crazy.

And he got lucky.

He did.

In dreams there is no past and future, only a shining endless now. In dreams there is no gravity, no hunger, no cold . . .

"Hey."

Boba groaned. In his dream he was riding a great beast around and around in an arena, trying to catch up with his father, but he kept slipping off . . .

"Hey!"

"I am," said Boba.

"You am what?" a voice said with a laugh.

"Holding on," said Boba. But there was nothing to hold on to. The beast was gone.

Boba sat up and opened his eyes.

He was in the dorm, the Orphan Hall. The noise was now a low hum, still obnoxious but bearable.

Most of the kids were playing games or sitting and rocking their toys or dolls. All but one, who was sitting at the foot of his bed.

"Wake up," he said — or was he a she? It was hard to tell. The kid at the end of the bed was a humanoid, like Boba, but with darker skin and shorter hair — and very merry eyes.

Boba smiled. He couldn't help it. "Who are you?"

"The only reasonably mature kid in this zoo. And I'm exactly what you need."

"Which is what?"

"A friend."

CHAPTER TWELVE

"I'm Garr," said the visitor sitting at the foot of the bed, extending a hand.

Boba took it cautiously. "Teff," he said, remembering the name he had conjured up for the Jedi. (He wished he had been more creative.) He sat up and rubbed his head. "I must have fallen asleep. How long was I sleeping?"

"Days," said Garr. "A standard day, anyway, according to the ship's chronos. We all notice when there's someone new. You had been in the bacta bath but you still smelled a little ripe. Where did they pick you up, anyway?"

"Raxus Prime," said Boba.

"Ugh. Is it as bad as they say?"

"Worse," Boba confided. He decided to change the subject. "Where were you, uh, picked up?"

"Excarga," said Garr. "My parents are ore traders. When the Separatists arrived to take control of our ore-processing facilities, they took everyone prisoner, so my parents hid me. Later, when the Republic counterattacked, they picked me up, but I couldn't find my parents. What about your parents?"

"My parents?"

Garr pointed around the Orphan Hall. "All of us are here because we were separated from our parents. Sometimes I think that's why they call them Separatists. What about your parents? Were they captured or, you know . . ."

Garr was reluctant to say the word. Boba wasn't. "Killed," he said. "My father was killed. Cut down. I saw it. I watched it."

Boba looked down and saw that his fists were clenched. He wondered if he should tell his new friend that it wasn't the Separatists who had killed his father — but the Jedi.

"I'm sorry," said Garr. "What happened to your mother? If you don't mind my asking."

"I don't mind your asking," said Boba, "if you don't mind my not answering."

"Fair enough." Garr got up and pulled at Boba's hand. "Let's go get something to eat. The commissary closes in a few minutes, and most of the space brats are finished, so we'll have a little peace and quiet."

For the next few days, and for the first time in his life, Boba had a friend. He could hardly believe it. He decided not to question it, but simply accept it as one of the surprises life was throwing at him. By nature — and by teaching — he was suspicious of anyone who came too close. But now he was . . . enjoying it.

Garr was good at having fun. When they weren't exploring the ship, the two played sabacc or simply lay on their bunks and talked, trying to ignore the chaos and craziness of the other orphans.

There were a few other kids their age, but Garr avoided them, and Boba did, too. They might ask too many questions. Because most of the orphans were much younger, Ulu was too busy with the "space brats" (as Garr called them) to worry about what his older orphans were up to.

All orphans were prohibited from roaming the ship unattended, but that's exactly what Garr and Boba did, telling Ulu that they were going to one of the ship's libraries for a book (not likely, since all they had were boring military manuals) when in fact they were exploring the ship's seemingly endless corridors.

Boba shared his discovery with Garr — that no one notices a ten-year-old. And it was true. The troopers or crew members they ran into in the corridors simply assumed that the two friends were someone else's responsibility, if they noticed them at all.

*   *   *

Politics didn't interest Garr, but starships did. "This is the most advanced assault ship in the Republic's fleet," Boba's new friend explained. "There are over fifteen thousand troopers, all with the most advanced weaponry. They are all alike — I think they're clones."

"Imagine that," said Boba. He wondered what Garr would think if he knew the clones' true origin.

Garr's favorite place was the rear docking bay, where the starfighters were lined up to be armed and serviced by busy tech droids.

"I could fly one of those," Boba said once. He regretted saying it immediately; it gave too much away.

"Really?" Garr asked. "Who taught you? Your father?"

Boba nodded.

"My mother would have had a fit," said Garr. "What did your mother think about you flying a starfighter so young?"

"I don't honestly know," said Boba. "I never asked her."

Boba knew his words sounded hollow. They felt hollow, too.

Boba's favorite spot on the ship was its rear observation blister, or ROB. A small, cold room under a clear plexi dome, it was usually empty, since the crew was too busy to look at the stars and the troopers didn't care about anything except war and discipline.

The ship was traveling through normal space, which meant that the stars didn't streak by (or appear to streak by) as they did in hyperspace. Even though the ship was traveling at thousands of kilometers per second, it seemed as though it were standing still, space was so huge.

Standing or sitting on a bench under the dome, Boba saw a sea of stars in every direction. There were no planets visible, only gas giants, dwarfs, quasars, and the occasional smudge that marked the location of a black hole. Distant galaxies were pinwheels of fire.

"Okay, we've seen space, and it's boring!" Garr was always more interested in adventure than astronomy. "Let's find something to do."

"Just a few minutes . . ." Boba liked the view, but he liked the dreams he had while staring into space even more. He was always dreaming of the day he would get *Slave I* back, and experience the stars on his own.

As they explored the ship's corridors, Boba and Garr often had to stand aside for formations of clone troopers marching to the mess hall or to the main docking bay for a battle sortie.

"I think they are creepy," said Garr.

"Me too," said Boba.

"If you see them without their helmets, they all look alike," said Garr.

The troopers marched from place to place, or sat in their dorms polishing their Tibanna-gas blasters. They never talked with anyone outside their ranks, and rarely talked to one another; and never noticed the two ten-year-olds who walked among them. They always traveled in groups of four, six, ten — always even numbers. They didn't like to be alone.

They paid no attention to Boba and Garr as they continued to go everywhere together. They saw the vast hydroponic farms, tended by droids, that turned waste into air and water, just like the forests and kelp beds on the planets. They saw the immense plasma engines, tended by droids and a few harried crew members. They saw the clone troopers, never excited, never bored, endlessly cleaning their weapons.

After a few days of exploring, they had covered almost every part of the vast assault ship, except for one area.

The bridge.

"I would give anything to see the bridge!" said Garr. "I even tried it once, but I couldn't sneak in. No kids allowed! The bridge is where the Jedi hang out, you know."

"Who cares?" said Boba. The less he saw of the

Jedi, the better. Luckily, they seemed to have lost interest in him after their surprise at finding him on Raxus Prime.

"I care!" said Garr. "I admire the Jedi. They are the guardians of civilization, willing to sacrifice all so that others can live in peace. I wish I'd be found to be Force-sensitive and trained as Jedi. Don't you?"

"Not me," Boba said. He thought about telling Garr the truth — that he hated the Jedi, and wanted to be a bounty hunter, like his father.

But he decided against it. There was a limit to how much you could trust anyone, even your best friend.

Garr had a secret too, at least as far as Boba was concerned. Or at least, a mystery.

The mystery was whether Garr was a boy or a girl. Boba had gone so long without figuring it out that now he was almost embarrassed to ask. But he knew enough not to let embarrassment hold him back. (That was part of wisdom, too.)

"Garr," he said one day as they were strolling down a long corridor, "do you mind if I ask you a question?"

"Not at all," Garr said. "As long as you don't mind if I don't answer."

"Fair enough," said Boba, recognizing what he'd

said when Garr had asked about his mother. "Are you a boy or a girl?"

"Like, male or female?"

"Yeah, you know."

"I don't know, actually," said Garr. "I mean, I know what you mean, but I don't know yet whether I am male or female. On my planet, it's not determined until age thirteen."

"Determined?"

"Somewhere around our thirteenth birthday, our bodies change, and become one or the other. Until then, it's sort of, you know, up in the air."

"Cool," said Boba. "I was just wondering."

"Does it make a difference?" Garr asked.

"Not to me."

"Good. I wish everybody was like you, Teff. Did you ever wonder why I don't hang out with the other ten-year-olds? They want to treat you one way if you're a boy, and another way if you're a girl, and there's no in-between. No way to be just a kid, just a person."

"Stupid," said Boba. But he wasn't surprised. He had always thought most people, including most kids, were a little slow. "Can't they treat somebody as just a friend?"

"Nope," said Garr. "But come on! Let's find something to do!"

They were off again.

The troopship cruised slowly (under light speed) through normal space, on the lookout for Separatist forces. There were no more battles, though they heard rumors of other battles taking place throughout the Republic.

"The ship will be warping into hyperspace soon," said Garr one day. "It will take us to one of the central worlds, probably Bespin, where we will be offloaded at some orphanage. I hope we will still be together."

"Me too," said Boba. He didn't want to tell his friend that it wasn't going to happen. Boba had no intention of going to an orphanage.

CHAPTER THIRTEEN

"Hey, Garr, check this out!"

They were in the rear docking bay, alone except for a few service droids humming and buzzing busily on the far side of the vast room.

"What?" Garr said. "It's just a door."

The door was marked EMERGENCY ONLY.

"I'll bet I can open it," said Boba. The system looked very similar to the one his father had used to teach him to hot-wire locks.

"So?"

"So this is our chance. You are always talking about wanting to see the bridge, the command center of the ship, right?"

"Yeah, sure," said Garr. "But this door doesn't lead to the bridge. This is an emergency airlock door. It leads to the outside of the ship. To outer space."

"Exactly," said Boba. "Come on. Follow me."

With a deft crossing of wires and simulation of code, Boba opened the door. On the other side was a small airlock, lined with space suits on hangers. It was like a closet with two doors. Boba knew that once the inner door was closed, and the outer door was opened, the air would rush out and the door would open into space.

The anti-grav plates were off inside the airlock. Boba and Garr both floated free, past the space suits.

"Yikes," said Garr. "I'm not used to this. What if I get sick and throw up?"

"Just don't think about it," said Boba. "Pick a space suit and let's go."

All the suits were slightly too large for ten-year-old bodies. The suits were for emergency evacuation only, so they carried only small air tanks and battery-powered heaters, enough for an hour and a half.

"One hour will be long enough," said Boba.

"Are you sure?" asked Garr, picking a suit. "What if something goes wrong?"

"What could go wrong?" Boba asked as he helped zip Garr into the suit. He put on his own suit, and selected two helmets from the rack nearby.

He spit on his helmet's faceplate and wiped it with his sleeve before putting it on. "Keeps it from fogging," he said.

"Whatever you say," Garr said, spitting on the faceplate and wiping it dry.

When both suits were on, secure and sealed, Boba tried the comlinks. He showed Garr the switch built into the wrist gauntlet.

"Can you hear me?"

"You're shouting!" said Garr. "Turn the volume down."

"Sorry . . ."

Boba made sure the inner door was closed and sealed. Then he pushed off the wall and floated across the tiny room to the outer door, which was thicker. Instead of a knob it had a wheel.

He looked at Garr, questioning. Garr gave him a thumbs-up.

Boba turned the wheel to the left.

One turn, two.

He was just beginning to think nothing was going to happen when, all of a sudden, there was a WHOOOOOOSH of air. Boba shivered as the icy chill of space rushed into the room.

Boba started to push the door open, then stopped. "Almost forgot!" He grabbed a ten-meter coil of safety line from the wall. He clipped one to Garr's belt and the other end to his own.

Then he opened the door and floated out into the emptiness of space.

Garr watched for a moment, swallowed hard —

And followed.

They were floating in an endless sea of stars.

It was like falling, down down down, into a hole as deep as all eternity. A hole so deep, they would never hit bottom.

The stars went on forever, and Boba and Garr floated among them like specks of dust.

No, thought Boba, it was the stars that were dust.

And Garr and I are dust's dust —

"Better now," said Garr, swallowing bravely. "Now what?"

"Now we find the bridge," said Boba. "We have over an hour. But we have to be careful."

"I'm feeling *very, very* careful!" said Garr.

"Good. We have to keep secured to the ship. If we float away from it . . ."

"What will happen?" Garr asked.

"Nothing will happen."

"Nothing?"

"Nothing forever. We will float forever, spinning off into space until we die. There's no way back, since these emergency suits don't have jetpacks. But don't worry, we have our safety line."

"Do I sound worried?" Garr asked.

Boba laughed. "Yes!"

"Good!" said Garr. "If I weren't worried, I would be crazy!"

Boba made sure Garr had a good hold on the hull of the ship. Then he floated forward ten meters until the line stopped him, and he found a handhold on the ship.

Then he secured the line while Garr went ahead.

They took turns that way, climbed "up" the ship toward the bridge, belaying for safety while the other forged ahead, finding the route:

— Over and around the huge ion engines, each trailing a kilometers-long exhaust of ghostly blue photons, like smoke.

— Up the sheer long cliff of the *Candaserri*'s dorsal fin, being careful never to look back and "down" into the well of stars.

— Across the traverse of the sheer hull side, staying on the steel strips between the rows of lighted windows.

"Secure!"

"Going ahead!"

The suit comlinks made the two friends' voices seem closer than when they were in atmosphere. They pulled themselves along, using every bolt, antenna, edge, and knob of the hull. Sometimes, through the windows, they saw crew members hurrying along a corridor, or clone troopers marching in formation toward the mess hall or the dorm.

"Careful," said Boba, tucking himself into a niche whenever they passed a window. "If anyone sees us, we're in big trouble."

"They'll raise the alarm," said Garr. "They'll think it's an attack!"

Boba and Garr were too close to the ship to see the shape or the size of it. Each ridge, fin, or bulge in the hull was a surprise, and hid another.

Finally, they saw the sleek pod that was the bridge tower module, perched atop a dorsal fin. It looked almost like a smaller ship hitching a ride on the *Candaserri*. It was windowless except for the wide plexi bubble-window at the front.

"They will have alarms," said Boba. "We'll have to move carefully."

The two made their way up the fin, then to the top of the pod. Standing roped together, and secured by their mag-soles, they cautiously worked their way forward until they had reached the top edge of the wide forward window.

Boba knelt, Garr beside him. They crept over the edge of the window and looked down. Boba felt totally exposed. If any of the crew looked up, they would see two helmeted heads looking in *from space!*

Every alarm in the ship would go off.

But no one was looking up. The bridge was quiet. Crew members sat at their control consoles, while officers circulated among them, checking the system coordinates.

"Awesome!" said Garr. "This is the main command center. Everything happens here first."

The captain and the first officers, in their brightly colored uniforms, were consulting with a robed Jedi at a holomap table. Boba recognized Glynn-Beti, the Bothan Jedi who had questioned him.

I'm lucky she got distracted, he thought. *If she*

had made me open that flight bag, I would probably be a prisoner right now.

"I wonder what they are talking about," Garr said. "Maybe they got word about some of the parents. I would like to see my parents again."

Boba didn't say anything. It was an awkward moment.

"Someday you will meet my parents," said Garr. "You will like them."

"Maybe," Boba said. *I doubt it,* he thought.

Boba was ready to go, but he was waiting for Garr — who liked watching people as much as Boba liked watching stars.

Garr lay facedown, looking through the window at the crew on the bridge.

Boba lay on his back, staring up. He loved the dizzy feeling he got, looking deep into a sea of stars and galaxies.

They had been on top of the bridge tower module for almost twenty minutes. Boba checked his air tank and it was still over half full. But his heater was running down. He could feel the chill of space seeping into his suit, especially at his feet and hands.

"We should be heading back," he said to Garr.

"Couple of more minutes," said Garr. "They're looking at another holomap."

"A map? Let's see." Boba rolled over and looked down.

"That's a weird map!" said Garr. "I can't tell anything about it."

"Uh-oh," said Boba.

"What?"

"We'd better get back into the airlock, fast!"

"What's wrong?" Garr's voice was sharp with fear.

Just then a siren wailed. The two could feel it reverberating through the hull.

"That's the ten-minute alarm!" Boba said. "That was a hyperspace map they were looking at. The ship is about to jump!"

CHAPTER FOURTEEN

Faster!

Down, down —

Faster!

Around, around —

Boba was no longer feeling the cold, even though the little heater in his suit was almost drained.

Garr was gulping air, spinning through the vacuum, grabbing at one handhold and then another.

Neither spoke. There was no time for words. They hurried toward the back of the ship where the big ion jets were staining the universe a pale blue.

How much time do we have left? Boba wondered. *Six minutes? Five?*

"What happens if . . . ?" Garr asked as they made their way down the fin from the bridge tower module.

"If what?"

"You know what! If we don't get inside the ship before the jump into hyperspace!?"

"At best, we will see a flash of light, and be fried

to a crisp in the plasma flare of the hyperspace warp."

"That's best? What's worst?"

"At worst we won't feel a thing or even see a flash of light. We will just look around and see no ship. It will be gone. And we will drift here all alone, endlessly, until we die."

The alert siren still wailed but they heard it only when they touched the hull, through their hands or the soles of their boots.

At the steepest part of the wing, Garr missed a step, and spun off into space. Boba grabbed a seam and held on for dear life. The safety line snapped tight — yanking Garr back into Boba.

OOOMMPPHHHFF!

"Careful," Boba said. He wanted to say "slow down" but he knew he couldn't. If they slowed down, they were lost.

"You idiot!" said Boba as he untangled the line and started down, over the rear of the wing.

"I'm sorry!" Garr said. "I missed a hold."

"I was talking to myself!" Boba said. "This whole thing is my fault. It was a stupid idea!"

I lost track of what was most important. A bounty hunter never does that.

Through the window Boba could see crew members running, security droids clearing the halls, and clone troopers scurrying in formation.

How much time left? *Three minutes? Two?*

The airlock was still at least five minutes away . . .

"This way!" Boba said. It looked like a shortcut.

He plunged down into a dark "canyon" — a slot between the rear boosters and the ventral hull fin — making his way hand over hand.

It was dark, and the handholds were far apart. Garr belayed Boba, and then Boba belayed Garr, so that one of them was always secured to the hull of the ship.

Boba grinned when he emerged at the other end of the slot. His gamble had paid off. There was the lighted airlock door, still open, waiting for them — only a hundred meters away!

Two hundred meters if they went around on the hull. One hundred if they took a chance and floated straight across.

"Let's try it," Boba said. "This last jump can be made in one leap if we both let go."

"But what if we miss?"

"Then we're dead. But we may be dead anyway if we don't try it. We're running out of time."

Boba looked at his friend. He wondered if he looked as frightened to Garr as Garr did to him. *Probably!*

"Well, then," said Garr, giving a brave thumbs-up, "what are we waiting for? Let's try it!"

*   *   *

The airlock door a hundred meters away looked tiny.

Boba gathered the rope into a coil, took Garr's hand, and said, "On three. One . . . two . . ."

He didn't remember saying "three" but he realized he must have said it, for they were floating free in space, unbelayed —

— drifting slowly, hand in hand, toward the lighted square of the airlock door.

Both were silent. Boba was hardly even breathing. It was as if a word, a breath, might make them miss their target, and spin them off into space.

Thirty meters, twenty, ten —

As they got closer, Boba saw that the target was even bigger than he had thought. The airlock door had handholds on either side, so he didn't have to hit it dead center.

And at the end of the hull, just past the door, there was an antenna.

At the last minute a slight spin turned Boba and he saw that he was, in fact, going to miss the airlock door.

No sweat. "Your move, Garr. Just grab at those handholds as we go by."

"Got it!" said Garr. "Well, almost . . ." Another spin had pulled Garr back, just short of the handholds. Now they were floating on toward the end of the hull.

Luckily the antenna was right in reach. Boba

let go of Garr's hand and uncoiled the rope. He reached out and grabbed the antenna as he floated past.

"Got it!" he said aloud, to himself and Garr.

Just as it broke off in his hand.

CHAPTER FIFTEEN

"Ooooph!"

The safety line went tight, jerking Boba and Garr together, then setting them spinning, like a kid's toy — a giant kid's toy that had been thrown away, down the deepest darkest hole in all the universe.

The deep dark hole that *is* the universe.

For they were spinning away from the ship, attached to each other but to nothing else, doomed to float on forever while the *Candaserri* disappeared into hyperspace.

They both were moving, falling, tumbling, head over heels away from the ship, toward the emptiness of space.

Deep into the Big Isn't.

Realizing the worst made Boba feel calmer. His panic was gone. His fear was gone. He remembered something his father had said: *The worse things are, the calmer you need to be.*

He felt as if he were standing still and watching the universe spin around him. There was the *Candaserri*; then there was Garr, at the other end of the safety line; then just stars until the ship came up again.

Each time the ship was slightly smaller. *How long before it's gone altogether?* Boba wondered. The hyperspace jump was due at any moment.

"Teff, you still there?"

"Yeah."

"It's been great, being your friend."

"Same here," said Boba. He almost wished he had told his friend his real name. Maybe it wasn't too late . . .

He caught sight of Garr, wheeling through his field of view.

Then the stars again, white except for one tiny orange one.

Then the ship, still there.

Orange star? Where had that come from?

Boba watched as the orange star came up again. It was exactly opposite the ship in his spin. If he had a jetpack, he could use the orange star for a fix: Aiming at it would stop his spin and guide him toward the ship.

No jetpack, though. And only a few minutes of air. When it was gone —

And that was when he got the idea.

"Teff? You still there?"

"Yeah."

"What're you doing? I hear a clicking noise."

"I've got an idea," Boba said.

"What?"

"Can't talk. Gotta save air. Just hang on to the line — and hope for the best."

Boba's emergency space suit had no jetpack, but it did have something that might possibly be used for a jetpack.

The air tank.

Boba disconnected his air tank and pulled it from his back. Now all he had to breathe was the air in his suit. It would last less than a minute.

Boba held the air tank against his stomach and waited for the orange star to appear in his wheeling, whirling field of vision.

There it was! He pressed the release valve.

SSSSSSSSSS

The universe slowed down, just a little. Boba waited until the orange star appeared again.

SSSSSSSSSSSS

Slowed more. And this time the ship was closer when Boba saw it swim into view.

SSSSSSSSSSSSSS

We're moving! Garr was still spinning at the other end of the lifeline. But Boba was stable. He could see the ship over his shoulder, getting closer, as he aimed the air tank at the little orange star and used the air like a rocket engine.

SSSSSSSSSS

For every action — like the air hissing out — there is an equal and opposite reaction — like

Boba floating backward toward the ship. He felt the line jerk tight, and knew he was pulling Garr with him.

"What's going on?" Garr asked.

Boba didn't answer. All he had to breathe was the leftover air in his suit, and it was getting stale.

SSSSSSSSSSSSSSSSS

The ship was getting closer. Closer. There at the bottom was the open airlock door.

Boba aimed at the little orange star again.

SSSSSSSSSSSSSSS

Closer and closer.

SSSSSSSSSSSSSSSSSSSSSSS

The air in Boba's suit was almost gone. He gasped for breath. SSSSSSSSSSS. He sprayed the air into space, but he needed it in his suit, in his lungs . . .

SSSSS SSSSSSS

The air was almost gone from the tank. Boba could see the ship over his shoulder, getting closer and closer. But not quite close enough.

S S SSS S S

Boba felt his head spinning. His lungs were burning, begging him for air.

Little orange star.

Garr at end of line.

Ship huge, close —

"Teff, are you there? Something is pulling us toward the ship! They must have seen us!"

SS SS SSsssss —

Last gasp of air. *Did we make it?*

"Garr, grab handrail!"

Did Garr hear? Boba hit the side of the door and bounced back, into space. He reached for the handhold by the airlock door, but it was out of reach. *Just* out of reach!

He was falling again, forever this time —

And that was when his father came to him, out of the tomb of death, out of the darkness of dream, grabbing his hand, and pulling.

Pulling and pulling . . .

Boba!

CHAPTER SIXTEEN

"Good job, Teff!"

Boba smiled. His father had covered him with a blanket made of stars, and praised him. But didn't he know his name wasn't *Teff*? That was a stupid made-up name for . . .

"Breathe, Teff!"

Who pulled the blanket away?

"Wake up."

Boba opened his eyes. He saw Garr's worried face.

They were in the airlock. Boba's helmet was off. He opened his mouth, took a deep breath, and it was like shaking hands with an old friend.

Air! Wonderful air.

"What happened?" he asked.

"You passed out," said Garr. "After you saved us. Using the air tank like a little rocket. That was brilliant."

"Every action has an equal and opposite reaction," said Boba. "I think that was one of my father's sayings. But what about the jump?"

"It happened. Feel it?" Garr placed Boba's hand

flat against the bulkhead, and there it was: the os-
cillating hum of the ship's null quantum field gen-
erators. "The jump came just after I grabbed the
handhold and pulled us into the airlock. We barely
made it!"

"Close call," said Boba as he hung up his space
suit. "But I guess a meter is as good as a kilome-
ter."

"Another of your father's sayings?" asked Garr
with a laugh.

"Where were you two?" asked Ulu Ulix when
Garr and Boba got back to the Orphan Hall. His
three eyes were flashing fire; he was angry. "You
know there's a general alarm before a jump. You
were supposed to report in."

"Sorry," said Boba. "It was my fault. We were at
the rear observation blister. I, uh, wanted to see
what the stars look like from hyperspace."

"I appreciate your honesty, Teff," said Ulu Ulix,
softening. "But rules are rules. You two are re-
stricted to the Orphan Hall for one day. No more
roaming around."

"No, please!" said Garr. "We're ten! We can't
spend all our time with a bunch of little kids."

"Apparently one of the airlocks was opened,"
said Ulu Ulix with a teasing smile. "You wouldn't

know anything about that, would you? You should be more careful. If you get caught breaking the rules, you'll get me in trouble with Master Glynn-Beti. And that's the last thing I want!"

"That's also the last thing *we* want," Boba said quite honestly.

After that sullen day, if Garr ever wanted to find Boba, Garr knew where to look.

The rear observation blister. The ROB.

Boba was watching and thinking. He knew he should understand what secret Dooku thought he possessed. He remembered how bothered Dooku had been when Boba called him Tyranus. Why was that so important?

Then suddenly — finally — Boba understood. Tyranus had hired his dad to help create an army of clone troopers. But now Count Dooku was fighting the army he'd helped create. Why would you make an army and then fight against it? Boba still had a puzzle, but he was now sure he held an important piece — the piece Dooku had wanted to destroy. As Count Dooku, the man was fighting against the Republic, but, as Tyranus, he had helped create an army for that same Republic.

Boba decided to hide that information deep inside him for the moment. He had his father's instinct for knowing it would come in handy later on. It was part of his father's legacy to him . . . for better or for worse.

"Boring," said Garr the next day, staring out.

Boba had to agree. Hyperspace looked like a clumsy child's drawing of a universe, a first draft.

"Those streaks are stars?" Garr asked.

"Stars smeared across space-time," said Boba. "When we drop out of hyperspace, they will look more like stars."

"Like the orange one?"

Boba looked up from his book *Operational Starfighters*. He had been watching the tiny, flickering orange star for days, almost lost amid the smears.

"It's not a star," Boba said to Garr. "If it's not a streak, that means it's matching our speed exactly. Following us, maybe."

Curious, he thought. He wished he could see it better.

"We'll find out soon enough," said Garr. "Ulu Ulix sent me to get you. We're getting ready to jump out of hyperspace, and we're supposed to be secured in our quarters."

"Let's go, then," said Boba. The last thing he wanted was trouble with Ulu Ulix or his Jedi Master, Glynn-Beti. "Gotta keep them happy!"

* * *

The jump was uneventful. Just a weird lurch, a moment's dizziness.

The orphan kids' moods improved immediately. Boba and Garr went to the commissary for their first untroubled meal. Lunch after hyperspace was like breakfast after a long sleep. Everyone was buzzing with excitement.

"We must be near Bespin."

The announcement would come from the bridge soon. Hyperspace jumps were a little unpredictable, but only a little.

After lunch, everyone went forward to the main obvservation blister, or MOB, to see the stars. Everyone except Boba. He went alone, back to the ROB.

That tiny star; there was something about it . . .

He picked up the viewer and scanned the sea of stars for the little orange light.

It no longer stood out, like it had in hyperspace.

But he found it, just where he had thought it would be, directly behind the *Candaserri*.

Boba zoomed in for a better look. It was a ship. It was tiny, and it was several kilometers away, but clearly matching speed and course with the *Candaserri*.

Following. Shadowing. *What for?*

The orange color came from the glint of starlight on the rusty, battered hull.

The familiar hull.

Boba wiped his eyes. Could it be that he was overtired, just seeing things? He dialed the zoom, bringing the little ship closer, until he could see the stubby wings, the scratched cockpit, the pitted sides. He could even see the pits that had been put into the ship while flying through the asteroid belt on its way to Geonosis.

He lowered the viewer from his eyes. They were filled with tears, at the same time that his fists were clenched with fury.

For the ship was one he knew well. It was his legacy from his father, and it had been stolen from him by Aurra Sing.

It was *Slave I.*

CHAPTER SEVENTEEN

"Hey, Teff, what's up?"

"Not much, Garr." Boba put down the viewer and turned to face his friend, who had just entered the ROB. *Keep your emotions to yourself.* "Just stargazing."

"See anything interesting?"

"Nothing much," said Boba. "Star dust, space trash, you know."

"Well, come on, then," said Garr. "Ulu Ulix has been looking for you. The Padawan wants us to help strap down the little ones for arrival."

"Arrival?"

"We're going into orbit around Bespin. Trip's over. Welcome to your new home!"

Home? Not if I can help it! thought Boba as he picked up his flight bag and followed his friend.

The forward observation blister was filled with crew members and orphans, gazing with wonder at the planet the ship was orbiting.

It was huge. It glowed orange in the light of its distant sun.

"Bespin is a gas giant, with its metallic surface so far under layers of atmosphere gunk that it's hardly been reached, much less explored!" Garr said excitedly. "The main industry is mining Tibanna gas from the atmosphere. Nothing lives on the surface. All the cities and mines and factories float in the clouds, and . . . hey!"

"Huh?"

"You're not listening, Teff!"

"Oh, sorry," said Boba.

"Daydreaming?"

"I guess."

Daydreaming? Not exactly. Boba's mind was racing; he was thinking about the startling discovery he had just made in the rear observation blister.

Slave I! He had seen it. The little starship he had inherited from his father, Jango Fett, was following the *Candaserri* — and being careful, Boba had noted, to stay in the shadow cone, where it would not be picked up by the assault ship's approach sensors, which were probably tuned to pick up flotillas, not solitary craft.

Boba was pondering this information silently while he stood beside Garr in the crowded forward observation blister watching stormy Bespin spin below.

"There you are!"

Boba and Garr saw Ulu Ulix pushing through the crowd.

"You two are determined to get me into trouble, aren't you! Don't you know you're supposed to stay near the Orphan Hall?"

"Sorry," said Garr, hiding a grin. While Ulu had been busy, they had the run of the ship, and they had taken advantage of it.

Boba didn't like Jedi, but Ulu was an exception. He decided to ask the Padawan about what he had seen — without, of course, revealing too much. "Ulu, have you ever heard of a bounty hunter called Aurra Sing?"

"Aurra Sing? Sure. She's —"

"Why do you wish to know?" asked a harsh, high voice. Boba turned and saw Glynn-Beti looking at him suspiciously.

Boba groaned. If he had known she was around, he would have kept his mouth shut. "Uh . . ."

"Speak up, orphan. *Teff*, isn't it? Why do you ask about Aurra Sing?"

"I was just wondering. I, uh, heard some crew members talking about her."

"She is an enemy of civilization, of galactic order," said the Bothan Jedi. "She is wanted for numerous crimes, high and low, including murder. That's all you need to know. Ulu Ulix —" Glynn-Beti glared at her Padawan. "What are these two doing so far from the Orphan Hall? Are you forgetting your duties? Take them there *immediately.*"

Ulu bowed. "Yes, Master Glynn-Beti."

"Gather the other orphans. And all of you, meet me in the docking bay as soon as you have packed your things. We're being ferried down to Cloud City."

"Yes, Master," said Ulu, bowing again to the departing Bothan's back.

"Whew!" said Garr, when Glynn-Beti had left. "What was that about?"

"Aurra Sing," said Ulu Ulix. "Don't mention her name around Glynn-Beti. Glynn-Beti condemns her, and for good reason. Aurra Sing kills Jedi for sport."

"I thought bounty hunters only worked for money," Boba said.

"Aurra Sing is different," said Ulu Ulix. "It is said that she has some sorrow in her past that causes her to hate the Jedi. Whatever it is, she attacks us every chance she gets."

"You mean, for fun?" asked Garr, shocked.

"Sick fun," said Ulu Ulix. "But come on, you two. Let's get moving."

That explains it, thought Boba, as he followed Garr and Ulix back toward the rear of the ship. *Aurra Sing is trailing the ship to get a crack at a Jedi or two. Good luck to her!*

I wonder what she would think if she knew I was on board.

*   *   *

The ship's corridors were filled with crew members hurrying to their stations. Planetary approach was an exciting event to all hands — except, of course, to the clone troopers. One planet or another, it was all the same to them.

Boba wouldn't miss them. His brothers — so much alike, and yet so different. They had no interest in where they were going, or where they had been. They were interested only in their weaponry, in their assignments, or in their chain of command. The clones were pure military.

So when he arrived at the docking bay, helping Ulu and Garr herd the younger orphans onto the lander, Boba was surprised to see his old friend CT-4/619 hard at work. He was painting out the emblems of war and the military numbering on the little lander that was going to take the orphans down.

"Remember me?" Boba asked.

"Not really," said CT-4/619. "Should I?"

"No, just wondering," said Boba. "What are you doing?"

"De-militarizing," said the clone.

"How come?" Garr, who was always curious, asked.

"Bespin," said CT-4/619. "They want no signs of war."

"The rulers of Bespin want to preserve their

planet's neutrality," said Glynn-Beti. The Bothan Jedi had approached unseen. As always, she made Boba nervous. "We are allowed to bring you orphans down, but not to carry any weapons or engage in any military activities."

"Not even your lightsaber?" Boba asked, indicating the Jedi's weapon hidden under her robe.

"The weapons of the Jedi Masters are not subject to local ordinances," Glynn-Beti said with a haughty scowl. "Now come aboard!"

CHAPTER EIGHTEEN

The lander dropped free of the *Candaserri* and
fired its retros, slowing it for atmospheric entry.
The twenty-one younger orphans, strapped into
their seats, shouted with glee and excitement as
the lander encountered the first wisps of air.

The faint whistling sound grew to a roar as the
little ship dove into the sea of clouds. It was terrifying and exhilarating. The orphans oohed and aa-
hed as the clouds whipped by, all reds and yellows,
oranges and browns.

Far off, Boba saw the flash of lightning. "A
storm," said Garr, who was, as usual, full of information. "The storms on Bespin are the deadliest in
the galaxy."

But the storm was soon left behind as the little
ship sailed down, down, down . . . into the middle
levels of the atmosphere, where the inhabitants of
Bespin all lived.

Boba usually liked planetfall — descending to a
new planet. But this time he had mixed feelings.

He was eager to begin the search for Aurra Sing,
who could not be far away.

At the same time, he knew he would miss life on the *Candaserri*. He had been forced to live a lie, as "Teff." But in return he had been granted, for the first and only time in his life, a friend. Someone to spend time with, to explore with, to talk to and share secrets with (only up to a point, of course).

It had all been a great pleasure — but now it was time for Boba to return to his real identity.

He was the son of Jango Fett, the toughest bounty hunter in the galaxy.

And he intended to get his ship back!

They landed at Portside, in the teeming central levels of the city. Uniformed officials appeared at the opened ramps of the ship and asked Glynn-Beti for documents.

Glynn-Beti handed over a holopad, pointing at the younger orphans who were lined up at the doorway — and then at Boba.

She whispered something to the officials, and they looked at Boba. One shook his head; another nodded.

What is she telling them? Boba was alarmed. He had planned to wait and make his escape from the orphanage as soon as no one was looking; but what if he never got there? What if Glynn-Beti was telling them to check his identity first?

Boba edged toward the open ramp. The Jedi and the officials had their backs turned. If he slipped out now he could disappear into the crowd before anyone knew what was happening. It might be several minutes before they even noticed he was gone.

There was only one problem. How could he leave without saying good-bye to his first, and still only, real friend?

The choice was between friendship and freedom.

Boba chose freedom.

CHAPTER NINETEEN

"Teff!"

He couldn't believe it — Garr had betrayed him! His best friend was yelling, alerting the Jedi!

Boba ducked his head and ran, darting through the crowd.

Portside was a maze of narrow alleys, lined with shops where stolen goods and weapons, illicit spice, and phony documents; all were on sale to anyone with credits.

It was a perfect place to disappear.

Boba looked back and saw an official running after him. But she was easy enough to lose — a couple of sudden reversals, a turn down a narrow alley, and Boba had faded into the milling polyglot crowd, where a hundred languages filled the air with a low buzz.

Made it! He slowed, and forced himself to breathe easily so that no one would notice that he was on the run. He was invisible, because nobody (or no creature) notices a ten-year-old.

Except another ten-year-old.

"Teff!" A hand caught his shoulder.

Boba turned, fists up, in a fighting stance, ready to defend himself against all the Jedi in the world, as well as their security droids, clone troopers, officials, or . . .

It was Garr.

"You forgot your flight bag," Garr said, handing Boba the precious legacy from his father.

Boba was amazed. Had he been that confused, that panicked? That was breaking the bounty hunters' code for sure, which was to remain calm in every situation.

Boba dropped his fists to his side. "Thanks," he said, taking the bag from Garr.

"Why are you running?" Garr asked. "They are going to send us to a nice place, I'll bet."

Boba didn't say anything; he didn't know where to start.

"Glynn-Beti is going to be mad now. We'd better get back, quick, before —"

"Garr!" Boba grabbed his friend by the arm. "Come."

"Where? What for?"

"Just come. I'll explain!"

Cloud City's central levels were open, at the edges, to the wind and air. Dragging Garr by the hand, Boba headed toward a park lodged up against a transparisteel barrier that looked down on a sea of streaming clouds. From here it was easy to see why Cloud City was considered one of the most beautiful cities in the galaxy.

"What's this all about?" Garr asked as Boba parked himself on a bench and pulled his friend down beside him. "Teff, talk to me!"

"In the first place," said Boba, "my name's not Teff."

"It's not? What is it then?"

Boba didn't want to tell another lie, but he didn't want to tell the truth either. "Never mind that," he said. "I have something more important to tell you."

"You're not an orphan?" Garr guessed.

"I'm an orphan all right. Just not a needy orphan wanting to be rescued by the Jedi."

"But why not? If they want to help out . . ."

"I told you my father was dead, but I didn't tell you how. He was killed by the Jedi. I saw it happen."

Garr gasped. "Was your father . . . bad?"

"Bad? He was *good*," said Boba, his voice rising.

"But the Jedi are good," said Garr. "They are the guardians of peace and . . ."

Boba began to see how hopeless it was. Garr would never understand.

"It was a misunderstanding," said Boba. "But because of it, I can't stay with the Jedi."

"You can stay with me!" said Garr. "My parents will be returning for me soon, I know they will! They will take you in. We can be brothers. Or brother and sister. Or whatever."

Boba shook his head. "You are truly my friend," he said, "but I can't afford to have friends. I have my own road to travel, alone. I must go my own way."

"But . . ." Garr's big brown eyes were filling with tears.

"We must say farewell," said Boba.

"Good!" came a voice that was at the same time familiar and frightening. For the second time that day, Boba felt a hand on his shoulder. Only this one was cold, with a grip like steel.

"Boba Fett."

Boba turned, slowly, because of the hand that pinned his shoulder. He saw bone-white skin, black eyes rimmed with kohl, a muscular but womanly figure in a red jumpsuit, and a shaved head topped with a single long lock of bright red hair.

And blazing angry eyes.

"Aurra Sing!" It was the bounty hunter who had captured him and stolen his ship. "I knew it! I saw *Slave I* following the *Candaserri.*"

Boba tried to twist away but Aurra Sing held his shoulder tight. Then Garr started kicking her. "Let go of him! Take your hands off him!"

"Who's this?" Aurra Sing asked, picking up Garr by the hair, so that the kicks only afflicted the air. "Do I kill it or just toss it over the side?"

She held Garr out over the railing, suspended by a lock of hair over a thousand kilometers of empty air.

"Neither!" said Boba, finally twisting free. He put his hands on his hips and faced Aurra Sing defiantly. "Garr is my friend. As you are not. What is it you want with me?"

"I want to make you an offer you can't refuse," said Aurra Sing. With a quick toss, she dropped Garr back on the bench.

"Ooooph!" said Garr. "What's going on here? Who are you? Who is Boba Fett?"

"Your little friend is too nosy," the bounty hunter said to Boba, without looking at Garr. "You and I have business, so tell him to make himself scarce."

"Go," Boba said simply to his friend. He tried to keep his voice cold. That was the only way to get Garr to leave. "I told you, I have no room for friends. You heard what she said. Disappear."

Garr resisted. When Aurra's hand moved to her blaster, Garr was convinced.

"Good-bye," Garr said sadly in farewell.

Boba allowed himself to say a heartfelt good-bye back. Though his heart felt real pain, that was it.

"What is this offer?" Boba turned to Aurra Sing and demanded as soon as Garr was gone. "All I want from you is my ship back."

"Then we're in agreement," said Aurra Sing. "That's what my offer is — your ship back."

"*Slave I*." Boba's eyes were wide with hope and excitement. "Where is it?"

"Not here." Aurra Sing's eyes scanned the other beings on the terrace. "Too many eyes and ears. There is a city called Tibannapolis, not too far from here. Meet me there at noon tomorrow."

"And if I don't?"

"You will, if you want to see *Slave I* again," said Aurra Sing. She tossed Boba a coin. "Here — a good faith offering. It will rent you a cloud car, which you will need to find Tibannapolis. Look for me near the ancient refinery known as Revol Leap. If you show up with Jedi or officials, the deal's off. You'll never see your precious ship again. Now I have to tend to business."

Then, with a flip of her topknot, and without a word of farewell, she was gone.

CHAPTER TWENTY

One hundred credits.

Boba checked the prices, and found out that he had barely enough to hire a cloud car, with enough left over for a meal, as long as it was a small one. He dragged it out as long as possible, wondering what he was going to do to pass the time until his meeting with Aurra Sing. He knew he'd have to avoid the Jedi who might be looking for him — and he wondered why Sing would want to give him back his ship. She must want something in return, or was it a trap? And what if she were caught by the Jedi? Unfortunately, he couldn't exactly turn her in himself.

Noon tomorrow — it seemed like a long time away. But it wasn't. Bespin turned so swiftly on its axis that the days were only twelve hours long. Boba barely had time to grab a nap on a park bench before it was time to go.

*   *   *

The cloud car was a neat little item: two open-cockpit cabs, or nacelles, attached by a three-meter-long shaft that held the repulsorlift engines. Boba chose to ride in the cockpit with the driver, a short and prickly Ugnaught, a native of Bespin — or so Boba thought.

"You from around here?" he asked, just to make conversation . . . and maybe learn a thing or two about the planet he was now stuck on.

"We were brought here by Lord Figg," said the driver. "He gave us our freedom, in return for our labor building Cloud City. We are eternally grateful to him for . . ."

The Ugnaught driver droned on, but Boba was more interested in studying the cloud car's simple controls: a ring that was pushed in for down and pulled out for up, or twisted for turns.

I could fly this thing better than him!

As Cloud City dwindled into the distance, and the cloud car darted in and around the multicolored towers of fog and vapor, Boba began to appreciate the exotic beauty and appeal of Bespin. The atmosphere was buoyant and thick, so it required little energy to fly or to float. Things fell slowly, when they fell.

Evolution had produced thousands of forms of small, colorful life, which fed on one another with happy abandon. Boba saw larger creatures, too. Great floating sacks, with amorphous forms and shifting colors. They were herded by men on batlike creatures.

"Wing riders," said the cloud car driver. "Riding on Thrantas. Not native to Bespin. But then few of us are. We Ugnaughts were actually brought here by . . ."

"You already told me," said Boba.

"Sorry," said the cloud car driver. "It's just that we have found our freedom here, and we are eternally grateful to the . . ."

"You already told me," said Boba. He looked out the window. "There. What's that?"

The cloud car was spiraling down through a scrim of clouds. Below, Boba saw a huge, round, rusted eeck of metal and plastic, floating at a tilt.

"Tibannapolis," said the driver. "I'm out here at least once a week."

It looked to Boba as if the entire abandoned city were scraps on a plate, about to slide off into the garbage can. "Why would anyone come here?" he wondered.

"Souvenir hunters," said the driver.

"Can you tell me where Revol Leap is?"

"I can do better than that," said the squat little Ugnaught. "I can take you there." Instead of weaving in and out of the ruined buildings, he dove under the city. Looking up, Boba could see rusted remains of the Tibanna processing factories and

mines. The flat bottom of the floating city was covered with algae, and plants that fed on the algae,
and floating beasts that fed on the plants, and
plants that fed on the beasts that fed on the
plants.

This is a harsh universe, Boba thought to himself. *I must follow my father's example and become
harsh also.*

Revol Leap was at the city's edge — a section
of tower as jagged as a broken tooth that hung out
over the emptiness.

Suddenly — a spot of orange, a sleek nose, a
stubby wing, a familiar beloved shape . . .

Slave I. There it was! Idling on a warpout deck
under the twisted spire of the Leap.

And standing next to it was Aurra Sing.

She looked as fierce as ever, with her red hair
gleaming in the dim light that filtered through the
clouds. *Mad at the galaxy,* Boba thought. *But why?*
That kind of anger seemed more of a hindrance
than a help.

Remain calm at all costs was Jango's way. *And
it will be my way, too,* thought Boba.

As the cloud car slowed, hovered, and landed,
Boba was suprised to realize that he was glad to
see Aurra Sing.

It had been nice to have a friend like Garr. But

what good was a friend you have to hide the truth from?

Aurra Sing wasn't a friend, far from it; but at least she knew who Boba was.

"Want me to wait?" the driver asked as he landed, the little cloud car scraping on the steel with a harsh sound.

"No," said Boba, pulling out his flight bag and throwing the driver his last credits. "Keep the change."

"Hey, thanks, pal," the Ugnaught said. Boba realized he had overtipped him. But what did it matter? *Slave I* was back!

He waved at Aurra Sing. She of course didn't wave back. Too busy scowling at the galaxy. Boba wondered what would happen if the galaxy scowled back —

And suddenly it did.

CRACK! CRACK!

Two laser bolts hit near Aurra Sing. Another hit near the cloud car.

The Ugnaught driver jumped out of the cloud car and ran for the safety of a nearby building. Aurra Sing stood her ground and looked up. Boba ran to her side and followed her glance.

A Bespin sky patrol skimmer was diving out of the clouds, firing at *Slave I*.

"You betrayed me!" Aurra Sing cried. She reached under her robe and drew out a blaster. Then she backed toward the *Slave I.*

"Wait!" Boba said, running after her. "I didn't tell them anything. How can you be so sure it's the Jedi anyway?"

Aurra Sing grinned as she opened the cockpit. "Who else would be trying to kill me? And failing so miserably?"

Boba scambled up behind her. "Now we can get away."

"Sorry, kid, the deal's off!" Aurra Sing said. "When you told the Jedi where we were meeting, you blew it."

"I never told anyone anything! It wasn't me!" Boba threw his flight bag into the ship. The engines were already idling. Aurra Sing grabbed Boba and hurled him from the vehicle. He hit the steel deck of the floating city so hard that it knocked the breath out of him. Before he could get back on his feet, she'd closed the ramp, fired up the turbos, and taken off.

Boba barely had time to jump free, dodging the blistering exhaust.

"Come back!" He looked up. *Slave I* was rising into the clouds, with the sky patrol craft close behind. The battle was on. Both ships were firing now, streaking the sky with tracer blasts.

Boba wanted to be part of the fight. He wanted to be at the controls of his ship again. *But how?*

With his eyes on the sky, he backed up, clenching his fists in frustration.

Then he remembered the cloud car.

Pull for UP, push for DOWN. Piece of cake.

Boba took off in hot pursuit of the sky patrol craft, which was in hot pursuit of *Slave I*. In space, he knew he wouldn't have a chance of catching up. But in the thick atmosphere of Bespin, all vehicles were relatively slow.

The cloud car was ridiculously easy for him to fly. And sweetly maneuverable. Boba felt his blood drumming an excited beat. It was great to be back at the controls of a ship, even a little tourist hauler.

Boba was falling behind, so he took a shortcut through a cloud. He had guessed right: he came out above *Slave I*, where Aurra Sing couldn't see him. She had slowed to a near hover.

She was planning something.

Boba watched as Aurra Sing slipped into a bank of clouds, as if to lie in wait. And soon he saw what she was waiting for.

The sky patrol craft cruised into view, circling the cloud, scanning the horizons for Aurra Sing. Little did its pilot know that the pursuer had become the pursued, and that Aurra Sing was preparing an ambush.

Holding his breath, Boba watched the sky patrol craft drift past the cloud. Any moment now, there would be a blast of laser fire, and the broken pieces and shattered crew of the patrol craft would fall slowly into the depths of Bespin's atmosphere, where they would all be crushed flat, lost forever in the toxic soup of heavy gases.

Good riddance! Boba thought. Then, as the craft drew nearer, he saw who was in it. There at the controls was a Bespin pilot while Glynn-Beti gave orders. Beside her was Ulu Ulix, and beside him, Garr.

So it was Garr who betrayed me! Garr must have told the Jedi everything! But still . . . my friend. No doubt thinking this would help . . .

A few more meters and they would all be in Aurra Sing's sights.

There was no time to think. Boba pushed the ring forward and dove, faster and faster. He cut in front of the patrol ship, surprising it and throwing it off course, just as Aurra Sing's laser bolt fired —

CHAPTER TWENTY-ONE

— and missed, by centimeters.

The little cloud car might have been small, but it was also amazingly fast. With the sky patrol craft in pursuit, Boba dove down under the city and threaded the cloud car into the forests of dangling algae, where it was all but invisible among the thousands of strands, some of which were hundreds of meters long.

The patrol craft was right behind. After a quick look around, though, it left, presumably to resume the search for Aurra Sing. *Wonder if they know I saved their lives,* Boba thought. He didn't regret it, though he wondered if it had been the smart thing to do. If he had let Aurra Sing blow them to pieces, he would perhaps be with her now, in *Slave I.*

Now, here he was in the weeds. Nowhere, with nowhere to go. A ten-year-old boy in a stolen craft. No money, no friends; he didn't even have his precious flight bag.

What was that?

Boba wasn't the only one hiding in the weeds.

Slave I was cruising through, slipping silently among the hanging fronds. Was Aurra Sing hiding from the sky patrol craft or chasing it? It was impossible to tell.

The cloud car had no comm unit. But what did it matter? Boba was sure Aurra Sing wouldn't talk to him anyway. She was convinced he had betrayed her — and even though she was wrong to think he had told the Jedi where to find her, he had betrayed her by spoiling her ambush.

If she sees me, she'll run. Or worse, blast me.

If only I could sneak up on her, Boba thought. And then, watching her drift slowly toward the edge of the platform, he thought of a way that he could.

Keeping the cloud car hidden in the hanging fronds, he followed *Slave I* across the underside of the abandoned city. It was clear now that Aurra Sing was hiding from the Jedi. She was hovering, barely using her jets. Had she lost her nerve?

Boba knew that as soon as the Jedi were gone, she would be hitting her turbos, blasting for space.

If this is going to work, I have to make my move now, he thought. It meant taking a chance, but Boba was getting good at taking chances.

She was drifting past. Boba waited, with his hand on the edge of the cloud car's open cockpit, until *Slave I* was directly underneath.

Then he stood up.

And stepped over the edge, into the open air.

As he fell, slowly at first, then faster and faster, Boba watched the ship below.

It was tiny; Bespin was huge.

If he missed, he would fall for a thousand kilometers, until his skull cracked in on itself like an egg.

If he missed, but he hadn't allowed for the sideways drift of *Slave I*. He only missed by a few meters. He saw the shock on Aurra Sing's face when she saw him fall past. He could only imagine the look of horror that she saw on his.

Then he heard the WHOOSH as she fired her turbos, and dove underneath him. He heard the *click/ whrrr* as she opened the entryway and positioned herself beneath him, like a net.

OOOMPH! Boba hit on the flight bag he had thrown in earlier; the battle helmet and the book made it hard as a rock.

The entryway closed.

Safe! Boba grinned — until he saw Aurra Sing's scowl.

"If I didn't know you were the son of Jango Fett," she said, "I would swear you were trying to keep the Jedi alive by spoiling my little surprises."

"I just want my ship back," said Boba. "I don't care who you kill." That was a sort of lie — Boba didn't want her killing Garr, or even Ulu. But it was close enough.

"Fair enough," said Aurra Sing. "So let's switch seats."

"Huh?"

"You know how to fly this thing, right? And I'm a better shot than you. We're going to have to work together to get out of here."

Boba didn't have to be told twice. Picking up his flight bag, he scrambled forward to the pilot's chair. It felt good to have his hands back on the familiar controls of *Slave I*.

"Now take us up and out. Let's see if our friends are still there."

They were.

K-RANG! KA-RANG!

Boba dodged laser bolts from two sides. The sky patrol craft had been joined by starfighters from the *Candaserri*. This was their chance to catch the bounty hunter who had attacked so many Jedi.

Aurra Sing fired back, but the shots were wild. Boba threw the little ship into a roll, and dove into a cloud.

"Let's grab some vacuum!" Aurra Sing said. "Head for space."

"Not with those starfighters on our tail!" Boba shouted. "There's no place to hide up there." He had counted at least four from the *Candaserri*. The Jedi had called for reinforcements, and gotten them.

"Well, we're not exactly invisible here!" Aurra Sing yelled back. "We're surrounded — and there's a storm coming. These Bespin storms are deadly."

Maybe that can work to our advantage, Boba thought.

He checked the radar imagery. There it was — a monster storm, towering from the bottom levels of the atmosphere, all the way to the lower reaches of space. It was streaked with lightning, and it spun like a supersonic top.

"Hang on!" Boba cried. He spun *Slave I* out of the cloud, into the middle of the waiting Jedi starfighters.

KA-RANG!

KA-RANG!

Boba threw the little ship into a shimmy, dodging laser bolts as it streaked across Bespin's cloud-stacked sky, with four — no, six — no, eight! — starfighters and a Cloud City sky patrol tight on its tail.

"Now you've done it!" cried Aurra Sing. "They've all seen us."

"Not for long," said Boba, thinking of his father as he headed straight for the lightning-stitched storm cloud. "Nobody follows where we're going!"

CHAPTER TWENTY-TWO

Total darkness.

Then blinding light.

Slave I shook and spun and creaked and groaned.

The turbos were useless. Nothing could match the power of the storm. The ship went where the storm sent it, which was down, down, down —

Slave I was designed to withstand the high vacuum of outer space, not the tremendous atmospheric pressures of a gas giant like Bespin. A crack appeared in the cockpit canopy; Boba smelled an acrid, toxic stench.

"We're breaking up!" cried Aurra Sing. "I thought we were heading for space!"

"Me too," answered Boba.

Both their voices were soon drowned out by the screaming of the wind. Boba stood the ship on end and hit the turbos, holding on for dear life. *Slave I* shook, it rattled, it rolled and spun and tumbled end over end. The lightning crashed over them in huge breaking waves, like a surf of light.

Boba saw Aurra Sing's face reflected in the

viewscreen, and for the first time she looked more terrified than angry. The sight scared him. He knew that he looked even more scared.

Then, suddenly, it was over.

The silence was more terrifying than the noise. Boba knew that he was dead — he saw stars everywhere.

Cold, tiny, silent stars.

"We made it," said Aurra Sing. "Good flying — for a dumb kid."

Boba didn't bother to answer. He was weak with relief. They had made it. *Slave I* was in space. The plucky little starship had climbed the spinning walls of the storm, all the way into orbit around Bespin. No one had dared follow.

"We need to talk," said Boba. He was exhausted, but he felt a new confidence. "This is my ship. I want it back. Now."

"Later," said Aurra Sing, laughing. "There are other planets in this system where we'll be less conspicuous. Unless you want to wait here for the *Candaserri* to spot us?"

CHAPTER TWENTY-THREE

"Your father and I were not exactly friends," said Aurra Sing, once they were in orbit around a small dark planet, a sister to Bespin, which was still visible as a tiny globe in the distance. "Bounty hunters don't have friends. But I respected him. He was the real thing. No sentimental attachments, no loyalties."

"Like you?" Boba asked.

"Sort of — and sort of like you," Aurra Sing went on. "You're developing some of his better qualities. Not that I care. Our paths have only crossed out of my necessity."

Boba wondered what this meant. "Let's uncross them, then," he said. "This is my ship. Pick a planet, and I'll put you off; we'll say farewell."

"And good riddance, too," said Aurra Sing. "But first we have a job to do together. You and me and your father, Jango Fett."

"My father?"

"He was richer than anyone realized. He left credits and treasure stashed all over the galaxy. It's yours, Boba. All you have to do is pick it up."

"Where?" Boba asked. His heart was pounding with excitement.

Aurra Sing smiled. "Several places. I happen to know where they all are. That's why we're a team. I have the coordinates and you have the codes."

"Codes? I don't have any codes."

"Your DNA and retinal scans are the codes. Your father made sure the treasure could only be accessed by his son."

"Why should I trust you? How do you know all this?" Boba asked. "You already stole my ship once, and betrayed me to Dooku."

"Trust me? You'd be a fool to trust me. Do you think I trust you?! You're Jango Fett's son, after all. We're going to get the treasure and split it, fifty-fifty. That's it, kid. Then you're on your own."

"Fifty-fifty? But it's mine!" Boba wondered if he would even see the fifty she was promising.

Aurra Sing smiled. "What choice do you have? Unless you want to wait for someone else to find the treasure."

Boba also wondered if Aurra Sing knew that Jango Fett had tens of thousands of sons. *Does she know that all she has to do is kidnap a clone trooper? But what was that his dad used to tell him? That he was the only unaltered clone?*

"Okay," said Boba. "It's a deal. We're a team — for now."

"Everything's 'for now,' kid," said Aurra Sing. "So let's head for the first site. We can catch some shut-eye in hyperspace. I'll punch in the coordinates while you look the other way. And I mean the other way!"

As soon as the jump was made and they were in hyperspace, Aurra Sing went to sleep, snoring loudly.

Boba sat on his flight bag and watched the stars streak by. He was tired too, but he felt cautiously good. He had his ship back and his flight bag. He was on his way to get the rest of his father's legacy. He had made a friend, even if it was a friend he would never see again.

He had escaped Count Dooku . . . but for how long? And in Aurra Sing's company, he would be doubly pursued by the Jedi.

Aurra Sing was certainly no friend. But she was useful. And at least he could trust her — to be untrustworthy!

Boba Fett knew he would have to remain on guard.

MAZE OF DECEPTION

MAZE OF DECEPTION

ELIZABETH HAND

PROLOGUE

The Dream is always the same. Boba Fett always thinks of it as *The* Dream, because it's the only one he ever remembers. The only dream he ever *wants* to remember.

In The Dream, his father, Jango Fett, is alive. He is showing Boba how to handle a blaster. The dull gray weapon is much heavier than Boba thought it would be.

"Like this," Jango says. He is not wearing his Mandalorian helmet, so Boba can see his father's brown eyes, coolly intelligent but not cold, not when he is looking at his son. When his father holds the blaster it looks weightless, a deadly extension of Jango's own hand. He hands the weapon to Boba, who tries hard to keep his hand steady as he holsters it.

"Always make certain your grip is tight," Jango goes on, "or else an enemy can knock it from you. Like this —"

A quick motion and the blaster falls from Boba's hand. Boba looks up in dismay, expecting a reprimand, but his father is smiling. "Remember, son — trust no one, but use everyone."

That's when Boba wakes up. Sometimes his father's message is different, and sometimes the weapon is different. A dartshooter, say, or a missile. But one thing never changes.

Boba always wakes from The Dream. And his father is still dead.

CHAPTER ONE

"Boba! Downtime's over! I need you — we're in final approach."

Boba looked up groggily from where he'd been asleep in *Slave I*'s cockpit. Beside him, where once his father would have sat at the starship's controls, the bounty hunter Aurra Sing was hunched over the console. She was staring at the screen. It was filled with symbols that were meaningless to Boba Fett — the coordinates of their precise destination remained scrambled.

"Yes!" Aurra Sing murmured triumphantly. "We're almost there."

She looked aside at Boba. Quickly he turned away. He wasn't supposed to know where they were going.

That was part of the deal. Aurra Sing would bring the two of them here, following the coordinates she had discovered in *Slave I*'s databank. The coordinates were part of a complex system — a treasure map, really — that detailed where Boba's father had stored a vast fortune in credits and precious metals, all across the galaxy.

Jango Fett had been a bounty hunter — an extremely *successful* bounty hunter. He had been an extremely clever one, too. Trained as a great Mandalorian warrior, Jango had learned the most important lesson of all: *Prepare for the worst.* And so he had made certain that his young son, Boba, would have access to his fortune after his death. The fortune could never be obtained by anyone else, because the access code was programmed so that only Boba's retinal scan and DNA could obtain it. Since Boba was the sole *unaltered* clone of his father, he and he alone shared Jango's pure genetic material.

But Boba did not know where the fortune was. Only Aurra Sing knew that, because she had accessed the records on his father's ship. The ship that should have been Boba Fett's now.

Boba looked warily at the person next to him. Her topknot of flaming red hair brilliant against dead-white skin. Her eyes blazing as twin suns.

"She is one of the deadliest fighters I have ever known," Jango had told Boba once, years before. "She was trained as a Jedi, but for some reason she hates them more than she hates anyone in the galaxy — and that's saying something! Don't ever cross her, son. And above all, don't *ever* trust her."

Boba Fett certainly didn't trust her. Who would? Aurra Sing was as thin and muscular and fine-boned as a Kuat aristocrat, but as deadly as a Mentellian savrip. She was a solitary hunter and a lethal predator.

Like my father. Like I could be, Boba thought. His glance turned admiring — though he was too smart to let Aurra Sing see *that*!

"Get ready for descent," she snapped as she punched in the final landing codes. "Soon you'll start making yourself useful to me, kid!"

The coordinates were still scrambled. But earlier, while Aurra Sing was momentarily distracted, Boba had peeked at the screen and stolen a glimpse of the itinerary data. They were somewhere in the Core Worlds. A long way from Bespin and Cloud City, where he'd met up with Aurra. Boba knew about the Core Worlds from overhearing his father's conversations. It was a good place to buy weapons — a good place to buy *anything*, now that he thought about it. Maybe a good place to outfit *Slave I* — once he got rid of Aurra Sing.

He didn't know the name of their actual destination, and he couldn't read the planet's coordinates, but he could see it on the monitor. A medium-sized planet, as gleaming and faceted as a green-and-gold jewel. He glanced at Aurra Sing, but she was busy with the landing program. He looked back at the planet on the screen. A string of unintelligible numbers and letters scrolled across it, and then a single phrase that he could understand.

AARGAU. LANDING ACCESS GRANTED.

Aargau. So that's where they were going.

Too bad I've never heard of it. Boba sighed. The landing restraints chafed his arms. When he tried to get more comfortable, Aurra Sing glared at him.

"You want to get out now?" she said, and gestured at the dumping bay. "It can be arranged!"

Boba gritted his teeth, forcing himself to smile apologetically. "Sorry."

Don't trust her, his father had said. But Boba had struck a deal with her. He had agreed — reluctantly — to split the treasure with her, fifty-fifty.

He had no choice. He had no money, no credits, no possessions except for his flight bag, his father's Mandalorian helmet, and *Slave I*. He had no friends out here, wherever *here* was. And he had no friends anywhere. Even when he had the chance of having a friend, he soon lost it.

He had only himself to rely on: an eleven-year-old with his father's training, his father's split-second reflexes, his father's fighting instincts — and his own talent for survival.

"Ready?" barked Aurra Sing. It was a command, not a question.

"Ready," said Boba, and he readied himself for their final descent to Aargau.

CHAPTER TWO

Aargau wasn't the first planet Boba Fett had ever visited, or even the second. For a kid, Boba had seen a lot of planets in a short time. There was gray, cloud-swept Kamino, his homeworld, where months could pass and you'd never see anything but sheets of silvery rain, and hear nothing but the pounding of wind and water. There was Geonosis, a vast desert planet that glowed beneath its orange rings, where Boba had buried his father; and Bogden, a small planet orbited by so many moons it looked like part of a gigantic game of Wuur-marbles.

And there was the *Candaserri*. The Republic troopship *Candaserri* wasn't a planet, of course, but it had seemed almost as big as one to Boba. On *Candaserri* he'd run into the hated Jedi, though not Mace Windu, the Jedi Knight who had killed Boba's father.

Still, except for the Jedi, *Candaserri* hadn't been so bad. It certainly wasn't as disgusting as Raxus Prime, the galaxy's toxic dumping ground, where Boba Fett had last encountered the Count. He always thought of him as "the Count," because the Count had two names — Tyranus and Dooku. Boba's father had always told his son, "If anything should happen to me, find the Count. He'll know how to help you."

As it turned out, the Count had found Boba first. The Count hired Aurra Sing to bring Jango Fett's son to him — for safekeeping, the Count assured Boba. Aurra Sing had kept *Slave I* as part of her payment, which Boba didn't think was fair — it had been his father's ship, and by rights it should be Boba's ship now.

But you didn't argue with the Count, any more than you argued with Aurra Sing.

Not if you expected to live, anyhow, Boba thought as he waited for *Slave I* to make its landing on Aargau. The Count was a tall, imperious man with icy eyes. Like Aurra Sing, he had been trained as a Jedi — although unlike Aurra Sing, the Count had finished his training and had once been a Master — which made him even more dangerous. And like Aurra Sing, the Count now hated the Jedi.

When Boba first heard his father talk about the Count, Jango referred to him as Tyranus. It was Tyranus who had recruited Jango Fett as the source for the great clone army created on Kamino. In appearance, every clone trooper resembled Jango Fett as an adult.

But only Boba Fett resembled his father as a real boy. Unlike the clone troopers, Boba's DNA had not been genetically enhanced. He grew at a normal rate, not at the accelerated rate that the clones did. Boba thought the clones were sort of creepy. They were cool, because they could fight better than any droid army, but they were strange, too, because they looked so much like his father.

The Count was even creepier. Especially since Boba knew the Count had two identities.

Tyranus had created the clone troopers now used by the Republic, while Dooku was on the side of the Republic's enemies: the Separatists. Two men on opposing sides — but they were both the same person!

And only Boba Fett knew that. He smiled now, thinking of it. *Knowing a secret is power*, his father had always told him. *But only if it remains your secret.*

"Ready," muttered Aurra Sing. Around them the

starship shuddered with the force of reentry. "And — *now!*"

Through the screen in front of them he had his first glimpse of Aargau. The planet's surface was invisible. All he could see was one single, impossibly huge pyramid, rising like an enormous shining steel spike from the mists of cloud far, far below.

"What's that?" asked Boba in awe. He had never seen an artifact that vast. "Is it — is that where people live?"

Aurra nodded. "Yes. Aargau is run by the Inter-Galactic Banking Clan. They're sticklers for organization and control. So a large part of the habitable portion of the planet is one gigantic pyramid. It's divided into seven levels. The upper level is the smallest, of course, so security can check all visitors coming and going. Then as you go down, you find administration, then the banks and vaults and treasuries. The merchant and living levels are below these."

Boba peered down. He could see lines zigzagging across the stepped levels of the pyramid. There were blinking lights, glowing canyons, and brilliantly colored tunnels everywhere across the pyramid's surface.

"Wow! It's like a big maze," he said admiringly.

"That's right. Droids are programmed to find their way around all the levels, but people can spend years memorizing the access codes and charts, and still get lost. They say that if you get off on the wrong level, you can spend your entire life wandering around and never find your way back to where you started."

Cool! thought Boba. He glanced furtively at Aurra Sing. Once he had his share of his father's fortune, maybe he could lose Aurra in this planetary labyrinth, regain control of *Slave I* — and regain his freedom, too. He felt in his pocket for the book his father had left him. It was the possession that Boba treasured above all else, except for his father's Mandalorian helmet.

The helmet was safe in Boba's sleeping area. But the book he had recently decided to keep with him always. It contained information and advice that his father had recorded for him. In a way, it was like having a link to his father, even though Jango Fett was dead.

But Boba didn't want to think about that. Once he had made certain the book was where it should be, he turned his attention back to the screen.

Slave I was approaching the top of the glittering pyramid. Far below, Boba could see flickers of light, green and red and blue. It made everything look like part of a gigantic circuit board. He pointed to where the deepest reaches of the planet sparkled brilliantly.

"What's down there?" he asked. "At the very lowest level?"

"That's the Undercity, kid. They say that anything goes down there — if you can find your way."

She leaned back in the command seat, grinning as the ship's computer finally made contact with the planet's security force. On the screen in front of her, green letters scrolled — not the scrambled coordinates, but letters that Boba could read clearly.

WELCOME TO AARGAU
YOUR ARE NOW ENTERING A
NEUTRAL ZONE

"Hah!" said Aurra Sing. She unfastened her safety harness and stood, shaking back her topknot mane of red hair. "Neutral zone! No such thing!"

"What do you mean?" asked Boba. He slid from his chair and followed her to *Slave I*'s docking bay.

"I mean nobody's ever neutral. Not really. Everyone and everything has a price — you just have to figure what it is." Reflexively she checked her weapons, then glanced at Boba. "I guess you're ready — all we need is *you*, after all. Let the bank check your identity and hand over the money!"

She grinned, then punched in the code to open the starship's outer doors. "Come on, kid — let's go get rich!"

CHAPTER THREE

Boba quickly decided that Aargau was definitely the cleanest planet he'd ever been on. The docking zone was like the inside of a gigantic holoscreen, with flashing lights and low, brightly colored buildings. The streets were broad and empty of any vehicles, except for a couple other airspeeders that had recently landed. There were few people or droids that he could see. Not even his father's spartan apartment on Kamino had been as clean as this!

And everything was bathed in red light — a harsh light that made Boba's eyes sting.

"Is the atmosphere this color?" he wondered.

Aurra Sing shook her head. "No. That's from special infrared rays," she explained, as they clambered out of *Slave I*. "Aargau has human-standard atmosphere. Every level is color-coded. It's supposed to make it easier to find your way around. It gives me a headache."

"Me, too." Boba rubbed his eyes. "So this level is red?"

"That's right. Infrared rays help disinfect incoming ships — and visitors. Aargau has a *lot* of rules."

Several uniformed soldiers walked among the other ships at the docking site. Even in uniform, with their faces hidden by their helmets, Boba recognized them. They were clone troopers, members of the clone army created by Count Tyranus. Aargau was part of the Republic, which would explain why the clones were here. In one of the other docking bays, Boba recognized a Republic gunship. That was where the clone troopers would have come from.

But why was a gunship here? Was it refueling?

Boba watched as the troopers drew nearer. It was a weird feeling, seeing the clones again. Boba knew that every one of them had his father's face. His father's eyes, his father's mouth — but not his father's smile. Because the clones rarely if ever smiled.

Boba could see Aurra Sing tensing as the troopers approached them. But they only nodded politely. They gave a cursory look at *Slave I*, then moved on.

"They didn't search us," said Boba in surprise. He glanced back at the troopers. "Or the ship."

Aurra shrugged. "Not really their job. They're

fighting battles, not checking cargo. Anyway, nobody bothers smuggling anything *into* Aargau. Too affluent. They've got a saying — 'Better poor on Aargau than wealthy anywhere else.' This is the bank for the whole galaxy. There's enough precious metals in vaults on Aargau to outfit an entire army a thousand times over."

"Really?" Boba grinned slyly to himself. If the bank here was that rich, would it even notice if a few bars of gold were missing?

As though she could read his thoughts, Aurra Sing added, "It's easy getting *onto* Aargau. Getting *off* is more difficult — you don't want to know what they do to people they catch trying to smuggle stuff off-planet." She turned and gave him a nasty grin. "Don't even *think* of double-crossing me, kid. All they have to do is suspect you of smuggling, and you're history. 'Cause who is an officer going to believe? An adult or a kid?"

Not just a kid — a bounty hunter's kid, thought Boba, and scowled. But he said nothing.

"So just you stay with me," Aurra Sing hissed as they headed toward a large, shining console desk. An immense holosign flickered in the air above it. The holosign had a scrolled message that repeated itself over and over and over again in a hundred different languages.

WELCOME TO AARGAU,
JEWEL OF THE ZUG SYSTEM!
OBSERVE THE FOLLOWING RULES:

I. NO UNLAWFUL REMOVAL OF
PRECIOUS METALS
II. NO POSSESSION OF WEAPONS
EXCEPT BY AARGAU CITIZENS
III. NO WILLFUL CONSPIRACY TO
DEFRAUD, DISCREDIT, OR DECEIVE
THE BANK OF AARGAU

THE ABOVE CRIMES ARE PUNISHABLE
BY IMMEDIATE EXECUTION

Boba glanced at Aurra Sing. She would have a little trouble with Rule Number II, he thought.

But Aurra Sing didn't bother to read the rules. She strode right through the holosign and into Customs Central. Boba hurried to catch up with her.

"Welcome to Aargau," said the attendant at the Customs Central console. She was humanoid, with the telltale gauntness and pallid skin that marked her as a member of the InterGalactic Banking Clan, from Muunilinst. She wore an expensive-looking, gold-and-silver plasteel suit. Its buttons looked like real platinum, with insets of blinking, emerald-colored gavril eyes. She held up a small retinal scanner, directing it first at Boba's eyes, then Aurra's. After the scan was complete, she glanced back down at the device's readout. Her expression betrayed nothing.

"May I ask the purpose of your visit?" she asked.

"I am this boy's guardian, appointed by his family to see that he gets the education he deserves," Aurra lied. Boba winced at the thought of being related to her. "We're here to check on the status of his High-Yield Universal Institutional Savings Account."

"Very good." The attendant smiled blandly. "And may I see proof of your investment?"

For a moment Aurra Sing said nothing. Then she slid a small shiny card across the desk toward the attendant. Boba's eyes widened: The card had to be encoded with the access information to his father's secret fortune!

Aurra Sing looked at the attendant and said, "I think you'll find everything you need there."

The attendant slipped the card into a new scanner. The scanner beeped and blinked. The attendant read the information display.

"Yes," she said. She looked over at Boba. "You are Boba Fett?"

Boba nodded and the attendant smiled. "With this kind of card, I'd guess you're quite a wealthy young man!"

"Yes," Boba agreed. But he certainly didn't feel — or look — wealthy! He glanced down at what he was wearing. Blue-gray tunic over blue-gray pants, knee-high black boots. Standard-issue stuff, not the way a rich kid would dress.

Would that make any difference to the security people here on Aargau? The security attendant certainly didn't seem to care. She glanced again at the shiny information card Aurra Sing had given her, still in its slot on her desk.

She said, "As first-time visitors to Aargau, you are cleared to visit Levels One through Three. That is where off-world banking accounts and precious metals are stored. Your own credits will be on one of those levels. Once you have withdrawn your credits or metals from your account, you may purchase clearance to Levels Four and Five. Level Four is where you can arrange for lodging, and Level Five is where you can buy supplies."

"What's on Level Six?" asked Boba.

"Entertainment and recreational facilities."

Boba grinned. "And Level Seven?"

The Customs attendant gave him a cool smile. "Level Seven is the Undercity. A young person like yourself would have no business there. We encourage free trade, of course, so we don't restrict merchants or traders from anywhere in the galaxy. As a result, you can find some very shady characters in the Undercity. It is terribly dangerous, especially with the recent skirmishes against the Separatists. The Republic has sent a peacekeeping force to make certain that its investments remain protected."

She continued to gaze at Boba, and went on. "You must also be sure not to exchange your money with anyone who is not a licensed member of the InterGalactic Banking Clan. There are black market money changers on Aargau. It is illegal to do business with them. If you're caught, you will be deported immediately. And you *will* be caught. Do you understand?"

Boba nodded seriously. "Yes," he said.

Beside him, Aurra Sing fidgeted impatiently. "Thanks," she said. She started to reach for the info card. "Now, if you don't mind —"

But before she could move, the attendant raised her hand. Seemingly out of nowhere, several

S-EP 1 security droids appeared and swarmed toward the desk. They were followed by a third droid that made Boba's heart pound in fear and amazement —

An IG assassin droid.

CHAPTER FOUR

Boba heard Aurra suck her breath in sharply. Behind the desk, the attendant made a slashing motion with her hand. The assassin droid stopped. Slowly it raised one arm.

Its lasers were pointed right at Aurra Sing!

Instinctively the bounty hunter went into a defensive stance. "Call it off!" she ordered the attendant.

But the attendant only shook her head. "I told you," she said in her calm voice. She was staring at Aurra's blaster."You'll have to leave your weapons here."

"Not on your life!" Aurra Sing said. She reached for her blaster. But she stopped abruptly when she saw the assassin droid reach for its concussion grenade.

"Oh," said Aurra. She withdrew her hand from her blaster. "Sorry! I guess I overlooked that detail.

I was so busy with everything else I was thinking about."

Aurra looked at Boba and smiled — a smile that was more like a grimace. "Right, Boba?"

"Yeah," said Boba. He hoped the grin he gave the attendant didn't look as fake as Aurra Sing's. "We were so excited about finally landing here, we just forgot!"

The attendant turned away from Aurra to smile indulgently at him. "I'm sure you did."

Boy, are grown-ups dumb! thought Boba. He knew that the weapons check was the only thing that could separate him from Aurra — right away.

"But you still must leave your weapons here," the attendant went on. She looked back at Aurra Sing — only this time she didn't smile. "The penalty is death. This is your last warning."

Aurra Sing scowled. "I never go anywhere unarmed."

"Didn't you read the planetary bylaws?" The attendant began to recite in a monotone. "'No unlawful removal of precious metals. No possession of weapons except by Aargau citizens —'"

Aurra cut her off quickly. "Can I leave them on my ship?"

The attendant nodded. "Very well. But you will have to be escorted by Security Personnel." She gestured to the uniformed security guards who stood watching from a few feet away. In the distance, Boba saw other uniformed figures milling about. Some had their faces hidden behind helmets; others were bareheaded.

"I need a Sigma Red escort," the attendant announced into her comlink. "She has permission to return to her ship," she said to the droids, and made another slashing gesture.

At the attendant's command, the droids retreated. At the same time, two of the uniformed security guards walked over to the desk.

"Is there trouble here?" one of them demanded. He looked suspiciously at Aurra Sing.

Boba felt his heart start to pound again.

What if they were *both* forced to leave Aargau before he got the fortune his father had left for him? He'd be as bad off as he was before. Worse, actually — because he'd be stuck with Aurra Sing!

But Aurra seemed to be thinking the same thing. Her expression suddenly grew calculating. She gave the security guard the same fake smile she had given the attendant a minute before.

"I'm cooperating, officer," she said. But the look she gave Boba was anything but glad.

The clone guard continued to watch Aurra suspiciously. The attendant looked at her, too. She pointed at Aurra Sing.

"Please escort her back to her ship," the attendant said.

The guards flanked the bounty hunter, one on either side.

"See that her weapons are properly stowed away on board," the attendant went on. She looked at Aurra. "Once you have done that, the guards will escort you back to this desk. Then I will give you your final clearance, and you can access the other levels here on Aargau."

Aurra Sing glared at the attendant. She looked at the attendant's uniform: She was wearing a blaster.

"What about you?" snapped Aurra. "You're armed!"

"Don't you listen?" the attendant asked in disbelief. "Citizens may carry arms. In fact, it is unlawful for citizens of Aargau to *not* carry weapons."

Aurra Sing turned to stare at Boba. "What about him?" she demanded. Aurra pointed at Boba angrily. "Why aren't the guards on him?"

The attendant looked at Boba. He made sure to appear as young and innocent as possible — this was the chance he'd been looking for. The attendant shook her head, almost in sympathy for the boy.

"He is not armed," she said in her calm voice. "On Aargau, free citizens may come and go as they please, once they have received clearance. This boy has received clearance. And he has broken no rules. He can decide for himself."

She turned to Boba. "Boba Fett. Do you want to accompany your guardian to the ship? Or do you want to remain here?"

Freedom! "I'll wait here," he said, trying not to let his excitement show.

For a moment he thought Aurra would lunge at him. But then she seemed to think better of it. After all, would a real guardian attack her charge?

"You better wait!" she snapped. "I'll be right back, so you better not move!"

The guards stood beside her, glaring. Aurra turned.

"Let's get this over with," she said. She started walking toward *Slave I,* a guard at either side.

But when they reached the docking bay she

looked back at Boba one last time. Her face was calm, but he could see the rage in her eyes.

Still, when she was out of sight, Boba couldn't help grinning to himself. At last. He was on his own.

CHAPTER FIVE

Boba stared at the shadow that was *Slave I*, waiting in the docking bay. He could no longer see Aurra or the guards.

But he liked looking at the ship — *his* ship. The Mandalorian helmet his father had left him was still on board, where Boba had stored it, safe from Aurra Sing. He wished now that he had thought to bring the helmet with him. It had saved his life when he wore it, back on Raxus Prime.

And, with the helmet on, he could be mistaken for an adult. That could be useful, sometimes.

But other times — like now — it was also useful to be a kid. No one expected a kid to be as smart as Boba was, or as self-sufficient. No one expected a kid to know that Dooku and Tyranus were the same person.

And no one expected a kid might have plans that didn't include a parent or guardian. Especially a guardian like Aurra Sing, who was only using him — and would get rid of him the moment she didn't need him anymore. He had no doubt about that.

Boba knew he only had a very short time until Aurra returned from the ship. When she got back, he would have to go with her to one of the lower levels to get his father's fortune. Boba knew she could not be trusted. If she had the chance, she would double-cross him.

And she has no right to the money at all, Boba thought angrily. *My father intended that fortune for me! Not some other bounty hunter — and especially not Aurra Sing!*

But without Aurra, he had no way of knowing where to find his father's treasure. It was somewhere here on Aargau — but where? The attendant had said it would be on one of the first three levels—but each level was enormous. Without any credits, Boba might as well be back on toxic Raxus Prime.

He sighed loudly. Then, remembering where he was, he turned a little worriedly and looked at the attendant in her boring Banking Clan uniform.

He expected her to be watching him. Isn't that what grown-ups did? Watched you all the time, so you couldn't move, or even think, on your own? Boba hated it, just as much as his father had hated any kind of supervision, by the Bounty Hunters' Guild — or anyone else.

But the attendant seemed to have forgotten all about Boba Fett. She stood behind the desk with her back to him. She was talking into a communicator and scanning a computer screen. Boba had just started to turn away again, when something shiny on the desk caught his eye.

The info card! Aurra Sing had forgotten to take it back!

It was still in its slot on the desk, gleaming softly in the harsh red light.

"Wow!" Boba whispered to himself in excitement.

If he could get it, he might be able to use it to locate his father's fortune!

Boba looked around furtively. Across the plaza, the security droids hovered near a bank of turbolift doors. On the other side of the plaza, a group of uniformed guards stood at ease, talking. Several people wearing clothes that identified them as members of the Banking Clan were walking toward the desk.

In a minute they would be here. The attendant would turn to greet them —

And Boba would lose his chance! Quickly, he reached across the desk. For an instant his hand hovered above the shining card. Then, quick as lightning, he grabbed it.

That was easy! he thought. He glanced at the desk. The attendant still had her back to him — but as he watched, she began to turn.

Quickly, Boba put his head down.

Don't run, he thought, even though every nerve in his body was firing *RUN!*

Don't look back — even though every second he imagined the attendant noticing and shouting at him to stop. He began to walk away, as fast and as silently as he could. He crossed the plaza, his head still down, his sweating hand clutching the shining card. He headed toward the turbolifts that descended to the lower levels.

Don't look back, he kept repeating to himself. *Don't look back!*

But more than anything, that was what he was dying to do — look back, and see if Aurra Sing was leaving *Slave I*.

Any minute now she would return.

He forced himself to keep going. It was one of the hardest things he'd ever done. Boba's instinct, always, was for action — to run, to fight, to outwit anyone who tried to stop him. But right now, only silence and stealth would save him.

And the ability to blend in. To *not* draw attention to himself.

Boba stared at the floor beneath him, cold and red and gleaming, clean as everything on Aargau was clean. Maybe twenty meters ahead of him was the wall, and the rows of huge turbolifts. What was it the attendant had said about them? Boba tried to remember.

As first-time visitors to Aargau, you are cleared to visit Levels One through Three. This is where off-world banking accounts and precious metals are stored. Your own credits will be on one of those levels.

Boba's hand tightened around the shining card he had snatched from the desk. If it gave him access to his father's credits, he could get it all for himself — and leave Aurra Sing out of the deal completely!

The thought made Boba hopeful. Then, suddenly, from behind him came footsteps.

"Hey," someone called. "You — !"

Boba's throat grew tight. His hope faded. He had forgotten one of the first rules of bounty hunters — stealth.

He had let himself be seen.

"You!" the voice came again — a familiar voice. "I said, wait!"

Boba's heart was hammering inside his chest. He looked straight ahead, to where the wall of turbolifts loomed. They were just a few yards off now. There were a lot of doors, but one of them should open soon. If he sprinted, he might make it — or he might be captured by whoever was behind him.

Boba didn't look back. His hand clutched the shiny card — the key to what was rightfully his. His heart was pounding so hard his chest hurt. A few steps ahead of him he could hear the grinding sound of more turbolifts moving upward. They slowed to a halt as they approached the Security Level.

"Hey — !"

The voice came again, directly behind him!

Run! thought Boba.

He sprinted the last few steps. Immediately before of him, a line of green lights blinked above another turbolift door.

"*Approaching Security Level One,*" a mechanized voice announced. "*Please stand back from the doors.*"

Boba jumped forward. In front of him, the green lights turned to red. Someone touched his shoulder. Boba stared straight ahead, his heart thumping. The turbolift doors slid open.

"*Security Level One!*" the mechanical voice repeated. "*Please let passengers out.*"

Dozens of people hurried from the turbolift. Boba darted between them, until he was inside. He was breathing hard. But he was alone in the turbolift!

"You!" shouted the same, strangely familiar voice.

Boba whirled.

"*Now leaving Security Level One*," said the mechanical announcement.

The doors began to slide shut. There were only inches left before it closed.

Boba let his breath out. He was safe!

With a cry a small figure lunged through the gap. The turbolift doors hissed shut. Quickly, Boba shoved the shining card into his pocket. Then he backed up against the wall and faced his pursuer.

He was trapped!

CHAPTER SIX

Boba had his back to the wall. His hands tensed to fight —

But fight who? Or *what?* Boba let his breath out in shock.

Because for a moment, he thought he was staring into a mirror. He saw his own face, his own body, his own hands raised protectively. Even the clothes were the same — same gray-blue tunic, same high black boots. The only difference was that the boy staring at Boba Fett wore a helmet.

But it wasn't a clone trooper's helmet, or a Mandalorian helmet. This was a tan helmet with gold-plated metal fittings. Boba had seen thousands like it, back on his homeworld of Kamino. It was a learning helmet, part of the equipment clone youth wore to enhance their training.

Boba was staring at his clone twin!

The two of them looked warily at each other,

keeping their arms raised in a fight posture. After a minute, the clone shook his head. He held his hand out to Boba. For the first time Boba saw that he held something.

"You dropped this," the clone said. He offered it to Boba. "Up there, by the security desk."

Boba looked at it in disbelief. It was his book — the book his father had left him. Boba shook his head. Finally he took it from the other boy.

"Thanks," Boba said. He'd been so busy trying to leave before Aurra Sing returned that he'd forgotten he had the book with him. He looked at the boy and ventured a smile. To his surprise, the boy smiled back.

"I thought it might be important," the clone said. "I'm glad I caught up with you."

Around them the turbolift descended smoothly, silently. Above the door a stream of blinking lines and numerals indicated that they were slowly approaching Level Two, thousands of meters below the first level. Boba put the book back into his pocket, beside the shining card. The boy clone looked at him curiously.

"You're not wearing a helmet," the clone said. He tapped at his own helmet. "Are you an odd or even?"

"An odd or an even?" Boba repeated. "What do you mean?"

Then he remembered.

All young clones were numbered. All young clones wore learning helmets like the one worn by the boy in front of him. The only difference was that some of the learning helmets had gold-colored hardware. Others had plain black metal hardware. Odd-numbered clones wore gold. Even-numbered clones wore plain.

This boy's helmet had gold plating. He was an odd. He was still staring at Boba, patiently waiting for a reply.

"Oh," said Boba at last. "I'm, uh, same as you. Odd."

The boy clone nodded seriously. "Is your helmet getting repaired, too?" He tapped his own helmet, making a face as a burst of static came out of the earpiece. The noise was loud enough that even Boba could hear it.

"That's why I'm here," the clone went on. "I should have remained on board with the others. But my helmet has been malfunctioning. Our commander said it would be faster to just get it repaired here, down on the Tech Support Level."

"Tech Support?" said Boba.

"Level Three. That's where all repairs are done." He looked at Boba and, for the first time, frowned slightly. "You should know that. Your helmet really *must* have malfunctioned."

Boba knew that the learning helmets provided a constant stream of data that the young clones absorbed. Some of the information was spoken through the earpieces. Some of the information was visual, streaming across the small screen that protruded from the helmet to cover this boy's left eye. Clones developed at twice the speed of normal humans. They grew twice as fast, and by using the learning helmets, their brains developed twice as fast, too.

"That's right," said Boba slowly. "I was on my way down to see if it's been repaired."

The clone nodded. He smiled again, and Boba wondered if his friendliness might be a result of his malfunction. Clones were usually not very emotional.

And even though there were hundreds of thousands of them, they were always alone.

Like me, thought Boba in mild surprise. For the first time he smiled back.

"I'm 9779," said the clone. "What designation are you?"

Boba thought fast. "1313," he said.

"I'm from Generation Five Thousand," the clone went on. "Is that your Generation, too?"

"Uh, yeah," said Boba. He hoped he wouldn't have to answer any more questions. Still, he was curious himself. He asked, "Why are all the troopers here on Aargau?"

"You mean us?" 9779 looked surprised. "You better get your helmet fixed if you forgot that! There are rumors that Separatists are here on Aargau. This is a neutral planet, but we clone troopers are supposed to keep an eye on them. Just in case of trouble."

Just in case, Boba repeated to himself. He wondered why the army would've brought a clone whose training was not complete. This had to be *part* of the training — going to a relatively stable world to learn how to patrol and defend.

"We are now approaching Level Two," the turbolift's mechanical voice intoned. "Please stand back from the doors."

9779 obediently moved aside. Boba started to head for the door before it opened, but the clone stopped him.

"Did you forget?" 9779 asked, his face serious. "We're going to Level Three. Got to get your helmet back!"

"Oh —" Boba stammered. "I, uh —"

But then the doors began to open. And Boba didn't have to worry about *just in case of trouble*.

Because trouble had found him. Standing outside the turbolift was —

Aurra Sing!

CHAPTER SEVEN

Boba darted to one side, behind 9779. The clone stood, oblivious, as a small group of people waited to get into the turbolift with them. In the front of the little crowd stood Aurra Sing, her face dark with anger. When she saw 9779, she gave a low laugh of triumph.

"Gotcha!" she crowed, and lunged for the clone.

"Hey — !" said 9779, confused, as Aurra Sing grabbed his arm.

"Sorry," said Boba under his breath to the clone. "But this is my stop."

Other people were crowding into the turbolift now. Before Aurra Sing could spot him, Boba squeezed between the newcomers, out onto Level Two. Behind him he could hear the clone's protests getting louder.

"— let go of me! I'll have you deported!"

"I told you to wait for me!" said Aurra Sing furiously. "Did you think you'd get that money for your-self?"

That's right! said Boba to himself. He moved quickly away from the turbolift. *That's exactly what I thought!*

The mechanized voice made its final announce-ment. Then the sleek metal doors closed, and the turbolift descended once more.

Boba was on his own again.

Just how he liked it!

He quickly checked to make sure he still had his father's book and the data card.

He did. He smoothed his hair, wishing again that he had his Mandalorian battle helmet to help disguise his appearance. He wasn't sure if he wanted to be mistaken for a clone again — next time he might not be so lucky. He turned and began to look around.

He was in a long, shimmering green tunnel. As a matter of fact, everything around him had a greenish glow — the walls, the floor, even the people.

And there were people everywhere. Thousands of them! He saw representatives of every race he could imagine — Gotals, Twi'leks, Dugs, Ithorians, and many more — as well as beings he didn't recognize at all. Mingled among them was an occasional clone trooper. They were easy to recognize in their sleek white body armor. Even they had a green glow on Level Two.

But mostly, he saw members of the InterGalactic Banking Clan. They were tall, thin figures in distinctive drab uniforms. Their faces were dead-white, their cheeks sunken like those of San Hill, who Boba had seen on Geonosis. Boba knew they never ventured outdoors. They spent their entire lives inside, managing their vast stores of currency.

If I was rich, I wouldn't waste my life indoors, Boba thought.

No — not IF *I was rich —*

WHEN *I'm rich!*

He put his hand in his pocket. He touched the smooth card that would lead him to the treasure.

If only he knew how to find it!

But where to start?

Boba frowned. Then he heard the mechanized turbolift voice behind him.

Now approaching Level Two.

Uh-oh. The first thing he better do was get away before Aurra Sing discovered his deception. He looked around.

Level Two was much bigger than Level One. There was a central area — that was where Boba was standing now. And, extending out from this central area, there were tunnels. Hundreds of them, shining green tunnels with moving walkways. A nonstop stream of people went in and out of the tunnels. They stepped onto the walkways, which led them away.

Where did they go?

Boba walked a safe distance from the busy turbolift area. He went toward one of the tunnel entrances. There was a sign above it.

FIRST ROYAL BANK OF M'HAELI

Boba turned and looked at the next tunnel.

BOTHAN INDEPENDENT TREASURY

"Huh," he said. He looked at another tunnel, and another.

N'ZOTH BANKS ONLY
REGISTERED BANK OF AMMUUD,
CORPORATE HEADQUARTERS

"Banks," murmured Boba to himself. "They're all banks."

That's what the tunnels were. Every tunnel led

to a bank, or treasury, that belonged to a particular planet. He turned slowly in a circle, looking at all the tunnels stretching in every direction.

There weren't just hundreds of them. The galaxy contained untold numbers of planets. Even if only some of these had representative banks on Aargau, there might be *thousands* of them!

How could he ever figure out which one held his father's treasure?

Boba fingered the card in his pocket. Around him a steady flow of people went by. No one paid him any attention. After a minute he put the card back into his pocket, and slowly took out his father's book.

It wasn't just a book, though. Boba walked over to a quiet spot a short distance from one of the tunnels. There he opened the black book.

Inside there were no pages. There was a message screen. The first time he had opened it, after his father's death, he had seen his father's face and heard his father's words.

"There are three things you need, now that I am gone," his father's image had said. "The first is self-sufficiency. For this you must find Tyranus to access the credits I've put aside for you. The second is knowledge. For knowledge you must find

Jabba. He will not give it; you must take it. The third and the most important is power. You will find it all around you, in many forms.

"And one last thing, Boba. Hold on to the book. Keep it close to you. Open it when you need it. It will guide you when you read it. It is not a story but a Way. Follow this Way and you will be a great bounty hunter someday."

Hold on to the book. Boba bit his lip in remorse and anger. How could he have left it up on Level One? If it weren't for Clone 9779 —

Boba shook his head. No time for remorse now.

But, he thought, *if I ever see that clone again, I owe him a favor. A really, really big one.*

CHAPTER EIGHT

Boba looked around. He could barely see the turbolifts from here — too many crowds. That meant Aurra Sing would have trouble spotting him, at least for a little while. He glanced from one tunnel to the next, all of them glowing silver-green in the eerie light of Level Two.

Did one of them hold the treasure?

It was like a puzzle. Or no — it was like a labyrinth. A maze. And beneath this level was another level, and then another, levels upon levels extending for kilometers to the surface of Aargau, where the Undercity was. Even if he ever claimed his credits, how could he find his way around? Would he be able to get back to Level One and his ship?

Mazes upon mazes. His father had told him once about being captured and imprisoned in an underground labyrinth on Belsavis and another time on Balmorra. A deadly scorpionlike kretch insect hunted him through the tunnels.

"How did you escape?" Boba had asked breathlessly.

"By keeping my head," his father replied. "Mazes are designed to confuse you. To disorient you. But mazes always have an inner logic. Someone had to design them, after all. If you can stay calm and think, you can always find your way out — if you have enough time."

Boba shook his head. He looked at the vast number of tunnels around him.

No one had enough time to check out every one of them!

He glanced down at the book, still in his hands.

Open it when you need it, his father had said.

Well, I sure need it now! thought Boba. He opened it.

The message screen was gray and blank. But slowly, as he stared down at it, letters appeared.

NEVER SEEK OUT HELP, the screen read.

Boba read the message over and over. Finally he closed the book and put it back in his pocket.

Never seek out help. He looked around at the thousands of silver-green tunnels. If he didn't ask for help here, how would he ever find his way?

"Excuse me," said a small voice beside him.

Boba jumped, his hands thrust out in a fighting posture. Next to him was a little figure, not even as tall as he was. It had a vaguely donkeyish face, pale yellow in color, with large pointed ears that swooped out from either side of its head like wings. It wore plain yellow homespun pants and a vest over a matching yellow shirt. Its hands and face were covered with short, soft fur.

It was a Bimm, Boba realized. A native of Bimmisaari.

"I could not help noticing that you seem a bit confused," the Bimm went on in its singsong voice. "May I be of assistance?"

"Uh," stammered Boba. Then he remembered what his father's book had said.

Never seek out help.

Boba glanced nervously, across to where the turbolifts were discharging more passengers onto Level Two.

Could that flash of red and white, fast as crimson lightning, be Aurra Sing? Or was he just imagining it?

The Bimm said, "I am Nuri. An independent money exchanger." Nuri gestured at the teeming crowds around them. "It is confusing, is it not? Especially when one is a first-time visitor to Aargau. Might this be your first visit?"

Boba looked at Nuri suspiciously. But the Bimm's

singsong voice was friendly, his small bright eyes warm and welcoming. Besides, Boba was a whole head taller than the little alien. Reluctantly, Boba admitted, "Ye-e-es — it is my first visit."

The Bimm nodded wisely. "I thought so. Much of my business consists of helping people like yourself. Making their time here easier. Visitors from all over the galaxy come to Aargau —"

Nuri swept his little hand out. A group of brightly dressed Mrissi swarmed past them, their brilliant feathers peeking from long robes. Close behind them a group of security guards paced watchfully in formation. Behind the guards were more members of the Banking Clan.

This group, however, seemed different from the others of the Clan. Boba stared at them, frowning. There were more heavily armed guards, for one thing. And a number of security droids — lots of S-EP1s. In the middle of them all walked a very tall, very thin man with a face lean and sharp as a razor. Two lieutenants flanked his sides.

"That is San Hill," said Nuri in a low voice. "He is the head of the InterGalactic Banking Clan."

"He looks like a big stick insect," said Boba, not wanting the Bimm to know he'd seen San Hill before.

Nuri tried to hide a smile. "Perhaps. But he is one of the most powerful men in the galaxy. His presence here, now, is very interesting indeed."

The two of them turned and watched as the procession disappeared into one of the eerie green tunnels.

When they were gone, Nuri said, "But enough of that!" The Bimm put a small, furred hand upon Boba's shoulder. "Tell me, what is the nature of your business on Aargau?"

Boba started to reply. But the words stuck in his throat. From the corner of his eye he had seen another flash of red and white, darting across the far side of the crowded level.

This time, there was no doubt that it was Aurra Sing.

CHAPTER NINE

The Bimm's face creased with concern. "What is it?" he asked.

Boba said nothing. He started to move very slowly back, going into a half-crouch. Nuri turned and let his gaze flick across the crowds moving everywhere around them. After a moment he drew his breath in sharply.

"You have made an impressive enemy, young man," he said in his fluting voice. On the far side of the great space, Aurra Sing's muscular figure could be glimpsed. She was standing near the turbolifts, scanning the area with her keen eyes. Nuri glanced at Boba, then took a step back to stand beside him. "A bounty hunter! And not just any bounty hunter, but the legendary Aurra Sing!"

Boba looked down at the Bimm. He was surprised to see that the little alien did not look frightened. Instead, he looked impressed.

That made Boba feel a bit better. "Yes," he said.

"I, uh — I had some business with her. You see, I'm a bounty hunter, too. Or will be, when —"

The Bimm raised one small, furred hand. "You need say no more. *My* business is your welfare. But I suggest we discuss that elsewhere!"

Quickly, the Bimm grasped Boba's arm. "This way," Nuri said. He pointed to a small, dark passage a short distance away.

Boba glanced back over his shoulder. Aurra Sing was gone. A security droid now stood where she had been.

"Oh, no!" Boba said under his breath. He felt a stab of panic. Aurra could be anywhere, behind anyone. . . .

He had been careless. And his carelessness could cost him his fortune — or his life.

"Quickly!" whispered Nuri. "Come —"

Boba hesitated. He didn't know anything about this small, pointy-eared alien. Nuri looked harmless enough, but —

But Boba had no choice. If he remained here, he'd be playing hide-and-seek with Aurra Sing, with a bunch of clone troopers for an audience.

"Okay," said Boba. He followed Nuri toward the dark passage. "I'm coming."

Unlike the other tunnels, this one was narrow and dim. It had a low ceiling and rounded walls.

There was no blinking sign overhead to identify it. A small panel was set into one wall beside the entrance. The panel had a lot of buttons on it. Nuri pressed the buttons in a pattern Boba tried to follow. An instant later the wall slid open to reveal a second, hidden passage.

"This way," said Nuri. He ducked into the passage, with Boba at his heels.

The door closed behind them. Boba straightened, blinking. They were in a small, circular room. Instead of the eerie green light that colored everything on Level Two, the light in here was soft and yellow. Soothing, like Nuri's voice.

"Where are we?" asked Boba.

The Bimm stared up at him. His bright black eyes narrowed. "I will answer your questions in a moment, my young friend," he said in a low voice. "But first, you will have to answer mine."

Boba swallowed. His hand moved protectively toward his pocket. The Bimm's gaze followed it. Boba fingered the card in his pocket, but did not take it out.

He didn't have to. Nuri had already guessed what it was. He looked up at Boba. A smile filled the alien's broad face.

"Ah! I see!" said Nuri. "You have a filocard. You have come here to convert currency — or to get currency that you have stored in one of the banks here. May I see your card?"

Boba shook his head. His fingers tightened around the card in his pocket. He felt sweat beading on his forehead. What was the alien *really* after?

He glared at Nuri. He was still bigger than the alien. Stronger, too.

But then Boba remembered where he was: in a strange tunnel, on a strange planet. Even if he did escape from the Bimm, where would he go?

As though reading his mind, Nuri raised his hands. His expression was mild. "You misunderstand, young sir! I am no thief! I am here to provide a service, that is all. I can help you get your credits!"

The Bimm looked pointedly at Boba's pocket. A shining corner of the card stuck out. It glinted in the dim room.

"That is what I do," Nuri continued. "I help visitors. For a fee, of course."

Boba hesitated. If the alien tried to steal his card, Boba could knock him down. He could force the alien to do what *he* wanted.

Isn't that what bounty hunters did? Capture people?

Yet Nuri did not look dangerous. He looked

friendly. He looked like he really did want to help Boba. *To* — how had the Bimm put it? — *to provide a service.*

Could Boba trust him?

Boba remembered the dream he had about his father. *The* Dream.

"Trust no one, but use everyone."

Boba looked at the Bimm's bright, friendly eyes. Slowly he pulled the card from his pocket and nodded.

"Okay," he said. He held the card out. His own eyes were hard. "But remember — I'm a bounty hunter. Just like Aurra Sing. You wouldn't make her angry, right? Well, you don't want to even *think* about double-crossing me."

CHAPTER TEN

The Bimm stared at Boba. Then he bowed respectfully. "Of course, young sir. I am here to help you — for the fee I mentioned earlier."

Nuri took the card from Boba. The alien's fingers felt soft, furry, and very, very warm. Boba frowned slightly. "How much is the fee?"

Nuri held the card up to the soft yellow light of the passage. He examined it carefully. "That depends," he said.

Boba moved closer to him. He tried to figure out what the alien could see in the card. "Depends on what?"

"On how much this is worth." Nuri held up the card. "I can arrange for you to procure your currency, without, er, complications."

The alien glanced meaningfully at the door leading back out onto Level Two. Boba knew that by "complications," he meant Aurra Sing.

Boba asked, "How can you do that?"

Nuri shrugged. "By avoiding attention. As I am sure you have noticed, there are many rules on Aargau."

Boba nodded. "I saw that," he agreed.

"Well, some of us — many of us — have made our own rules. Now, I have shown trust in you, young sir, by telling you my name. But before I check this —" Nuri held up the shining card "— I must be able to trust *you*. I must know you are not dangerous, or a wanted man. I must know *your* name."

Boba nodded slowly, thinking.

He had to admit it. He liked the idea that someone thought him dangerous. It made him feel powerful. It made him feel that he had a secret.

Which, of course, he did. He knew that Count Tyranus and Count Dooku were the same person. That was a dangerous secret — but it gave him power.

And he was the only one who knew.

Also, of course, he *was* wanted — wanted by Aurra Sing!

Boba looked at Nuri. The Bimm still held his card up, waiting.

"My name," said Boba proudly, "is Boba Fett."

The Bimm stared at him. After a moment he

bowed. "Boba, sir," he said. "I am proud to meet you."

Boba bowed back, a little awkwardly. "And you — Nuri."

The Bimm straightened again. Suddenly he was all business.

"Now," Nuri said. He opened his pale yellow vest. Under it he wore a thick leather belt. On the belt was a small rectangular object: a computer of some sort.

Nuri fiddled with the computer, and it blinked to life. He held up the card, then inserted it into the top of the computer. The computer beeped and blinked. A small silvery screen lit up. There were numbers and letters on it which Boba could not understand.

Must be in Bimmsaarii, he thought.

Nuri peered down at the screen, reading it. His furry eyebrows raised in surprise. He looked up at Boba and said, "Well! You are quite a fortunate young bounty hunter, Boba, sir! You are worth a great deal."

Boba nodded. "I know."

"It says that this fortune was acquired for you by someone named Jango Fett," the Bimm went on. "Your father?"

"Yes," said Boba.

"Is he with you, then? He is the only other person allowed access to this treasure."

Boba shook his head. "N-no," he said. He could not keep the sorrow from creeping into his voice. "He's — he's not with me."

The Bimm looked up at him. His eyes were sympathetic and understanding. "I see," he said. He seemed to think for a minute, staring first at the card, then at Boba.

At last Nuri said, "This Aurra Sing. She is not someone I would want pursuing me. She has killed many people. Many powerful people. Here on Aargau, we are neutral. But we are not stupid. And we are not without sympathy for those in need."

He smiled at Boba, then held out the card for him to take. "Here, Boba, sir. I will help you retrieve your treasure. There will be a fee for my services, but you do not have to pay me in advance. I will deduct it from your card."

Boba looked at him. "Thank you," he said. He took the card and put it back into his pocket. "Could you tell which bank has the treasure in it?"

"No." Nuri rubbed his chin. "To get that information, you would have to go back to Level One, to the security desk."

Boba's heart sank. He looked at the door that led onto Level Two.

Somewhere out there, Aurra Sing was looking for him.

And, knowing Aurra Sing, she would find a way of obtaining a weapon — whether it was allowed or not.

Boba turned to Nuri. "Isn't there any other way?" he asked. "Besides going back up there?"

The little alien smiled. He put a reassuring hand on Boba's arm. "Boba, sir, I have told you that here on Aargau, some of us have made our own rules. Well, we have made our own place, too. A place where the other rules don't apply — and our rules do."

He turned and gestured toward the dim passage behind them. "I will take you to this place now, if you wish."

Boba looked at the Bimm, and then at the passage. He felt his neck begin to prickle with fear and excitement. "What is this place called?" he asked.

Nuri gazed down the passage and smiled — a strange, knowing smile.

"It is called," he said, "the Undercity."

CHAPTER ELEVEN

"The Undercity?" Boba echoed Nuri's words. "But —"

He stopped, remembering what he had been told on Level One.

You can find some very shady characters in the Undercity, the attendant had warned him. *It is terribly dangerous, especially with the recent skirmishes against the Separatists.*

And now Nuri wanted to take him there!

Just the thought scared Boba. But then he remembered what his father used to say —

Fear is energy, Jango had taught him. *And you can learn to control it. If you concentrate, you can change your energy, from fear to excitement. Then you can use that energy, instead of being used by it.*

Boba concentrated now. He closed his eyes. He could feel his heart pounding. He could feel his own fear.

He took a deep breath. He held it while he counted to three, then exhaled slowly.

This is energy, he thought. *And I can control it.* Breathe. Exhale.

Already he could feel his heart slowing down. Growing more calm. More in control.

Not afraid, but excited.

"Okay!" he said. He opened his eyes and saw Nuri a few feet ahead of him. "I'm ready! What are we waiting for?"

Nuri smiled. "This way," he said, and pointed down the passage.

Boba followed him. The passage twisted and turned. Tubes of glowing yellow lit their way. Now and then he saw small holosigns, covered with symbols he did not recognize. The images shifted and changed, from red to green to blue to purple. They made his eyes hurt to look at them. After a while he concentrated on staring at Nuri's back and nothing else.

After about five minutes the Bimm stopped. Set into the ground in front of him was a heavy, round, metal door. Nuri stooped and, with an effort, yanked the door open. He straightened, catching his breath, and stared at Boba.

"In a moment we will begin our descent to the lowest level of Aargau," Nuri said. "The actual surface of the planet. It is the remains of a vast city. It was built by the original natives of Aargau millions of years ago. The pyramid has grown out of it, layer by layer, level by level, over thousands of years. Aargau is a highly civilized planet now. As I told you, it has many rules. But it was not always so."

Here Nuri's expression grew serious. "In the Undercity, individuals are not as well-behaved as they are up here. It is dangerous to visit there. Sometimes fatal."

Boba swallowed. He tried to look brave — although he certainly didn't *feel* brave.

But that was okay. He felt excited. He was doing something he had never done before! And he was doing it on his own.

Well, almost. He looked at Nuri and smiled. "I can handle it," he said.

Nuri cocked his head. "You are not frightened?"

Boba shrugged. "Yeah. I am. But I haven't changed my mind. I still want to go."

Nuri looked pleased. "That is good. To admit fear is a good thing. It makes one careful. And carelessness has killed more visitors to the Undercity than anything else."

Nuri rubbed his chin, regarding Boba thoughtfully.

"And besides," said the little Bimm. His smile

grew even wider. "A visit to the Undercity is an important part of any bounty hunter's education!"

That made Boba feel good. He grinned back.

"Well then —" Nuri gestured at the opening in the floor in front of him. Boba took a deep breath, then stepped alongside him.

"I'm ready," he said, and looked down.

"Ready for anything?" asked Nuri.

Boba nodded. "Ready for anything!"

CHAPTER TWELVE

As Boba looked down, he saw what had been hidden behind the round door in the floor. A capsule, big enough to hold two people. It had clear sides, so you could see out of it. It had a control panel but no steering mechanism. It reminded him of the cloud car he had flown in Cloud City, only smaller, and with no way to change direction.

"What's that?" he asked.

Nuri bent to press a button on the capsule's side. Its top hatch opened. "Hop in and find out," he said.

Nuri climbed into the front. Boba slipped in behind him. The top closed again. Boba looked around and saw that the capsule was inside yet another tunnel — like a sort of tube, or slide, that curved and swirled and twisted ever downward.

"Is this how you get to the Undercity?" he asked.

Nuri nodded. "It is one of the ways. There are thousands. Many are only known to a handful of people. Many have been hidden for so long that they've been forgotten. Of course, there are *official* routes to the Undercity — turbolifts and such — but one needs special clearances for those. And money."

With no warning Nuri flicked a switch on the control board and the capsule plummeted downward with a sudden *whoosh*.

"Whoa!" Boba shouted. It was as though the entire floor had dropped away beneath them. The capsule shot almost straight down, then curved abruptly to the right. It corkscrewed around and around — like going down a gigantic, kilometers-long slide. Boba braced himself with his hands and looked out.

Everywhere he saw lights. Shimmering, blazing flashes of red and orange and blue and violet.

"Those are the other levels," Nuri explained. He had to shout to be heard over the rush and roar of their descent. "We are traveling at a rate of kilometers per minute — but in realtime, not in hyperspace."

"Cool!" said Boba. He wished this thing had controls!

He stared out again. He had glimpses of huge leaping flames, of tunnels that seemed to be filled with molten gold. One level was like a giant aquarium, where huge dianogas floated, their tentacles waving.

Boba wrinkled his nose. "Smells bad here," he said.

"Sanitation level," said Nuri. "We're almost there."

Suddenly everything went black. Not the kind of black you see at night when you go to sleep. Not the kind of black inside a closet, or a darkened ship. Not like the darkness of space, which was not darkness at all, but spangled with stars and planets and distant galaxies.

This was darkness like Boba had never seen. Like he had never imagined. It was like a huge, smothering hand pressed upon his face. Boba couldn't see Nuri in front of him. He couldn't see his own hand. For a heart-sickening second Boba imagined that he himself had disappeared. That he had somehow been transformed into antimatter. That he was —

"Here!" exclaimed Nuri.

An explosion of light surrounded them. Purple, green, deep blue. Boba blinked. The light flickered. It was not an explosion now, but flashes of color. Shapes. Buildings. Moving waves that were people. The familiar figures of droids, creatures, men, and women. Above them all was that terrible, strange darkness. It was like a cloud or a huge black curtain.

The capsule began to slow down. Boba let his breath out in relief. "That was great," he said. "Kind of creepy at the end, though."

Nuri nodded. "That was the emptiness between the Undercity and the upper levels. Sunlight never comes here. Only artificial light. And darkness."

Boba shivered. The capsule came to a halt. He gazed out at a teeming city. It was more crowded than anyplace he had ever seen. A disorderly mass of living things, more like a hive than anything else.

The capsule lid popped open. Nuri jumped out. He bowed to Boba.

"Welcome to the Undercity," he said.

Boba had thought that Level Two was crowded. He had thought that Coruscant was crowded, and the *Candaserri*, too.

None of these compared to the Undercity. There were so many people, so many beings, so many droids, so many *everything*, that his head whirled.

"Stay with me!" said Nuri. "If you get lost, you'll never find your way out."

Boba scowled. "Don't bet on that," he said. "I've got a good sense of direction."

"That might not be enough to help you here," replied Nuri.

Boba hated to admit it, but he had to agree with the Bimm. High above them, the sky that was not a sky was crisscrossed with thousands of shining objects. They looked like ribbons, or rainbows. But they were actually other chutes, or slides, like the one Boba had taken down here. He could see capsules speeding through them, up and down. The air was filled with bright airspeeders, swoop bikes, robo-hacks, even Podracers. On the ground, streets and sidewalks wound around tall, crumbling buildings. The streets were filled with rubbish, broken stones, mangled airspeeders.

And everywhere he looked, he saw people — nonhumans, mostly, but a lot of humans, too. None of them looked friendly. A lot of them looked dangerous.

"Hey, watch it!" someone snapped at Boba. A tall, angry-looking Caridian glared down at him.

"Sorry," said Boba. The Caridian jostled past him. Boba looked around: Nuri was gone!

Ulp. Boba swallowed. A group of swaggering space pirates went by him, laughing. Boba stared back at them, trying to look unimpressed.

"Young sir!" Nuri's voice carried from a few meters away. "This way!"

Boba hurried to join him. Past shops and markets, through abandoned structures that looked like ancient starships, under a vast broken glass dome. They passed food vendors, too. Some of what they were selling looked disgusting — things with claws and tentacles and too many eyes. But some of the food looked and smelled delicious. It made Boba's mouth water. He couldn't remember how long it had been since he had eaten. He was pretty sure it hadn't been today.

At first he tried to keep track of the way they were going. But after a while, Boba gave up trying to keep track. Their path wound in and out, back and forth. Once he was certain they were backtracking. He wondered if for some reason Nuri was trying to fool him. Keep him from being able to find his way back on his own.

And no matter where they went, there were crowds. Despite the rule against nonnatives being armed, most of those he saw carried weapons of one sort or another. Vibroblades, stun batons, blasters, wrist rockets. Boba was pretty sure most of them *weren't* citizens of Aargau.

And he was pretty sure he would not want to bump into *any* of them, alone and unarmed.

"Where do all these people come from?" Boba asked.

Nuri led him down the street, toward an alley. "They come from all over the galaxy," he said in his high, singsong voice. "They are drawn by the fortunes to be made on Aargau, trading currency. And here in the Undercity, anything goes. Betrayal. Murder. The black market is busy here. Smugglers trade and sell gold, credits, data, droids, jewels, weapons, ships. But the single most valuable thing is *information*."

"Information?" Boba frowned. "That doesn't seem very interesting." *Not compared to weapons, or ships*, he thought.

"Trust me," said Nuri. "I know what I'm talking about. And stay near me — it's risky just coming down here. Especially for a first-timer."

I trust nobody, Boba thought angrily. At that instant, a figure rushed from the dark alley.

"Get back!" commanded Nuri.

"No!" said Boba. He reached for a broken brick to throw at the figure. It had nearly reached them, its arms outstretched. It was too dark to make it out clearly —

But not too dark to see that it was holding a blaster. And the blaster was pointed right at Boba Fett.

CHAPTER THIRTEEN

Boba swung his arm back, ready to hurl the brick. But before he could, Nuri stopped him.

"Stop!" the Bimm said. "Wait —"

The figure drew up beside them and halted, panting. It was a fur-covered Bothan, her pointy ears pressed back against her head in fear. "Nuri!" she exclaimed.

Nuri stared up at her in concern. "What is it, Hev'sin?" he asked.

"I have been searching for you!" She turned and looked at Boba. Her blaster was still pointed at him.

"Who is he?" she asked Nuri in a low, accusing voice.

Boba stared at his feet. Nuri glanced at him, then shook his head. "Only a boy," he said to the Bothan quietly. "You will not need your weapon with him. Tell me, Hev'sin — what is wrong?"

The Bothan hesitated. Then she slipped her blaster back into her belt. She stepped next to Nuri, and the two of them turned away slightly. It was obvious they were not worried about Boba overhearing them.

After all, Boba thought, *I'm only a boy. Not a serious threat.*

Or so you think.

Boba knew about Bothans. They were the greatest spies in the galaxy. They left their homeworld, Bothawai, and traveled everywhere. And everywhere they went, they found work — at undercover jobs, as independent operatives, or part of the Bothan Spynet.

And what was it Nuri had just said?

The single most valuable thing is information.

Boba pretended to stare at the alley nearby. But in fact he was listening to what the Bothan was saying.

Boba was spying.

Two can play this game, he thought. *And maybe only one can win — but that one will be me.*

He could hear Hev'sin talking, in a low, urgent voice. "They say he has come here to raise currency for the Separatists. That is why he is down in the Undercity. He is pretending to make a standard visit to the Banking Clan offices on Level Four, but his real business is down here. He doesn't want to draw the attention of members of the Republic."

"Are you sure of this, Hev'sin?" asked Nuri. He looked extremely interested, but not too alarmed.

"Positive," hissed the Bothan. "I saw him with my own eyes. He is surrounded by clone troopers — he never travels anywhere without a full guard now. Besides, I would know San Hill anywhere."

San Hill! Boba remembered — he had seen San Hill just a little while ago, up on Level Two — the man who was skinny and ugly as a stick insect. The Head of the InterGalactic Banking Clan.

San Hill was a Separatist. Boba learned this when he was on Geonosis, and he had seen San Hill meeting with Count Dooku. Boba wondered if San Hill knew that Dooku was the same person as Tyranus — Tyranus, who had created the clone troopers that were now attacking San Hill's allies!

I'll bet he doesn't *know,* thought Boba.

And then he had another thought.

Maybe he'd like *to know . . . for a price.*

Information was very valuable here on Aargau.

"Where did you see him?" Nuri was asking Bothan.

"Near the Hutts' gambling palace. You can be

certain San Hill is up to no good, if he is doing business with the Hutts."

Nuri nodded. "That is so."

Boba's eyes widened. *The Hutts!* He knew who they were — one of the most notorious clans in the galaxy! They ran smuggling and gambling houses all through Hutt Space, and beyond. Now it seemed that they had some sort of operation here on Aargau. An illegal one, too, since it was in the Undercity.

Boba's father, Jango, had done business with Jabba, the Hutt clan's ruler.

"The Hutts value a good bounty hunter," Jango had told his son. "They pay well, too — better than almost anyone."

For knowledge you must find Jabba, his father's book had said. Could Jabba the Hutt be here on Aargau?

Boba glanced over at Nuri and the Bothan, then quickly turned his head again.

"I must go now." The Bothan looked over her shoulder. She stared right past Boba. It was as though he was invisible to her. Another advantage of being young! "I knew you would want to know this, Nuri."

The Bimm nodded. "Yes. Thank you."

He handed her a coin. The Bothan looked at it,

disappointed. For a moment Boba thought she was going to argue — but then Boba remembered.

Bimms were expert hagglers.

And this Bothan didn't have time to waste on haggling. She gave Nuri a farewell that was more of a snarl, then turned and walked quickly away.

"Interesting," Nuri said, more to himself than Boba. "Most interesting."

He looked up, and it was as though he saw Boba for the first time. A small smile crossed the Bimm's face.

"Well, my young visitor," said Nuri. He gestured to the alley behind him. "Shall we go and get your money?"

Boba said nothing. He didn't move. Something about the Bimm seemed different. Maybe it was that smile. Maybe it was just that Boba was tired and hungry. He waited, and finally nodded.

"Okay," he said.

He followed Nuri into the alley. It was dim, but not too dark. It curved slightly, though, so Boba couldn't quite see what was ahead of him. A few more space pirates passed them, laughing loudly. Boba tried to stand as tall as he could when they walked by him. He'd give anything to be back on *Slave I*! He'd give anything to be off this planet, and on his own. . . .

"Here we are," said Nuri suddenly. He stopped in front of a metal door. There was a small window in the door, with bars in it. At the bottom was a narrow opening. Behind the barred window stood a very old, worn-out Admin droid.

"Can I help you?" it asked in a grating voice.

Nuri turned to Boba. "May I have your card, please?"

Boba thought for a moment. If the Bimm had meant to rob him, he could have done it before now. After a moment he shrugged. He pulled the card from his pocket and handed it to Nuri. The Bimm would still need Boba's DNA to get the credits.

Or would he?

"I'd like to have my fee deducted from this young man's account," said Nuri. He slid the card through the opening in the barred window. "Six hundred thousand mesarcs should do it."

The droid picked up the card. "As you wish," it said. It swiped the card across a shining red screen.

Boba watched the droid suspiciously. It hadn't bothered to question Boba at all. It hadn't even looked at him. And suddenly the words of the security attendant on Level One came back to him.

You must also be sure not to exchange your money from anyone who is not a licensed member of the Banking Clan. There are black-market money changers on Aargau.

This was an illegal banking machine.

"Hey!" yelled Boba. "What are you doing? That's *my* money!"

He lunged for the banking machine, jamming his hand through the narrow opening, reaching for the card and hitting at buttons to stop the transaction. He managed to halt things—but it was already too late.

"Five hundred thousand mesarcs have been taken from your account," the droid said in its rusty voice. It dropped the card back into the opening. "Have a nice day."

Boba grabbed the card. He turned furiously to Nuri.

"You!" Boba began to shout. But then he stopped.

Nuri was morphing. His face went from yellow fur to silver to green. He grew taller, his arms grew longer, until he towered above Boba.

He wasn't a Bimm at all.

"You're a shapeshifter!" gasped Boba.

CHAPTER FOURTEEN

"You're a clever young man," the Clawdite shapeshifter said. It was a *young* shapeshifter, with a menacing, oozing voice. Its body seemed to melt and re-form before Boba's eyes. Its body took on muscle, sinew, strength. Its head grew dark thick hair. Its eyes grew dark as well.

"But not quite clever enough," it said.

Boba stared at it in amazement. "But —"

"Consider yourself lucky, young sir," said the shapeshifter that had been Nuri. "I could have taken your precious card and kept it all for myself. I could have killed you."

The shapeshifter smiled — the same unpleasant smile Boba had last seen on the Bimm's face.

"But I admire your courage," the Clawdite went on. "You're young and learning, just like me. And I hate Aurra Sing. She is my rival. It seems you and I have that in common. I could have left you up on Level Two. She would have found you there, very soon. But finding you would have pleased Aurra Sing. I hate her far too much for that."

Boba stared furiously at the Clawdite. "You have no right to claim what's mine!"

The Clawdite laughed. "Well, you did take the card out before I could get everything. If you can somehow find your way back to the Upper Levels, you will find there is enough money left for you to buy a way to get off-planet. But only if you are clever enough, Boba. You will have to avoid being found by Aurra Sing. You will have to find a way to the Upper Levels. And then you will have to find your way to what's left of your inheritance."

The Clawdite tilted his head. "I said that the Undercity is part of any bounty hunter's education. I know it's a big part of mine. I hope you have enjoyed your lesson, Boba."

And with a mocking bow, the Clawdite turned and hurried down the alley.

Boba stared after him. *How could I have been so careless?* he thought angrily. *I forgot the number one rule of bounty hunters —*

Trust no one.

The Bimm — no, the *Clawdite* — had betrayed him. Still, the shapeshifter was right. Boba had learned an important lesson. Next time he wouldn't be so quick to accept help.

If there *was* a next time.

But what to do now? Boba turned and looked at the droid behind its barred window. Hmmm. Nuri had been able to get money from Boba's account. Why not Boba himself? He walked over to the window.

"I'd like to get the rest of my money," he said. He slipped the card through the opening.

The droid looked at him with its unblinking eyes. It took the card and slid it into a slot in its arm. "Sorry," it said. "You do not have permission to use this terminal."

It slipped the card back to Boba. Clearly, the Clawdite had known an access code that Boba couldn't even guess at.

"What?" Boba said angrily. "You mean —"

"Sorry," said the droid. "Shall I call security to assist you?"

"No," Boba said hastily. He began to walk away.

Then he stopped. Before, when the Clawdite had given Boba's card to the droid, the robot had said something — something about a bank.

Boba still had the card. If he knew exactly where his money was, he could get it himself — without Aurra Sing!

He went quickly back to the window. "What bank did you say that money was in?"

The droid tilted its shining chromium head. "InterGalacticBank of Kuat. Level Two. Shall I call security to assist you?"

"No!" Boba said quickly. "I mean, no thanks!"

Nuri had been right — information *was* valuable!

But he had no time to celebrate his good luck. Behind him came the sound of footsteps and more harsh laughter. Boba looked back and saw several tall, heavily armed figures. More pirates, no doubt.

Time to get out of here! He turned and ran soundlessly down the alley.

It ended on another street. This was one was even busier and more crowded than those he'd been on earlier, with Nuri. Boba stood for a minute, catching his breath. He felt no fear whatsoever. He felt anger, and excitement, and determination. He wasn't too worried about Aurra Sing down here. What were the odds of her finding him in all this chaos?

Still, where should he go?

He looked up and down the street. As far as he could see in every direction, there were shops. Some were brightly lit and filled with bustling service droids and well-dressed humanoids and aliens. Others were dim, with only one or two grim figures standing guard by the entrance. Some were in buildings that were little more than piles of rubble. All seemed to be gambling dens of some sort. Many had signs that blinked or scrolled messages in brilliant green or gold or silver letters.

ALL CURRENCIES CHANGED HERE
ALL COIN ACCEPTED
NO SUM TOO SMALL!

Boba began to walk. Excited, noisy crowds spilled from doorways into the street around him. Robo-hacks — airborne taxis — hovered in front of gambling houses, waiting to take new customers away to spend the riches they had just won. Evil-looking figures lurked in alleyways, waiting to pounce on unsuspecting passersby. High above, the air was crisscrossed with glowing tubes. Shining capsules sped up and down between the Undercity and the Upper Levels. In between, swoop bikes and airspeeders flashed.

That's what I'm going to get! Boba thought as he watched a swoop bike whoosh by. Once he figured out how to get his money, maybe he could hire one to take him back to *Slave I* — although flying one himself would be better!

"Pagh! Human scum! Out of my way!" a voice snarled.

Boba looked up, startled. A figure blocked the street before him. It was tall, with orange eyes in a pale fungoid-looking face, and a long trunklike appendage wrapped around its throat. A Twi'lek.

"Didn't you hear me?" the Twi'lek repeated fiercely. Its hand moved threateningly beneath its robes.

"Sorry," Boba said hastily. He stepped aside. The Twi'lek gave him a sneering look, then pushed him aside and strode past him. Boba watched him go, thinking.

"Wait a minute," he said softly to himself.

He had an idea!

His father had told him once about a Twi'lek named Bib Fortuna. The grub-faced alien had served as Jabba the Hutt's right hand, helping run his gambling operations on Tatooine and other places across the galaxy. Here on Aargau there was a Hutt gambling palace. Was there a chance that *this* Twi'lek was the one his father meant?

Boba stared after the retreating figure. If it *was* Bib Fortuna, he might be heading toward the Hutt's den.

Boba knew the odds were against it — but then, everyone in the Undercity seemed willing to gamble. He'd take a chance.

Boba began to hurry after the Twi'lek. He was

careful to stay out of sight and to always keep him in his view. Sometimes this was hard, as the alien ducked in and out of narrow alleys and tunnels. Still, Boba followed him tirelessly through the maze that was the Undercity.

Check this out, Boba thought with a grin. He was stalking his prey through incredibly dangerous terrain — just like a bounty hunter!

CHAPTER FIFTEEN

The Twi'lek had reached the end of a long, narrow winding street. He halted in front of a large building with a rounded roof that had spikes on it. The building was shaped like the head of a gigantic krayt dragon. The dragon's open mouth was the door. Inside, Boba could see a bustling throng of aliens, humans, and droids. Between the krayt dragon's teeth, a shimmering holosign flashed green-and-gold Huttese letters.

The Twi'lek walked up to the sign. Without hesitating, it went inside.

Boba watched him go. His heart was beating hard now. He had seen a lot of people, a lot of aliens, and a lot of droids since he'd been in the Undercity. But there was one thing he *hadn't* seen.

He hadn't seen a single kid. He hadn't seen a single person his own age.

The last thing he wanted to do was draw attention to himself. Silence and stealth were a bounty hunter's greatest weapons.

But there was no way he could sneak through that krayt's mouth and into the gambling palace unnoticed. A bunch of burly guards stood just inside the entrance — Gamorrean boars, by the look of them. Boba watched as the Twi'lek strode right past them. They bowed to him slightly, but otherwise paid him no notice. Yet when two Wookiees approached moments later, the Gamorrean guards frisked them before waving them inside.

How could Boba get past them?

Boba glanced behind him, down the winding street. He could see two more groups of people heading toward the Hutts' gambling palace. If he remained where he was, he'd be seen. At best he'd be told to leave. At worst —

He couldn't afford to think of that now. A few yards away, a pile of rubble loomed. Quickly, before the approaching groups could see him, Boba ran and ducked beside it.

The first group grew nearer. Boba could see them clearly now: half a dozen small Jawa scavengers. All wore the Jawas' distinctive hooded robes. All spoke one another in the Jawas' usual babble. As they passed, their eyes glowed from within their hoods like tiny torches.

"Hey," whispered Boba to himself.

He had another idea — a good one.

He turned and quickly began searching through the rubble. Bricks, broken glass, shreds of leather. A melted ruin that had once been a blaster. Broken spear-points. Exploded grenades. Something that looked alarmingly like a human hand.

The Hutts' gambling palace was a popular place. But it probably wasn't a good idea to stick around it too long.

Suddenly, Boba found what he was looking for. He bit his lip to keep from crying aloud in triumph. It was only a rag — a long, grayish-yellow piece of cloth, dirty and full of holes.

But it was good enough for him. Boba glanced back to make sure no one had sighted him. The Jawas were just approaching the entrance now. One of them appeared to be talking to the Gammorean guards. Swiftly, Boba pulled the cloth over his head. It smelled bad — it stank, as a matter of fact — but he gritted his teeth and tried to arrange it properly.

He pulled part of it over his face. He tugged it forward, till it covered his face like a hood. The cloth fell to just below his knees. He removed his belt from his tunic and tied it loosely around his waist. That was better. He was a little taller than the Jawas, so he bent his knees. It was hard to walk that way, but once he was inside, maybe no one would notice if he straightened up.

He peered around the pile of rubble. Another group was nearing the gambling palace. They were too far away for him to see clearly, but they were tall, and vaguely humanoid.

And there were a lot of them.

I'd better get inside, fast.

Boba looked down at the gambling palace. The Gammorean guards were nodding and waving the Jawas inside. Boba waited until the last Jawa had disappeared into the krayt dragon's mouth. Then he took a deep breath, and began to hurry toward the entrance.

But when he got there he stopped. One of the Gammorean guards glared down at him, grunting in a questioning tone. It held a tall spear, and waved it menacingly.

Its partner peered through its piggy little eyes at Boba, skeptical.

Boba bent his knees a little more. He tugged the folds of cloth around his head, praying his face didn't show. He pointed toward the entrance, miming that he wanted to go inside.

Just then, one guard nudged the other, grunting and pointing behind Boba.

"Aarrrgh!" snarled the other guard. It gnashed its tusks angrily and stared where the other had indicated.

Boba wanted to turn and look behind him — but he didn't dare. He stood, wondering if he should make a dash for the entrance.

Without warning, one of the Gammoreans swung his spear through the air high above Boba's head. He gestured Boba inside.

Boba nodded eagerly. Gathering the folds of his cloak, he ducked his head, then walked as fast as he could through the krayt dragon's mouth — and into the domain of the Hutts.

CHAPTER SIXTEEN

Inside the gambling palace, the noise was deafening. Laughter, angry shouts, howls of triumph and disappointment — all mingled with the jingle of coins, the rattle of dice, the clack of Kenoballs, the cries of card dealers and money changers. The Hutts' gambling palace was yet another maze, all smoke-filled rooms and arcades, so crowded with gamblers that Boba could hardly squeeze through. Gamorrean boars lumbered around, keeping order and throwing out the most unruly customers. Boba saw the Jawas he'd seen outside, haggling with a Bimm over a game of Outlander. Boba wondered if it was a real Bimm or another shapeshifter.

"Watch the Podraces!" a voice shouted. Boba looked up and saw a huge screen. Podraces were being broadcast from Tatooine. "No bets refused!"

Boba fingered the card in his pocket. He was too smart to waste his money on betting. His father had warned him against gambling.

"A bounty hunter gambles with his life every day," Jango always said. "Only a fool would gamble with money, too."

Boba tugged his ragged hood closer around his face. He had only one aim now — to find some way back to the Upper Levels. To find some way of locating his treasure. To get back to *Slave I* and leave Aargau — without Aurra Sing.

He put his hand in his pocket and touched the book his father had left him.

For knowledge you must find Jabba.

Find Jabba. Boba had always assumed that to locate the notorious gangster, he would have to go to Jabba's homeworld of Nal Hutta. Or to Tatooine, where the powerful clan leader had created a smuggling empire.

But what if Jabba were here, on Aargau? The Hutts were involved in every kind of illegal activity in the galaxy. Maybe Jabba was actually here, in the Undercity — in this very gambling palace!

But how to find him? Boba thought hard. He'd have to find the Twi'lek again — the one he thought might be the famous Bib Fortuna. He pulled the ragged cloak back a little from his eyes, straining to see through the dim, smoky room.

A deep voice snarled behind him. Boba looked

up and saw one of the Gamorrean boars. A spear was raised threateningly in his huge hand. The message was clear. *If you're not spending money, get out of here!*

Boba nodded apologetically. He started to turn away, when the guard suddenly grabbed his shoulder.

Ulp! If the guard pulled off his disguise, there'd be no Boba, either! Quickly he dug into his pocket and held up his card, careful to hold it in his sleeve, so his hand wouldn't show. It flickered gold in the dim light.

The Gamorrean's ugly pig face grew even uglier with disappointment. With a grunt the guard turned away and began to hassle someone else.

Whew, thought Boba. *That was close. Got to be more careful!*

He began edging through the crowd, looking for the Twi'lek. Once he thought he saw him, but it turned out to be a tall alien wearing a fur coat. Once he thought he heard a Wookiee's deep, hooting voice. But it turned out to be a small armored droid, rolling through the crowd.

Boba watched it curiously. Then he looked around. There were a *lot* of droids here — more than he would have expected.

Why were they here?

As he looked around, he noticed that these weren't protocol droids, or service droids. They weren't servomechs, either.

They were sentry droids. And security droids, and powerful police droids. Boba felt the skin on his neck prickle. He glanced up, and saw a guard droid hovering on the other side of the room. It turned slowly in the air, its sensors scanning the den. Its three weaponry arms were poised to fire if necessary.

"What's going on?" Boba whispered. Whatever it was, he didn't like it or trust it — one bit.

As if in answer to his thoughts, two tall women in pilot uniforms passed him. They were talking in low voices. Boba pulled his ragged cloak around his face and turned away. But he was listening.

"Rumor is that Dooku sent him," one of the pilots said quietly. "Raising more funds."

"There aren't enough credits in the galaxy to overthrow the Republic," the other woman retorted. "Dooku is mad."

"I assure you, that is the one thing he is not," countered her friend. "And there may not be enough money in the galaxy to fund a rebellion — but there certainly is enough in the Hutts' pockets!"

The women pilots laughed softly. They walked around a corner, out of Boba's earshot.

Count Dooku! Could the sinister Count be here as well?

No — the pilot had said, *Dooku sent him.*

Who would the Count have sent?

Boba thought fast. And he remembered.

San Hill. The head of the InterGalactic Banking Clan, and one of the most powerful figures in the galaxy. But just a little while ago the Bothan spy had told Nuri that San Hill was here, in the Undercity —

San Hill was raising funds for the Separatists. Raising money for Count Dooku. And at the same time, the clone troopers were here as a security force of the Republic — clone troopers who had been bred at the command of Tyranus.

The two sides were set to oppose each other, Republic and Separatists. Clones and droids. But behind each side was the same person: the man Boba knew as the Count.

Count Tyranus.

Count Dooku.

It was all part of some terrible plot, Boba was sure of that. He was also sure that, if his father were still alive, he would find a way to make use of this information — especially with San Hill on the same planet.

Boba could make use of it, too. He just had to

figure out how. Maybe the pilots would have more information. He turned and began to move stealthily after them, across the crowded floor.

But when Boba turned the corner, the pilots were gone. Instead, he found himself face-to-face with three tall, vicious figures. Armorlike scales covered their bodies, and their broad, lipless mouths were full of sharp teeth. Long tails protruded from beneath their tunics, lashing the air threateningly as they argued and laughed in deep, throaty voices.

Reptilian Barabels!

"Care to join us?" one hissed at Boba. They were in the middle of a game of three-handed solitaire. "The stakes are high, Jawa — your money, or your life!"

The Barabel jabbed at him with one long, pointed claw, and the others laughed.

Boba shook his head. He began to back away. But before he could, fast as lightning, the Barabel's clawed hand grabbed him by the shoulder. Boba ducked, kicking out at the Barabel's ankle. The tall reptile gave a shout of rage and pain. He snatched his hand back, his claws closing tightly around Boba's ragged cloak. Boba dove for the floor. The cloak hung from the Barabel's claws like a ribbon of gray mist.

"That's no Jawa!" one of the other Barabels hissed.

That's right, thought Boba grimly. He rolled across the floor, landed on his stomach, and immediately pulled himself under a table. Above him the Barabels stared at the ragged cloak. They all looked around, nostrils flaring as they peered in vain for Boba.

Meanwhile, Boba hunched back as far as he could into the darkness beneath the table and held his breath. One of the Barabels shook its heavy, lizardlike head. He snorted, snatched the ragged cloak from his friend and tossed it over his shoulder.

"Forget about him! Scavenging scum! Back to the game!"

Once again, the Barabels clustered together, jaws clacking as they looked hungrily over the cards in their hands.

Boba let out a sigh of relief. He was safe.

For the moment . . .

CHAPTER SEVENTEEN

He rested for only a few minutes.

Now what? he thought. He no longer had his disguise. If he tried to move, he'd be spotted and thrown out of the gambling palace. Probably his card would be confiscated, too. Then he'd be on his own, with no money and no way out of the Undercity.

And that was the *best* that might happen.

The worst was that he'd be killed. Or captured by slavers.

Boba clenched his jaw grimly. That would never happen. He wouldn't *let* it happen. A good bounty hunter never gets caught.

And he was going to be one of the best.

Still, he needed a plan. *If* he could find the Twi'lek — *if* the Twi'lek really was Bib Fortuna — it might lead him to Jabba the Hutt. *If* Jabba the Hutt was actually here — and *if* the gangster would help him get back up to Level Two.

That's a lot of ifs, thought Boba.

He began to crawl toward the other side of the table. From down here, the Hutts' gambling palace was a forest of legs. Boba scanned the room for a pair of legs that belonged to a Twi'lek. He didn't see them — but he saw something else.

On the far side of the room, in a shadowy alcove, a familiar shadowy form stood, arms crossed. The figure was clad in a tight-fitting crimson suit. Its long legs were encased in high brown leather boots. A leather weapons vest covered its chest. Its skin glowed dead-white even in the darkness of the gambling den. A long topknot of brilliant red hair cascaded down its back. Blazing blue eyes scanned the room, missing nothing. Seeing everything.

Aurra Sing.

Boba's heart raced. He had imagined things couldn't get worse — but they just had. There *was* one thing worse than being captured or killed — and that was being captured or killed by the galaxy's most vengeful bounty hunter. Aurra Sing would show no mercy. She wouldn't care that he was a kid, or Jango Fett's son. To her, he was a double-crosser. Someone who'd cheated her out of her share of the fortune — even if the fortune wasn't rightly hers.

Well, this was no time to *stop* deceiving her. Boba watched as Aurra continued to scan the room. Abruptly, she spun on her heel and began walking — right toward where he crouched beneath the table.

Boba held his breath and froze. He watched as the supple brown boots strode past him — just inches from his nose. A few feet away they came to a stop. He heard the hiss of the Barabels whispering in their own language. Then he heard Aurra's low, powerful voice.

"I'm looking for a boy," she said. "About this tall. Brown hair, brown eyes. Wearing a blue tunic and black boots — though he might be in disguise. I wouldn't put it past him," she added grudgingly.

"We've seen no one," a Barabel hissed. "Now leave us, unless you wish to join our — *ach!*"

Boba edged forward, just enough to peek out. One of Aurra Sing's powerful hands was wrapped tightly around the Barabel's throat. Her other hand held a dagger warningly before her.

"I'm not here to waste my time with filth like you," she spat. "Answer! Have you seen a boy?"

"Yesssss," hissed the Barabel. His clawed hand gestured wildly. "Minutes ago — right there —"

Boba sucked his breath in sharply. There was no time to lose. He turned and scrambled toward the back of the table. A wall was there — solid wood. Boba felt around on the floor, searching for a weapon — a stick, a brick, anything he might use to defend himself. His hand closed on something cold and hard. A heavy metal ring, bigger than his hand. He pulled at it as hard as he could. It weighed a ton, but he kept pulling, until at last it moved.

To his shock, the floor moved, too. Boba stared down in astonishment.

The ring was bolted to the floor. It was not a ring, but a handle. When he had tugged at it, he had lifted a panel off the floor.

It was a trapdoor.

"You better not be lying." Aurra Sing's harsh voice rang across the room from just meters away. "Otherwise I'll carve new scales on your ugly faces."

Boba heard footsteps — Aurra's feet, heading toward the table. He pulled harder at the ring, trying to pry the entire panel up from the floor. The steps grew closer. The wood squeaked and grated as the panel edged up. The sound seemed deafening to Boba. Now the panel was a few centimeters above the floor. He slid his hands beneath, and with all his strength pushed it up, up, until there was a space large enough for him to squeeze through. He shoved his feet in, kicking wildly at open air.

What if there were no floor? What if the trapdoor opened onto — nothing?

"All right, kid — this is it!" Aurra's gloating voice echoed from the room directly above him.

Boba took one last deep breath. He forced his legs through the trapdoor, then his chest and his shoulders. He slid down, his hands holding the wood panel above him. Beneath him he felt nothing, just raw empty space, black as the air above the Undercity. For an endless horrible moment he hung there, suspended between the floor above and nothing below. Then, with a gasp, he tugged the floor board back into place. It shut without a sound. His fingers slipped from the bare wood. His arms flailed at the air. And without a sound, Boba fell.

CHAPTER EIGHTEEN

It seemed he fell forever in that close, hot darkness. In reality, it was just seconds.

"*Ow.*" With a dull thud, he hit the ground. For a moment he lay there, catching his breath. He stared up. Perhaps three meters above him, he could just make out a black square bounded by four thin, weakly shining lines.

The trapdoor.

Would Aurra notice it? Boba wasn't going to wait and find out. Very carefully he stood, blinking as his eyes tried to adjust to the darkness. From overhead he could hear the sounds of the Hutts' den, somewhat muffled now. As his eyes grew accustomed to the dark, he found that he could see a little bit. The faint light from around the trapdoor showed him that he was in a tunnel. It stretched before him and behind him. He turned and peered into the blackness.

Which way should he go?

Above him he heard the scrape of booted feet upon the floor.

Aurra.

Boba chose to go forward — and fast. As quickly and carefully as he dared, he walked, his hands held before him. Now and then he shuddered as something dank and stringy touched his face or hands.

Cobwebs — at least, he *hoped* they were just cobwebs. Sometimes he thought he heard something skittering underfoot, a dry, rasping sound as of many tiny legs. And after several minutes of feeling his way through the dark, he heard something else as well.

Voices.

They came from somewhere ahead of him. Boba noticed that the tunnel seemed to be growing lighter. Instead of blackness, he was now surrounded by dark gray, like smoke. And now he could see that there were other tunnels branching off from this one. All stretched off into utter blackness. From some of them faint scurrying and chittering sounds echoed.

Boba shivered. If he had taken one of those paths by mistake, he might have wandered down here forever. He didn't want to think about what might live in them. And behind him he heard no footsteps following. There was no sign that Aurra Sing had come after him. He had managed to escape her again.

Maybe his luck was holding out, after all.

The light came from straight ahead, directly in front of him. Boba hurried toward it. He was so intent on getting there that he did not hear the soft clatter of many tiny feet in the tunnel behind him.

Just a few feet before him the passage abruptly ended. A pale square of light glowed on the floor. Boba looked down, and saw a small grille set into the ground at his feet. Through it he could make out dim shapes in a room below him.

"You are certain we are safe here?" a voice asked in the room below.

"Absolutely," a very deep, slow voice responded. It laughed, a horrible, hollow sound. "Hoh, hoh! My uncle himself has seen that this place is secure. No one can get here without our knowledge."

Boba's eyes widened. He was gazing into a secret chamber! The grille must have been put there to aid in spying. Boba slowly lowered himself, until he was kneeling and peering over the very edge of the grille. He was careful to stay back, in case someone happened to look up at the ceiling.

"That is good," the first voice said. Boba blinked. After the darkness of the long tunnel, it was hard to get used to the light again. But after a few seconds he could see more clearly.

And what he saw made his breath catch in surprise.

In the room below, a tall, skeletally thin figure sat in a large chair. To either side of him, armed guards stood. They were not clone guards, or droids, either. These were muscular humanoid figures, in drab gray uniforms with blasters slung at their sides. The figure they guarded was San Hill.

"It is in your uncle's interest to support our cause," said the head of the Banking Clan. "Count Dooku has assured me of that."

Boba had to squint to get a good look at the other figure in the room. It was big — huge in fact. A vast, mounded, sluglike body, reclining upon an even vaster chair like a throne. It had tiny, weak-looking arms and a long, fat tail. Layers of fat cascaded beneath its wide, froglike mouth. It was surrounded by guards as well. Boba swallowed nervously.

Was this Jabba the Hutt? If so, he was even more disgusting than his father had described him as being.

The sluglike creature shook its head. "My uncle will make up his own mind," he said in his booming voice. "He will not be hurried, even by Count Dooku."

"Why is your uncle not here?" asked San Hill in a soothing but irritated tone. He looked angry and impatient. "I wish to do business with Jabba himself, not some underling!"

"Gorga is not an underling!" boomed the Hutt. His tiny arms beat against his vast slimy chest. "My uncle is busy tending to our interests on Tatooine. If you desire, you may visit him there. But I would advise against it," Gorga added with a long, rolling laugh.

Boba grimaced. So this was Jabba's nephew! He had a hard time imagining something more repulsive than Gorga. But it seemed like he would have to, until he could see Jabba himself.

Boba felt a stab of disappointment and nervousness. He had hoped that Jabba would be here, to give him the advice — the knowledge — that his father had said the old crimelord possessed.

But Jabba was not here. He was on Tatooine.

I have to get to Slave I, Boba thought grimly. *I have to get to Tatooine.*

He had wasted enough time here in the Undercity. He had the information he needed about his father's fortune. It was in the Kuat Bank vaults on

Level Two. He had his card. *Slave I* was waiting for him, back on Level One. All he had to do was get to the bank, get his credits, and he would have enough to get off of Aargau, and on to Tatooine.

Just the thought of flying again made Boba feel better. He would trace his way back through the tunnel, back to the trapdoor. He'd figure out a way to open it again and climb out. Then he'd figure out how to get back to Level Two. He'd come this far on his own, right?

He could do it.

As silent as a shook, Boba began to inch away from the grill. Then he turned and started running back up the tunnel. It curved and curved, and once more Boba saw all those side passages, black and yawning like huge mouths.

Don't look at them. Keep your eyes on the tunnel!

Ahead he could just make out the sliver of light that fell from the trapdoor. He began to run even faster —

And suddenly, he stopped.

"No!" he whispered.

In the middle of the passage, something was crawling toward him. It was more than a half-meter long, with many black, jointed legs and a long, jointed body. Two long, clacking pincers were raised above its mandibles. Its small beady red eyes were fixed on Boba, and its jaws clashed together as it skittered toward him.

A kretch!

Boba kicked at it. He heard its claws clack, then felt them brush against his leg as it lunged for him. He jumped to one side, but the kretch was too fast — it followed, brushing up against his boot.

Boba kicked it again. This time he felt a satisfying *thump* as his foot connected with the scorpion-like creature. The kretch went flying, and with a loud crack struck the tunnel wall.

But now Boba heard more sounds — other small, clacking creatures skittering up the passage.

He turned to race toward the trapdoor —

And ran right into a tall figure. It was a man, wearing the same drab gray uniform as the guards he had seen surrounding San Hill in Gorga's hideaway.

But this man was no guard or underling. He wore the dress uniform of a high-ranking official in San Hill's employ, a broad decorative belt, and an expression that was equal parts suspicion and command. He smiled grimly down at Boba.

"Going somewhere?" he asked.

CHAPTER NINETEEN

Boba stared at the official in dismay. Behind him the kretch insects chattered and clacked. He glanced down at them. Then he grabbed Boba by the arm, turned, and pressed his own hand against the wall. Immediately, a hidden door opened. The official pulled Boba after him. The door closed as the kretch insects hissed and chittered, furious at losing their prey.

"So." The man gazed down thoughtfully at Boba. "It seems we *do* have a spy in our midst. But not a very careful one. Let's get a look at you."

He shone a torch into Boba's face. The boy shaded his eyes with his hand as the man stooped to stare at Boba intently. He had long, reddish hair, a rugged face. A jagged scar ran from below one eye, across his cheek and to his chin.

"Who are you?" Boba ventured.

"Vice-chair Kos of galactic accounts," the official replied. He held Boba's chin in his hand. Boba stared back at him defiantly, saying nothing. The man continued to look at him. Finally Kos shook his head. His eyes narrowed, as his expression changed.

"I know what you are," he said. "You're that Clawdite spy we heard about." A slight, almost admiring, smile creased his face. "Disguised as a boy — very clever."

Boba began to shake his head no. Then he stopped.

A Clawdite shapeshifter could look like anyone, or anything his size. The vice-chair thought he was Nuri!

"That's right," said Boba slowly. He looked warily up at the official.

The man's smile hardened. "Well, San Hill has his own methods of dealing with spies." He began to pull Boba toward him.

"And so does my master," said Boba.

Kos stopped. He stared at Boba suspiciously. "What do you mean by that?"

Boba hesitated. He had the kind of information a spy would have — real, possibly deadly, information. Out of everyone here on Aargau — out of everyone in the galaxy — only Boba knew that the Count was playing a deadly game. The Count was pretending to be two people, on opposing sides of a great, galaxy-spanning conflict.

It was information worth staking one's life on. And right now, that's what Boba was going to do.

"San Hill only knows part of the story," said Boba. He tried to keep his voice calm.

"And you know the rest?" snapped the vice-chair. But he looked uneasy. He glanced over his shoulder, then drew Boba close to him. "What have you heard?" Kos asked in a whisper. His gloved hands held Boba so tightly the boy's arm ached. "There have been rumors, a thousand rumors."

Boba's heart hammered inside his chest. He was in great danger — but with danger comes opportunity. If he was clever, he could use this official to escape from the Undercity; maybe even to escape from Aargau. . . .

"I know nothing of rumors," Boba said at last. He held his head up proudly and gazed straight into the vice-chair's eyes. "I know only the truth — but the truth comes at a price."

Kos stared fixedly at Boba. He seemed to be weighing his choices.

"I don't have all day," said Boba. "And neither do those I serve." He looked knowingly past the vice-chair, as though he saw someone else there.

Kos stiffened. His hand touched his weapons

belt, as though for reassurance. "Your price?" he said. "Your miserable shapeshifting skin should be price enough! You tell me what you know, and I'll let you go free — for now."

Boba fought to keep his voice steady. He could sense Kos's fear — if Boba could control his own fear, *he* would have the upper hand. "No. That's not enough. I will share my information — but first you have to bring me to Level Two."

"Level Two?" The vice-chair started laughing. Then his laughter turned to restrained fury. "I could break your neck right here — but after San Hill hears your news, he will devise more entertaining ways to kill you."

"After they hear my news," said Boba softly, "he will kill *you* for not taking me to him sooner. But by then my master will be here, and . . ."

He let his voice trail off threateningly.

The official stared at him. His face grew dark with anger. His hand moved toward Boba's neck.

Boba took a deep breath. If he was going to die right now, he would die fighting. He gazed unafraid and defiant up at his captor.

But then Kos stopped. He looked at the boy. His scarred face seemed to regard Boba with more respect. At last he nodded.

"All right," he said. "We'll do it your way. Trouble is brewing, that's for sure. Might as well be out of this place when the storm breaks."

He pushed Boba roughly ahead of him. There was the click of a blaster being loosed from its holster. "But don't even dream of escaping. I'll bring you to Level Two —"

"To the Kuat Bank," said Boba quickly.

For a moment the guard was silent. Then he laughed. "Kuat, eh? Well, someone must be paying you well for your services. But I guess you must be worth it, eh?"

You don't know the half of it, Boba thought, as the lieutenant marched him down the dark passage.

CHAPTER TWENTY

They walked in near-darkness for what seemed like hours, the torch's beam guiding them. But in reality, only a short while had passed — Boba had to remind himself that the darkness was deceptive, like everything else on Aargau.

At last they reached a spot where the tunnel widened. In front of them was a wide metal door. And in front of the door was an airspeeder.

"Get in," Kos snapped. He kept his blaster trained on Boba.

Boba clambered inside. He couldn't keep from smiling. Just the sight and feel of a cockpit made his blood race with excitement!

"What are you grinning at?" the official said suspiciously.

Boba composed his face into a calmer expression. "I am thinking that you made the right choice," he said.

This seemed to satisfy the vice-chair. He climbed into the pilot's seat, positioned himself behind the controls, and pressed a button. The wide door slid up, revealing a huge empty airshaft. It stretched up into dark, seemingly limitless space. Boba craned his neck and stared up.

Not limitless. High, high above them he could see a glitter of green.

"A shortcut," said the vice-chair. He allowed himself a smile. "This ventilation shaft opens directly onto Level Two. And — lucky for you! — the Kuat vaults are not far at all."

Without warning he grabbed the controls. The power generator roared to life. With a shudder the airspeeder bucked forward. Then, as Kos hit the throttle, the craft zoomed straight up.

Boba grabbed hold of his seat. This was more like it! He eyed the airspeeder's controls longingly. The craft rocked back and forth. It rose so quickly Boba's ears hurt from the abrupt change in air pressure. He looked aside at Kos piloting the craft.

I could fly this thing better than he can, Boba thought disdainfully.

Still, he had to admit, the vice-chair did go fast. Mere minutes passed, as they flew up, up, up.

Sooner than Boba could have imagined, the speeder came to a halt.

"Well then," said Kos. The speeder hovered in the air of the shaft. A few feet away was a wall, and a door with a sign on it.

LEVEL TWO, it read in glowing green letters.

A small metal platform extended from the door, hanging out over empty space. Boba turned and looked behind him. More emptiness. He looked up, squinting in the darkness.

He could barely make it out, but there it was. Far above him was a faint red shimmer: Level One. He looked down. He gulped. They must be miles and miles above the Undercity.

"Now." Kos turned to Boba. His eyes had grown even more intent, even more menacing. "You see that door there? I will open it, and allow you to enter Level Two — but not until you tell me what you know."

Boba's gaze shifted from the man to the platform. If he jumped from the airspeeder, he might be able to make it. But even if he succeeded, the door was locked.

And if he fell —

Boba swallowed. He thought of his father: No matter how Jango felt, he would always appear brave.

A lot of the time I'm scared, Boba, he had once said. *But if an enemy ever knows you're afraid, you're finished.*

Boba imagined he was as strong and powerful as his father. He imagined himself looking un-afraid — even though that was not how he felt.

He said, "San Hill is raising money for the Separatist cause. The Separatists are united behind Count Dooku —"

The vice-chairs's face twisted angrily. "That's not news! Everyone knows that —"

"I'm not finished," said Boba coolly. "Did you know that a man named Tyranus recruited a bounty hunter named Jango Fett for the Kaminoans to use to create a clone army for the Republic."

"I'd heard things like that," Kos admitted, growing more interested.

"Well, I know this: Dooku and Tyranus are the same person."

The official stared at him in disbelief. After a moment he started to laugh. "You really had me going for a minute," he said. Then his face darkened. "But I have no time to waste — tell me the truth! What do you know?"

Boba hesitated. He knew he was putting his own life in danger by sharing this secret. But it was the only weapon he had.

"He is helping to build two armies," Boba went on slowly. "He has spent millions — billions — on both the droids and the clones. And in the end, only he will benefit from a war."

Boba thought how foolish his own words sounded. But, strangely, the vice-chair seemed to hear them differently.

"Tyranus . . . is Dooku?" he said in a low voice. "But —"

He shook his head. He looked stunned and disbelieving, but Boba could tell that the seeds of doubt had been sown.

"Are you certain of this?" Kos asked after a minute. "This is treason. The highest kind of treason."

Boba nodded. Kos stared, thinking, at the control panel. Finally he said, almost to himself, "I must tell San Hill."

Without another word he steered the airspeeder over to the platform. The craft rocked gently back and forth in the air. The official reached forward and pressed a button. The door onto Level Two slid open.

"Get out," he said curtly. "Before I change my mind and kill you."

Boba jumped out, his heart pounding. It took him a second to get his balance. Then he raced toward the open door.

"Wait —" the vice-chair called from behind him.

Boba turned. The man half-stood in his airspeeder, his blaster drawn.

"You took too long," Kos said in a low voice. "I changed my mind."

CHAPTER TWENTY-ONE

With a gasp Boba turned and sprinted for the door. But before he could reach it, an explosion sounded behind him. He looked back and saw Kos turning to stare at something below his airspeeder. There was the drone of a hoverbike, and another explosive burst that shook the speeder. An instant later, the hoverbike itself came into view. Riding it was a familiar, red-haired figure.

"Aurra," said Boba in disbelief. As he stared she raised her blaster, her blazing eyes fixed on him.

"Got it in one," she said, and fired. There was a second blast as the vice-chair returned her fire, and the hoverbike rocked slightly.

Without hesitation Boba lunged for the airspeeder, diving inside just as the craft shot away from the landing platform. Kos glanced down at him, one hand on the controls, the other on his blaster.

"That's Aurra Sing," the man said grimly. "If she's part of all this . . ."

His voice trailed off. It seemed as though Aurra's sudden appearance made him take Boba even more seriously. The speeder veered and then swooped into a heart-stopping dive. "Take the controls!" Kos shouted as another volley of fire surrounded them.

Boba nodded and jumped into the control seat. The vice-chair turned to monitor Aurra's pursuit. "There are security forces all over Level Two," he said, shaking his head. "There's no way she can get away with this."

"That's not gonna help us if we're dead," retorted Boba. He steered the speeder around a sharp curve in the airshaft, then yanked back on the controls so that the vehicle abruptly shot up, up, into darkness. "I'll see if we can lose her."

Boba stared at the vast space around them, lines of windows and doors reduced to smears of white and green by their speed. Behind them the bike's hum rose to a furious roar. Blasts of white-hot plasma spun past the airspeeder, giving off a scorched smell. As Aurra Sing scored a direct hit, the speeder gave a violent twist to the left. Boba corrected it quickly. He let the speeder go into a dive as Aurra swung in right behind them, then pulled out and soared up again, the bike screaming in pursuit.

"Are we damaged?" Boba yelled above the roar of the engines.

"Not seriously," Kos shouted back. His blaster moved furiously back and forth, trying to get a fix on Aurra Sing, but she was too fast. "I'm going to call for reinforcements —"

Boba swallowed. If the vice-chair called for help, other soldiers would arrive. They'd take Aurra into custody — but they'd take him, too. He'd be questioned about what he had told the official, and —

Boba swallowed. He didn't want to think about what would happen to him if he were brought in for questioning. If what he knew about Dooku and Tyranus became known to San Hill. If it became known to the Count . . .

He couldn't let the lieutenant talk. He hunched over the controls, his hands like ice as they grasped the throttle, then punched commands into the panel.

"There's a price on her head," Boba said. "You'll be well-rewarded by my master for bringing her in. I'll set the comm unit to make a distress call," he lied, pretending to press a small panel of red lights. He glanced back to make sure the vice-chair's eyes were still on the hoverbike whipping through the air behind them. Then he looked up.

Ahead of them, gaps of deeper darkness appeared, more airshafts or maintenance tunnels. Boba kept his sights on one of these, a triangular opening that yawned bigger and bigger as the speeder raced toward it.

"Now!" breathed Boba. He hit the controls, and the speeder swerved suddenly, disappearing into the lightless tunnel.

"What are you doing?" Kos demanded.

"Evasive action," said Boba. Behind them, Aurra's bike swept past the tunnel's entrance. Boba held his breath.

Sure enough, moments later the bike reappeared, barreling up the dark passage after them.

"Get her in your sights now," Boba said, pointing at the figure on the bike, a black shadow against the brilliance of the tunnel's opening. "I'll keep the speeder steady."

Kos fumbled with his blaster. "Hard to see her in this," he muttered. "It's so dark."

"That means it's hard for her to get a fix on you, too," said Boba.

But that was another lie. Aurra Sing had a predator's mind and instincts. She also had a predator's skills. She could see in the dark as keenly as a tuk'ata —

But Kos could not.

Boba held his breath. He slid down as low as he dared, hoping the vice-chair wouldn't notice. But the official was squinting into the darkness, still trying to get his aim fixed on Aurra.

"There she is," he murmured. Boba heard the soft click of the blaster's loading device. Kos raised his arm.

Boba ducked as an explosion ripped through the air beside him.

But it wasn't the official's blast. It was Aurra's.

"Got him!" she crowed triumphantly. Boba grimaced as Kos's tall form toppled over the side of the speeder, to fall soundlessly into the vast and empty shaft. Too late Boba thought of the vice-chair's weapon — it was gone with him into the depths.

And now Boba was alone with Aurra Sing.

"Thought you could betray me? Think again!"

With a dull whine the hoverbike swept toward Boba's airspeeder. He glanced around, hoping to find something he might use as a weapon.

Nothing. He kept his hands on the controls and stared defiantly across the empty darkness at Aurra.

"Everything is for sale on Aargau," she said with a cruel laugh. "I bought myself citizenship. Too bad you won't live long enough to do the same."

Her laughter died, and she stared at Boba with hatred. "No one escapes from me, Boba. I'm the best at what I do."

"My father was better," said Boba in a low, calm voice. His gaze locked with hers as he continued to stare at her, unafraid. As he did, his hand moved slowly, silently, across the control panel. "My father didn't kill for fun. Or out of fear."

"*Fear?*" Aurra's voice rose almost to a scream. Her eyes blazed, and two crimson spots bloomed on her dead-white face. "You think *I'm* afraid? I think it's time I introduce you to the real thing!"

Her face twisted into a mask of rage. She raised her blaster before her face, the bike steady beneath her. "Good-bye, Boba," she said.

Boba ducked. He jammed his hand onto the controls, hitting the REVERSE DIRECTION command. A flaming pulse from Aurra's blaster zoomed a scant meter above his head. At the same moment, the speeder shot backward. He'd hoped it would slam directly into Aurra's bike. Instead it sideswiped it. Aurra shouted furiously as her arms swung and her next blast went wide. Her bike rocked wildly, and she clung to it to keep from plummeting into the abyss.

"Yes!" cried Boba in triumph. The speeder veered back and forth through the passage, barely missing the walls. He finally got control of it, whipping it around so that it soared out from the tunnel and into the vast main shaft. Behind him he could hear Aurra's angry yelling, and the dull thrum of her bike throttling down. He pointed the speeder in the direction he'd come. With a low roar it began to rush back toward the entrance to Level Two.

CHAPTER TWENTY-TWO

Boba knew better than to think he'd lost Aurra for good. She was like a mynock clinging to her prey, difficult to pry loose.

But not impossible. As his speeder drew closer to the entry to Level Two, Boba flicked on the comm unit. Immediately a voice came through the speaker.

"Sir, we've been unable to contact you for some time. Are you all right?"

Boba cleared his throat. "I'm fine," he said, trying to make his voice sound as deep and muffled as possible. "But there's a renegade noncitizen loose on Level Two. She's armed. There may be some casualties —"

And I don't want one of them to be me!

Behind him came the abrupt high drone of Aurra's bike and another explosive burst. The comm unit went dead. Boba leaned over the controls, not taking his eyes from what was ahead of him: the entry to Level Two.

Closer, closer . . . He could see the familiar sign, and the door behind it. Sparks of orange and scarlet flame whistled through the air around him as he drew the speeder alongside the landing platform. Keeping his head low he jumped out, turned, and bolted for the door. He shoved it open, and raced through, onto Level Two.

Immediately the world around him changed color. Instead of darkness, everything shone with a soft green glow. He was in yet another tunnel, but this one was well lit. At one end a sign blinked on and off.

EXIT

Boba whirled. At the other end of the tunnel was another blinking sign.

INTERGALACTICBANK OF KUAT
ENTRANCE ONLY

"That's it!" Boba said aloud. He began to run. From behind the door he'd just left he heard the hoverbike's drone suddenly shut off. He didn't need to look back to know that Aurra Sing was at his heels.

Ahead of him a security droid stood beside the entrance to the bank. "May I see your card, please?" it asked in its mechanized voice.

Boba dug into his pocket. For a second his heart stopped: He'd lost the card!

But no, it was still there. He yanked it out and handed it to the droid. The droid raised the card before its infrared eyes and scanned it. Then it took Boba's hand. There was a flicker of heat as it read his DNA. Then it nodded.

"Very good," it said. "You may enter."

"Stop him!" Aurra's voice raged from the far end of the tunnel.

"You better check her citizen papers," Boba said breathlessly to the security droid. "She's armed and I think her papers are forged."

He pushed open the door and hurried into the bank. Behind him he could hear Aurra's boots racing up to the entrance. Then he heard the droid's calm voice.

"May I see your citizen papers, please?" it asked. The door slammed and locked behind Boba. He grinned as he heard Aurra's voice rise in frustrated rage.

"May I help you?"

It was another droid, this one neatly clad in gold-and-silver hardware. It stood before an immense black wall. Set into the wall were thousands upon thousands of small boxes, each with a number.

"I want to get what is mine," Boba said, gasping. "My father — he left something for me here when he died."

"Of course," said the droid politely. "May I see your card, please?"

Boba handed the card to him. The droid turned and rolled along the front of the wall. Finally it stopped. It punched the card into a slot in the wall. One of the boxes slid open. One of the droid's mechanical arms withdrew something from it. It closed the box, turned, and rolled back to Boba.

"This closes your account," he said, and handed Boba a small leather pouch. The robot stuck the card into another slot inside its chest. There was a hiss and a wisp of smoke. The card had been destroyed.

Boba looked down at the pouch. It seemed awfully small. He opened it, and poured a handful of shining, multicolored credits into his hand.

"Is this all?" he asked. He shook his head. "My father left me a fortune!"

"There was a large withdrawal made from this account today," the droid said in its calm voice.

"Five hundred thousand mesarcs. That is what remains. Your account is now closed," it said with finality, and rolled away.

Boba stared after it in disbelief. Then he looked at the money in his hand. From the passage behind him, he could hear voices.

"Let go of me! I tell you, these papers are legal! I'm allowed to carry a blaster!"

It sounded like Aurra Sing was having a hard time with Aargau security. Even as Boba turned to look, a side door opened. Heavily armed soldiers wearing uniforms identical to the vice-chair's poured into the corridor. He watched as they ran toward where security had detained Aurra Sing, their boots echoing loudly. Moments later he heard Aurra Sing's shout of rage as the soldiers surrounded her.

"No — let me go, you'll never —"

Boba fought back a shiver. He felt no pity for Aurra — she would have killed him as easily as she'd killed the lieutenant, and with more pleasure. But he knew that losing her freedom would be far worse for Aurra Sing than losing her share of his father's fortune.

Still, she probably wouldn't be imprisoned or detained for long. Boba would bet his life on that.

But not right now. Right now, Boba planned to

hang on to every bit of currency he had. He looked at the money in his hand — not a huge fortune, maybe, but still enough to outfit a ship. Still enough to get him off Aargau. He put the money back into the leather pouch and closed it. He put it carefully into his pocket, along with his father's book. Then he turned and began walking quickly down the corridor, back to Level One.

CHAPTER TWENTY-THREE

No one questioned him when he bought the fuel and provisions for his ship. And no one questioned him when he climbed aboard, after obtaining clearance to depart Aargau. Money might not buy happiness, but it bought a lot of other things that were useful.

Boba settled himself in the cockpit of *Slave I*. It felt like coming home again — for the first time. He strapped himself in, hit the controls, and settled back. A moment later he felt the familiar rush and roar of takeoff.

Within moments Aargau was far, far behind him. Boba gazed out the screen at the glittering planet. He wondered briefly about the people he'd seen there. The young clone 9779. The Clawdite Nuri — if that was really his name. The manipulative San Hill.

What would become of them all, Boba wondered? And what would become of the Separatist cause, led by the double-crossing Count Dooku?

And Aurra Sing?

Aurra Sing might be in custody for now, but Boba knew she wouldn't stay there for long. She was too smart for that. And when she got free, she'd come looking for him.

Boba smiled with determination. When he next met up with Aurra Sing, he'd be ready for her. For now, he had other things on his mind.

Boba knew where his immediate future was — with the notorious gangster Jabba the Hutt!

With a grin, he leaned over the control panel and punched in the coordinates for Tatooine.